JUSTICE

KERRY KAYA

First published in Great Britain in 2023 by Boldwood Books Ltd.

Cover Design by Colin Thomas

Cover Photography: Colin Thomas

A CIP catalogue record for this book is available from the British Library.

Paperback ISBN 978-1-83751-270-6

Large Print ISBN 978-1-83751-266-9

Hardback ISBN 978-1-83751-265-2

Ebook ISBN 978-1-83751-263-8

Kindle ISBN 978-1-83751-264-5

Audio CD ISBN 978-1-83751-271-3

MP3 CD ISBN 978-1-83751-268-3

Digital audio download ISBN 978-1-83751-262-1

Boldwood Books Ltd
23 Bowerdean Street
London SW6 3TN
www.boldwoodbooks.com

For Riley

1

The sound of the front door slamming shut, closely followed by a tirade of angry shouts, was all it took for an all too familiar shard of fear to shoot up the length of Terri Tempest's spine. Her body trembling, she curled her slim frame into a foetal position and yanked the duvet tighter around her as though the action would somehow save her from her uncle's wrath, not that it ever had in the past. Her uncle Michael despised her, he'd told her so enough times, and she believed every insult and every sickening taunt that spewed out of his cruel mouth. The menace in his dark eyes whenever he looked in her direction was more than enough to alert her to the fact that he wanted to bring her harm, that one day his hatred of her would spill over and cause him to do the unthinkable and actually kill her, or at the very least seriously maim her. The burning question at the forefront of Terri's mind was: would anyone care if she was dead or alive? Oh, her mum may have a few choice words to say on the matter, she may even shed a tear or two, but she would never view the loss of her only daughter as gut wrenching.

One ear half-cocked, Terri listened for the sound of Michael's heavy footsteps on the stairs. In a wild panic, her gaze flew to the wooden desk chair that she jammed underneath the door handle on a nightly basis. If nothing else, her attempt to barricade herself in would slow her uncle down, but it wouldn't be enough to permanently keep him out. No, if Michael Murphy wanted to get into her room, he would do so without a moment's hesitation, kicking the door off its hinges if need be and not caring one iota about the destruction and terror he left in his wake.

Her heart in her mouth, Terri gingerly sat up and brought her knees to her chest, the thin cotton nightdress she wore doing nothing to keep out the cold chill that resonated throughout the house and as she shivered, a lone tear slipped down her cheek. At best, her home life was what could only be described as dysfunctional. Raised by her grandparents, she had first-hand experience of their haphazard parenting. In her early years she'd barely known her mother, despite the fact Bianca Murphy had tried to keep in touch whenever she could, or rather as often as she was allowed considering both she and her brothers were serving lengthy prison sentences for human trafficking.

It wasn't until Terri had turned sixteen that her mother and uncles had been released from prison, and four years later, Terri could honestly say she'd never known a moment's peace since that day. Instead, her entire mind and body felt as though it were constantly on edge these days, as though she were waiting with bated breath for her uncle to unleash his fury upon her. No matter how much she tried to avoid Michael, which in all fairness was far easier said than done considering the small council house Terri's grandparents rented was barely large enough to swing a cat, let alone house a family of six adults, there was no way to escape from him. From the moment Michael had stepped out of prison, he'd made his contempt for his niece known. His cold, hard eyes had looked her up and down with disgust, his thin lips curled into an ever-present scowl. 'She looks like him,' he'd snarled. 'You even named her after the bastard.'

The 'him' Michael was referring to was Terri's father, Terry Tempest. A man Terri had never met, nor was likely to meet considering he'd been murdered weeks before her mother had even found out she was pregnant. Over the years she'd thought of her father often, wishing that he would miraculously return from the grave and whisk her away from the family she had the misfortune of being born into. Much to Terri's shame, the Murphy family were well known on the estate where they lived, and they were regarded as scum, a title that followed Terri around like an albatross hanging from her neck. And those who looked down their noses at the Murphys were right to do so. Deep down in her heart Terri knew that her family was different to other families, that it was only fair they be treated with a measure of both hostility and suspicion.

Time and time again her uncles, mother, and even her grandparents had proven themselves to be the lowest of the low. They were well known to be thieves and liars with no morals whatsoever. They lived off government benefits and knew exactly how to play the system. For as long as she could remember, her grandfather had been claiming disability benefits, not that there was actually anything wrong with him other than being bone idle and allergic to doing a day's work. In fact, her family's only aim in life as far as she could tell was to inflict as much fear and damage on the local community as they could possibly muster. And if that wasn't bad enough, there were the whispers and rumours to contend with, the most popular being that her uncle Kevin had escaped from a mental institution and that in his spare time he liked to slice people up and devour on their flesh, and that her mother and uncles participated in incest. Of course, none of it was true, or at least Terri didn't think it was. Yes, it would be fair to say that Kevin was unhinged and that he did keep knives in his room, big ones – she'd seen them with her own two eyes – but to her knowledge he didn't kill people, let alone eat them. And as for her mum and her uncle Michael, they may have been close but she'd never witnessed anything untoward between them, at least nothing that would have sent alarm bells ringing in her head.

As she hugged her arms around herself, Terri thought back to her father and his family she'd never met. She had two elder brothers, her dad's sons, and although she'd never been officially introduced to them, she knew who they were. She'd even caught glimpses of them over the years, albeit from afar, not that they had ever acknowledged her or given her so much as a second glance, and if she was being entirely honest with herself she wasn't so sure that she wanted them to. Ricky and Jamie Tempest scared her. They had reputations as hard men and if the rumours about her family were bad, then the whispers she'd heard about her half-brothers were even worse. They worked as enforcers, were known to be ruthless and were personally responsible for knee capping those who didn't repay their debts; she'd even heard that they'd killed people and the mere thought was enough to make her shudder.

'Where is she, the bitch?'

Michael's loud voice drifted up the stairs, making Terri's body tremble that little bit more. She could hear her mother trying to placate him, her voice soothing as though she were speaking to a child. It was just a pity Bianca had never spoken to her own child in such a manner. If truth be told, Terri had only ever been viewed as a disappointment. Bianca had wanted a son, a strong son who had both Tempest and Murphy blood running through his veins. Instead, she'd been lumbered with a daughter, one who she viewed as being worthless.

The scent of cannabis assaulted Terri's nostrils, and she took a deep breath, hoping, praying, that the worst was over, and that her uncle would soon forget all about her, and that the booze and weed he'd consumed in large quantities would be enough to make him fall into a deep sleep. With a bit of luck she wouldn't have to endure his hatred until she crept down the stairs early the next morning.

About to lie back down, a loud crash from the room below was more than enough to make Terri sit bolt upright. Her mother's scream, followed by her grandmother shouting at her eldest son to leave the girl alone, was all it took for Terri to scramble out of bed. Breathing hard and fast, Terri kept her eyes firmly fixed on the door. She may have been considered weak by the rest of the family but that didn't mean she was prepared to stand by and do nothing while Michael took his anger out on her. He barely even knew her; he'd been locked up for the majority of her life and had done nothing since his release to try and build any form of a relationship with her, other than to grunt with displeasure whenever he was within her vicinity. As far as Terri was concerned enough was enough, everyone had their limits, and Michael's mistreatment of her had gone on long enough. She was as much a part of the family as he was and as far as she was aware she'd done nothing to warrant his loathing. She'd only ever been nice to him, not that her efforts had got her very far. No matter how she behaved towards him Michael did everything in his power to make her suffer, it was almost as though he got a kick out of treating her abysmally, as though it were some sick game he was playing. Well not any more, Terri was done with being nice, done with being his punching bag so to speak, the one he used to take his anger out on. She was determined to fight back, to prove to him once and for all that she wasn't going to allow him to abuse her.

Footsteps bounded up the stairs, and as Terri's body shook, she looked around her, desperately searching for a weapon, something, anything, as long as it stopped Michael from hurting her.

'It's because of her,' he roared from outside the bedroom door. 'Because of her I was banged up.'

'She wasn't even born,' Bianca's shrill voice retorted. 'How could it be her fault?'

'That's right,' Michael snarled. 'And that's how it should have stayed. You should have got rid of her. But oh no, not you; you wanted to keep that lowlife Terry Tempest's kid. I know you,' he continued, his voice rising. 'You only kept it because you thought you'd get your hands on Tempest's money, that having his kid would give you a rep, would make people even more wary of you.'

'So what if I did?' Bianca screamed back at her brother. 'I was owed money; it was my due for carrying his baby. And it could have worked, I could have had everything I'd ever wanted if it hadn't been for his stuck-up bitch of a wife.'

Terri's heart lurched. There were days that she wished for the same, wished that she didn't exist, or at least didn't exist in a world where she was related to Michael Murphy, or any of the Murphys for that matter. Grabbing her hair dryer from on top of her chest of drawers, Terri curled her fingers around the length of cable. It wasn't heavy and she highly doubted it would even do that much damage, but with a bit of luck it would startle her uncle just enough so that she could escape from his clutches.

A hard kick to the bedroom door splintered the wood and Terri jumped back in fright, her heart hammering in her chest. 'Go away,' she screamed. 'Just leave me alone.'

Again another kick, and within a matter of moments, Michael was standing in the doorway, his face contorting with rage. The pale pink knotted scar that sat just above his right eye was a stark reminder that prison hadn't been easy for him – something else he blamed her for. Why, Terri had no idea?

'Mum.' Terri's voice broke as she cowered away from her uncle and she was in half a mind to dive back under the duvet, screw her eyes shut tight, and cover her ears in the hope that her uncle would disappear and leave her alone.

'For fuck's sake Michael,' Bianca huffed. 'What's this going to achieve, eh?' she implored, tugging on his arm. 'Just leave her be. Come back downstairs with me and we can have a smoke, put on some music and talk about the old times.'

The cold look in Michael's eyes sharpened. 'What old times? We were banged up for sixteen years,' he yelled into his sister's face, spraying her with spittle as he did so. 'What exactly is there to talk about?' He flashed Terri a glare, his shoulder blades becoming rigid, and the murderous expression across his face intensifying. 'And all the while this little bitch was living the life of Riley, walking around without a care in the world. Well, what about me eh?' He poked himself in the chest. 'I was the one who paid the price because of her old man's greed. There wouldn't have even been a whore house if it wasn't for Tempest; it was all his idea and he dragged me, dragged us,' he corrected, 'down with him.'

Terri's mind reeled. Michael was lying, he had to be. He'd never made it a secret that he despised Terry, that he resented him. So why now, why would he feel the need to accuse her dad of something so sickeningly awful. If her dad had been involved then why had Michael never mentioned anything before now, it wasn't as though he hadn't had the opportunity to say something because he had, he made it his mission to tarnish her dad's reputation and did so frequently. For as long as she could remember her father had been the only good thing she had in her life to cling on to. She'd dreamt of him so often over the years that she had convinced herself that he'd played an integral part in her life, that the mental images she'd conjured up of him were more than just a figment of her imagination. She was certain that she'd even spoken to him once, that he'd stood in front of her and had smiled down at her. The memory was so hazy that she couldn't recall where she'd been at the time, all she could remember was speaking to a man with dark hair and bright blue eyes. He'd smelled nice too, clean like the

Matey bubble bath she'd loved so much. To learn her father had been as depraved and as evil as her mother and uncles chilled her to the very bone. In her mind Terry had been nothing more than a hero; she'd put him on a pedestal, had loved him, or at least had loved the version of him that she'd always imagined he would be like. In her dreams he was strong, well respected, loving, a man who would always be there for her, someone she could rely on. Not a monster, and certainly not someone who she should be afraid of.

As Michael took a menacing step into the room, Terri grasped the length of cable even tighter, her fingernails digging into the palm of her hand as she did so. 'Stop,' she screamed at him. 'Don't come any closer.'

'Or what?' Michael sneered, a smirk spreading across his face. 'What are you going to do, eh?'

Terri opened her mouth to answer and, quickly snapping it closed again, she threw her mother a pleading look.

'Yeah, I thought as much,' Michael taunted. 'You're just like him, that tosser you call a father. You're pathetic, a mistake, you should have been flushed down the toilet like all the other bastards your mother aborted out of her belly.'

Terri's entire body bristled. She'd always known she hadn't been wanted, that her mother hadn't cared one iota about her, but to know the rest of her family felt the same way, that they would have been far happier if she'd never existed, hurt.

Tears sprang to her eyes and she angrily swiped them away. 'Fuck you Michael,' she shouted.

Michael's smug grin froze. 'What did you just say—'

Before he could finish the sentence, Terri swung her arm forward, the plastic hair dryer bouncing off the side of Michael's head with a loud crack.

A shocked silence fell over the room, and as Terri's eyes widened to their utmost, the severity of what she'd just done hit her full on. For the first time since his release from prison she'd actually dared to stand up to him, not that Michael had given her any other choice. It was either fight or allow him to continue taking his hatred out on her. Despite her new found bravery the colour drained from Terri's face, and the only sound in the eerily quiet bedroom was her ragged breathing. 'I'm... I'm sorry,' she pleaded. 'I didn't mean to do that.'

Michael curled his hands into fists, the scowl across his face deepening. 'I'm going to kill you,' he spat. 'I'm going to knock you from here to kingdom fucking come and believe me I will love every second of watching you suffer.'

With the threat looming heavy in the air, Terri ducked past her mother and uncle, almost sending her grandmother careering to the floor as she shoved her out of the way in her haste to escape. Without even daring to look behind her, she raced down the stairs, pushed her feet into a pair of scuffed trainers, and with trembling fingers yanked open the front door.

'I'm going to have her,' Michael roared as he hurtled down the stairs after his niece. 'I'm going to make the no-good bitch wish she'd never been born.'

Dressed in nothing but a short nightie, Terri bolted out of the house and ran as though her life depended on it. Where she would go, she had no idea; she had no other family, she didn't even have many mates, at least none who she could call a real friend. Her school friends had only wanted to hang around with her because of who she was, a Murphy. And she'd lived up to her family's surname, had been a trappy kid, every teacher's worst nightmare. She'd acted out, answered back, been disruptive, had played truant, and had pretty much done everything in her power to get herself kicked out of school. Looking back on it now, her behaviour had been a way of disguising just how unhappy she really was, a cry for help. Not that anyone had ever come to her aid, nor had they ever taken her aside and asked her if there were any problems at home, but even if they had Terri highly doubted that she would have ever told anyone the truth. Even as a child she'd known when to keep schtum. From an early age her grandparents had ingrained it into her to treat anyone and everyone in authority with suspicion. In the end the teachers had been glad to see the back of her and Terri didn't blame them, not in the least. If the roles had been reversed, then she too would have heaved a sigh of relief.

As she turned on to the main road, the public house situated on the corner of the street beckoned to her as though it were a refuge, a safe haven. For all his faults, even Michael wouldn't be daft enough to attack her in public, would he? He wouldn't want to risk the police being called, perhaps even being sent back to prison if they were to conclude that he'd violated his probation. With tears streaming down her cheeks, blinding her vision, Terri continued to run. The only thing she knew for certain was that she had to get away from Michael, had to get away from all of the Murphys. If she didn't, then the consequences of her actions didn't bear thinking about.

2

Rina Taylor stepped outside the back entrance to The Merry Fiddlers pub in Dagenham and gave an involuntary shiver. Wishing that she'd had the sense to put on a coat, she hastily lit a cigarette and, pulling the smoke deep into her lungs, she stamped her feet on the ground, not that the action was likely to bring her any warmth considering it was a bitter cold night. Looking upwards, she squinted through the curling cigarette smoke. Unless she was very much mistaken, she had a feeling that snow could very well be on the horizon; it was certainly cold enough, she knew that much.

A sudden movement to the left of where she was standing made the hairs on the back of Rina's neck stand up on end. 'Who's there?' she called out.

When she received no response, Rina glanced behind her to the pub. If nothing else, the sound of music and customers chatting brought her some comfort. With one eye still trained in the direction of where she'd heard the noise, she continued to smoke her cigarette, all the while willing her heartbeat to return to its normal rhythm. It was bound to have been a fox, or, she gave a little shiver,

God forbid, a rat. Even so, a rat scurrying in the undergrowth had to be a lot better than an actual intruder, or someone lying in wait to rob them of the takings. Time and time again she'd told her husband, Archie, that they needed to have cameras installed, especially around the back of the pub, seeing as this part of the property couldn't be seen from the road. Not that the silly old bugger ever listened to a word she said, he was his own worst enemy and thoroughly believed that his reputation would be enough to ward off any potential intruders. Only that was half the problem. Archie wasn't as young as he used to be, neither of them were, and more than once in recent months they'd had problems with a firm thinking they were easy pickings. Protection money they called it, but in Rina's mind it was nothing more than a piss take, an excuse to extort ridiculous amounts of cash out of them.

Taking one last puff on her cigarette, Rina dropped the butt to the floor and ground it out beneath her high heeled shoe. She was about to slip back inside the pub when she heard the distinctive sound of someone crying. It was so low that she wasn't entirely sure if it was real or a case of her mind playing tricks on her.

Rina stole a furtive look around her and, wrapping her fingers around the neck of an empty beer bottle, she ever so quietly lifted it out of the crate and took a tentative step forward. 'I said, who's there?' Despite her small stature, Rina's voice held a note of authority, the type of authority that only came from being the landlady of busy East London boozer. Again, she was met with silence, and lifting the bottle above her head, she charged into the darkness, her long peroxide blonde hair flying out behind her.

'Jesus fucking Christ,' she all but screamed as she stumbled upon a young girl crouching against the wall with her arms wrapped around herself. 'What the fuck are you doing out here? I almost caved your bleeding head in.' Almost immediately, Rina's forehead furrowed and, placing her hand upon her chest, she raked her gaze over the short cotton nightdress, the bare arms and legs that were almost blue with cold, and then the young woman's fear-stricken, pale face. Lowering the bottle, she looked back at the entrance door, half expecting her scream to have brought out the entire pub. 'What are you doing out here?' she asked, her voice becoming gentler. 'You'll catch your bleeding death dressed like that.'

The girl shook her head, her eyes brimming with fresh tears.

As she studied the girl, Rina bit down on her bottom lip. 'Well you can't stay out here all night. So sling your hook and get yourself off home.' She was about to turn on her heel when she looked over her shoulder and sighed. The girl didn't move and she was just a girl, if her small, slim frame was anything to go by. 'Where are your parents? They must be worried sick about you.'

At the mention of her parents, the girl scrambled to her feet and, swiping away the tears that wet her cheeks, she lifted her head, her eyes flashing with defiance. 'I'm not a little kid,' she barked out. 'I'm almost twenty-one. I can take care of myself.'

Rina resisted the urge to laugh out loud. She didn't have the heart to tell the girl that twenty was still a child in her book. Placing her hands on her hips, Rina pulled herself up to her full height, all five feet, two inches of it. 'Well in that case, you should know better. Now get yourself off home,' she repeated. 'Before you end up freezing to death.' About to turn on her heel, Rina came to a halt and abruptly spun back around. 'Hey, I know you.' She caught hold of the girl's wrist, jerked her closer and peered into her face. 'I've seen you somewhere before.'

'No... no you haven't,' the girl croaked back, her voice surprisingly low and husky as she desperately tried to prise Rina's fingers away from her. 'You don't know me.'

As she continued to stare at the girl, Rina cocked her head to one side. With a heart shaped face, a tiny mole at the corner of her full lips, bright blue eyes framed with long eyelashes, and thick, dark hair that fell just past her shoulders, the girl was truly beautiful, and certainly not one she would forget in a hurry. Biting down on her bottom lip, Rina was in a quandary. To stand by and do nothing while the girl walked the streets dressed in nothing but a thin nightdress that barely covered her backside was asking for trouble, especially at this time of night when the pubs would be chucking out soon. Who knew whose hands she could fall into? 'Let me call you a taxi to take you home. If nothing else, it would give me peace of mind to know that you got home safe.'

The girl vehemently shook her head, the fear in her eyes enough to stop Rina dead in her tracks.

'I can't.'

Rina let out an irritated sigh. She should have seen this one coming. 'Don't worry,' she grumbled. 'I'll pay the fare.'

'No, you don't understand,' the girl cried, her slim frame trembling. 'He's going to kill me if I go home.'

Rina narrowed her eyes until they were mere slits. 'Who will?' she demanded.

'Please.' Ignoring the question, the girl pulled herself free and rubbed at the indentations Rina's fingers had left upon her wrist. 'Please… I can't go back there, he's going to really hurt me this time.'

Huffing out a breath, Rina lifted her eyebrows. By rights she should send the girl packing, back to wherever it was she had come from. It wasn't as though she was Rina's responsibility; she had enough on her plate without poking her nose into the girl's business. Only, deep down in her heart, Rina knew she couldn't just walk away and leave the girl out in the cold to fend for herself. She cast a glance over her shoulder back at the pub. Archie would go ballistic if she was to usher the girl inside, and as much as she loved the old fucker, he could be a hard bastard when he needed to be; he didn't take fools gladly, and certainly wasn't in the habit of taking in waifs and strays. But what if the girl really was in danger, what if she came to harm? Did Rina want that on her conscience?

'What's your name?' she asked.

The girl took a step backwards, her gaze darting around her as though looking for an escape route.

Fast on the way to losing her patience, Rina set her lips into a straight line. 'I can't help you if I don't even know your name.'

A glimmer of hope sparked in the girl's wide eyes. 'You'll help me?'

Against her better judgement, Rina nodded. She'd deal with Archie as and when the time came; it wasn't as though she wasn't able to wrap him around her little finger when she needed to. 'What's your name, and don't even think about spinning me a tale, because believe me, I'm not as daft as I might look,' she said, crossing her arms over her chest, the hint of a grin tugging at the corners of her mouth to take the edge off her words.

The girl hesitated, then swallowing deeply, she answered, 'Terri… Terri Tempest.'

There and then, Rina's blood ran cold and as the enormity of the situation became apparent to her, she sucked in a breath, wishing more than anything that she hadn't come outside for a cigarette and more importantly, that she hadn't stumbled across the girl. Of course she should have recognised her; she knew the girl's family well enough to know that they were trouble and she should know, considering she'd barred each and every one of them from the pub more than once over the years. And if that wasn't bad enough, the girl's surname was enough to make the tiny hairs on the back of Rina's neck stand upright.

Her hands ever so slightly shaking, Rina forced a smile across her face and motioned towards the pub. It was on the tip of her tongue to tell the girl that she'd changed her mind, that she was old enough to fend for herself. Only one look at Terri's face was enough to tell Rina that she was desperate, that whatever horrors lay in wait for her at the Murphy's family home didn't bear thinking about. How could she turn her away now, she'd already agreed to help and like hell was she going to go back on her word.

'Let's get you inside and out of the cold, shall we?' Placing her arm protectively around Terri's thin shoulders, Rina ushered her through the staff entrance and up a steep staircase that led to the living quarters, all the while her mind was working overtime. Seeing as she'd inadvertently brought trouble to their door, perhaps Archie was going to kill her stone dead after all.

* * *

Archie Taylor was raging. He'd taken one look at Terri and had shaken his head, his hard eyes warning Rina that she'd overstepped the mark. What the fuck was going on inside the woman's mind? Didn't he have enough to contend with, what with Frankie Gammon shouting the odds, demanding protection money from him? He wouldn't mind but he was more than capable of taking care of his own business and didn't need the likes of Gammon threatening him with all and sundry if he didn't pay up.

'Just one night,' Rina mouthed at him as she led Terri into the lounge.

Once Terri was settled on the sofa, Rina backed out of the room, gently closing the door behind her.

'Have you lost your mind?' Archie barked out.

Placing her finger to her lips, Rina tugged on Archie's arm and guided him towards the kitchen so that they could speak in private.

'What was I supposed to do?' she pleaded with him. 'It's

freezing out there, and she's just a kid, she's not even twenty-one yet.'

'And how is that my problem?' Archie huffed. 'Send her home to her family, let them deal with her.'

Rina shot a glance towards the lounge. 'I can't, she's terrified of them. She reckons that they'll hurt her if she goes home.'

Archie gritted his teeth. 'And like I've already said,' he snapped. 'How exactly is that my problem?'

As she placed her hand on Archie's chest, Rina ran her fingers over an imaginary crease in his shirt. 'That's the thing,' she said, looking up at her husband. 'She's a Murphy, or rather a Tempest. She's Terry Tempest's daughter.'

Closing his eyes in distress, Archie lifted his head towards the ceiling. 'Tell me this isn't true,' he cried, letting out an exasperated sigh. 'Tell me you haven't brought a fucking Murphy into my pub, into my home.'

Rina arched an eyebrow. 'Technically she's a Tempest.'

'Rina,' Archie warned.

'Okay.' Holding up her hands, Rina gave the door to the lounge another cautious glance. 'What did you expect me to do? I couldn't just leave her outside,' she said, pleading to his better nature. 'It's freezing out there and if something were to happen to her, would you really want that on your conscience because I know I wouldn't,' she said, stabbing her thumb into her chest. 'And what about the Tempests? I don't think Ricky or Jamie would take it too kindly if something were to happen to their sister, their baby sister might I add.'

Thinking it over, Archie rubbed at the back of his neck. Rina was right, she always was. How could they kick the girl out in this weather? Snow had been forecast, and he'd seen for himself that she wasn't dressed for the elements. She'd likely freeze to death and the amount of aggravation that would cause didn't bear thinking about. But to have a Murphy in his home was asking for trouble. He wouldn't be surprised if they woke up in the morning to find that she'd cleared them out. And then there was the other issue to contend with: her surname. The Murphys he could deal with; they were nothing but bullies, but when it came to the Tempests, did he really want to feel the full force of Ricky and Jamie's wrath if something were to happen to the girl? Not that they were particularly close if the rumours were anything to go by.

'Just one night,' Rina crooned as she stood on her tiptoes to plant a kiss on her husband's cheek.

In two minds, Archie scratched his chin. 'One night,' he growled. 'Then I want her gone.'

Rina beamed, and flicking the switch for the kettle to boil, she took out a mug from the cupboard then reached up to collect a jar of hot chocolate.

'I mean it Rina,' Archie said, narrowing his eyes as he watched his wife make their guest a hot drink. 'One night.'

When his wife didn't answer, Archie sighed. He could feel the start of a blinding headache beginning to form above his right temple and rubbed the heel of his palms over his aching eyes in an attempt to relieve the pressure. What with having Frankie Gammon to contend with, the last thing he needed was the added stress of having the Tempest brothers breathing heavily down his neck, not that they had ever needed an excuse to throw their weight around. No, if he knew the brothers as well as he thought he did then he knew for a fact they wouldn't hold back when it came to dishing out their own form of retribution if something were to happen to the girl. They would view their sister's predicament as a personal afront to themselves. Despite her being raised by the Murphys, she was still a Tempest, and it was Terry Tempest's blood that ran through each of their veins.

Wearily, Archie made his way back down the stairs, thankful

that the bell for last orders had already been rung; he wasn't in the mood for pleasantries, let alone plastering a smile across his face, a smile that he didn't believe he had in him. The only thing Archie knew for certain was that something had to give and fast before he ended up blowing a gasket.

3

Mason Tempest was laughing so hard that he was almost bent over. At the age of twenty-four, he was a handsome man with dark hair, startling blue eyes, and a tall, solid physique. It was often said that he was like the spit out of his father Ricky's mouth, but that was where the similarities ended. When it came to personality, Mason took after his uncle Jamie. And just like Jamie, he was reckless and had a quick temper on him, one that had repeatedly landed him in trouble over the years, much to his parents' chagrin.

'Is this prick for real?' Mason dragged the back of his hand across his eyes, all the while resisting the urge to smash a screwdriver into the gaunt, pockmarked face of the man before them.

'It would appear so.' Lounging back on a leather high backed office chair, Jamie Tempest looked incredibly bored as he slowly twirled the seat from side to side. Unlike Mason, he'd been in the enforcing game for a great number of years and had been a lot younger than Mason was when he'd first been introduced to the life by his dad, Terry Tempest. And during those years, he'd heard every excuse known to man as to why a debt couldn't be repaid on time.

'I… I swear to you,' Kane Watson stuttered as he looked between Jamie and Mason, terror resonating across his face. 'On my kids' lives I was going to bring you your money, I swear to God I was.'

Jamie narrowed his eyes. As a father of two young daughters himself, the fact Watson had brought his own children into the equation was enough to make Jamie see red. Getting to his feet, he took a menacing step across the taxi cab office that he and his brother owned and pulled back his fist. 'Don't you ever,' he snarled, 'use your kids as a reason to piss me off even further, have you got that? The piss poor, pathetic excuse of a life that you live is on you and if I so much as hear you even refer to your children in my presence again, I swear before God that I will cut your fucking tongue out,' he roared.

'I'm sorry,' Kane screamed. 'I didn't mean to, honest I didn't, but I'm telling the truth. You have to believe me.' Squeezing his eyes shut tight, he brought his skinny arms over his head in an attempt to protect himself from Jamie's onslaught. The pus encrusted track marks that dotted his forearms were bright red and weeping under the fluorescent light.

Jamie wrinkled his nose in disgust. The stark sight of Watson's drug abuse was enough to make him want to recoil, or at the very least make a mental note to remind himself to disinfect everything Watson had touched. And as for actually putting his hands on the dirty bastard, the mere thought was enough to make Jamie internally shudder. His gaze snapped down to Kane's tattered trainers; what was the betting his feet were dotted with the same scabby track marks?

'I swear to you man, I'm not lying. I had every intention of bringing you the money but he nabbed me off the street before I could get here.' As he cautiously opened one eye, Kane's body continued to convulse, his need for a fix outweighing the fear he felt at being in the Tempests' company, which by rights, given their reputations, should have been enough to make him feel more than just a little bit terrified. 'He told me to tell you that he said hello.'

It wasn't the first time Jamie had been given the exact same excuse as to why someone couldn't pay up, but there was something about the quiver in Kane's voice that told him he could actually be telling the truth.

'Fuck this shit, the dirty skank is trying to have us over.'

As Mason made a grab for the screwdriver, Jamie slammed his hand over his nephew's, stopping him from following through with the assault. 'Who?' he snarled. 'Who took the money?'

Kane swallowed deeply. His protruding Adam's apple bobbed up and down while his fearful gaze bounced between Jamie and Mason. 'It was Frankie... Frankie Gammon.' Tears sprang to his eyes, and he subconsciously began to scratch at his arms, his grimy fingernails ripping the paper-thin skin to shreds in a matter of moments. 'He threatened to pull my teeth out with pliers if I didn't hand the cash over, and I need my teeth man, I need to be able to eat.'

'The no-good fucker,' Mason hissed.

Without answering, Jamie lifted his eyebrows. Considering Kane's teeth resembled that of a burnt-out fuse box, perhaps Frankie would be doing him a favour. If nothing else, it would stop others from having the misfortune of Watson's rancid breath being forced upon them. Tearing his eyes away from the smears of blood that covered Kane's nicotine-stained fingers, Jamie took a step backwards and crossed his arms over his chest. 'And Gammon specifically told you to mention his name?'

Kane nodded so furiously that Jamie wouldn't have been surprised if he gave himself whiplash.

'I told you I'd heard rumours Gammon was throwing his weight around,' Mason said, screwing up his face. Pulling his mobile phone from out of his pocket, he nodded down at the device. 'I'll get on the blower to Dad and let him know the score.'

Thinking the situation over, Jamie continued to study Kane. Despite the fact his gaunt face was littered with fresh bruises, bringing further testament to the fact that he could very well be telling the truth and that he had been robbed of their money, he was still a junkie and it was no secret that they would sell out their own grandmothers for the price of a fix. 'If I find out you're lying to me,' he warned.

'I'm not,' Kane was all too quick to answer. 'Hand on heart,' he cried, placing his grubby hand on his stained T-shirt. 'I swear I'm telling the truth. I wouldn't lie to you man.' He swallowed again, the sound loud in the small confines of the office. 'I'd have to be some kind of an idiot, wouldn't I, if I thought that I would get away with trying to mug you off.'

Motioning for his nephew to pass across the mobile phone, Jamie jerked his head toward the office door. 'Get out,' he hissed, his steely gaze not wavering from Kane's gaunt face. 'And seeing as I'm feeling generous, you've got twenty-four hours to bring me my cash before I end up losing my temper. And trust me,' he said, thrusting a stiff finger forward. 'If I have to come looking for you then believe me when I say this, I'm going to hunt you down like the rabid dog you are and I will do more than just hurt you, I'll have you screaming so fucking hard that you'll beg me to end your sorry excuse of a life.'

Kane almost fell over his own two feet in his haste to escape from them and as he ran to the door, he steepled his hands in front of his chest. 'Thank you, Mr Tempest,' he cried, averting his face in a bid to disguise the glint of excitement shining in his eyes at the prospect of his next fix.

Not bothering to answer, Jamie kicked the door closed then

brought his nephew's mobile phone up to his ear. 'Bruv,' he sighed. 'Looks like we might have a bit of a problem.'

* * *

Bringing his car to a screeching halt outside the taxi firm he and Jamie had owned for a number of years, Ricky Tempest jumped out of the motor and bounded across the pavement. The business was a nice little earner, not that supplying taxis was their main source of income; it would be fair to say, however, that it was a good, legitimate cover for their real business dealings. Debt collecting.

'What's going on?' Ricky asked as he entered the office.

Jamie looked up, and lifting his eyebrows, he flicked his head towards the window. 'Some dough that should have been working its way into our hands was intercepted.'

The nerve at the side of Ricky's jaw pulsated. 'How much money are we talking about?'

'Not a lot,' Mason answered with a shrug. 'A few measly quid, hardly worth us losing any sleep over.'

'And we wouldn't have,' Jamie conceded, 'if it wasn't for the fact Frankie Gammon had the audacity to take what is ours.'

'Gammon?' Ricky's eyes narrowed. 'Since when did Gammon become an enforcer?'

'Since now, by the look of things.' As he stared out of the window, Jamie toyed with his mobile phone. 'None of this is sitting right with me,' he said, turning to look back at his brother. 'Why would he use Watson to deliver the message? The man can just about remember his own name. He injects that much shit into his veins, I'm surprised he can even function let alone string a coherent sentence together. And you're right about one thing,' he added, nodding in Ricky's direction. 'This isn't Gammon's game, so why is that slimy fucker stepping on our toes?'

For a few moments, Ricky was quiet then, pulling out a chair, he sank down, his mind going into overdrive. 'Are you sure Watson wasn't trying to pull the wool over your eyes?'

Jamie groaned. 'Do I look stupid?' He paused for a moment then shook his head. 'Actually don't bother answering that.' Sitting forward in the chair, he rested his forearms on the desk, mulling the situation over. 'Gammon made a point of ensuring his name was mentioned; the question is, why? He's bound to know that we're not going to sit back and let him walk all over us.'

'Maybe that's what he wants,' Mason volunteered. 'He wants us to retaliate.'

'Yeah maybe.' Running his tongue across his teeth, Jamie gave an irritated sigh. 'But why would he want that? Let's face it, Gammon is small time. The last I heard, he was peddling pills and popping them out at the school gates, two for a tenner. And that right there should tell you everything you need to know about the man, that he's scum. So how has he gone from that to trying to muscle in on our territory?'

'He could have backing?' Mason lifted his shoulders in a shrug and looked between his father and uncle. 'It's a possibility.'

Jamie waved his hand dismissively. 'Who in their right mind would back Gammon? Nah,' he said, flopping back in the chair and chewing on the inside of his cheek. 'There's more to this than meets the eye and believe me, when I get my hands on the little scrote, he's going down.'

Ricky couldn't help but laugh out loud. With his brother on the warpath, then all he could say was fuck Gammon's luck. On a good day, Jamie had little to no patience and the fact Frankie Gammon had had the audacity to try and tuck them up was a good enough reason for Jamie to give him a pounding that he wouldn't forget in a hurry. It would even be fair to say that Ricky had a feeling things were about to get downright nasty, at least for Gammon anyway.

And as Jamie had already pointed out, Frankie Gammon was scum, the type of man who in any normal circumstance they wouldn't have given the time of day let alone willingly had any interaction with. But seeing as he was now on their radar, it would be a case of when not if they caught up with him. 'I'm actually looking forward to having it out with the ponce.'

Lifting an eyebrow Jamie laced his fingers together and cracked his knuckles. 'Not as much as I am bruv.' He winked. 'It's been a long time since we had a tear up. In fact, I've got a feeling' – he grinned – 'that Frankie Gammon will soon see the error of his ways, especially once I've beaten seven bells of shit out of the no-good bastard.'

Ricky didn't doubt Jamie in the slightest; when his brother lost his temper, it was a sight to behold, so much so that he almost felt sorry for Gammon, but only almost. After all, it was no secret that Jamie was ruthless and only loyal to a select few. He'd even murdered someone who by rights should have been untouchable, someone whose blood matched their own, not that their half-brother Raymond Cole had ever deserved their loyalty. Right from the off Raymond had done nothing but plot and scheme against them. He'd wanted to tear them apart and see them suffer, and he'd almost succeeded too, but not before he and Jamie had been left with no other choice than to end his life. To this day Ricky didn't know what had become of his half-brother's corpse, and if he was being entirely honest with himself, he didn't want to know either.

As the years had gone by, he and Jamie had scarcely discussed Cole's demise; the subject had almost become taboo between them, and was a part of their past that neither one of them wanted to revisit any time soon. The only thing Ricky knew to be a fact was that Jamie had been the one to dish out the final blows, and had then disposed of Cole's body, someplace he would never be found. And good riddance to the bastard too. If Cole had had his way, he would have murdered them all, including his and Jamie's mother, Tracey, and Ricky's wife, Kayla. Even his son Mason wouldn't have been off limits, and he had only been a small child at the time, an innocent. Was it any wonder that Mason had grown up to be as ruthless as his uncle? Not only had he witnessed the murder of his paternal grandfather but his uncle had also plotted his demise along with the rest of the Tempest family. Popping an ever-present piece of nicotine replacement gum into his mouth, Ricky chewed thoughtfully before returning Jamie's grin. 'I can't wait,' he said, lounging back in the chair as if he didn't have a care in the world. 'The quicker Gammon has been dealt with, the better it will be for everyone concerned.'

4

From out of the corner of his eye, Archie Taylor studied Terri. Everything about her was dainty, from the way she nibbled on a slice of toast, to the way she nervously pushed a lock of dark hair out of her eyes. If he hadn't known any better, he would have sworn there was no way she could be related to the Murphy family. From what he was able to make out, they were like chalk and cheese. While the Murphys were loud mouthed thugs, the girl sitting across from him at the kitchen table gave the appearance of a rabbit caught in the headlights of a car.

Not taking his eyes away from the girl, Archie cleared his throat. 'Rina tells me you're Bianca Murphy's daughter.'

Terri's head snapped up and for the briefest of moments Archie saw fear reflected in her blue eyes before she timidly averted her gaze and nodded.

'Well...' Taking a large bite of his toast, Archie chewed before swallowing. 'I expect your mother will be expecting you home soon.'

Terri nodded and, dropping the piece of toast back onto the

plate, she gave an involuntary shiver. 'I expect so,' she answered, her voice low and her shoulders drooping.

'Well, whenever you're ready.' He jerked his head towards the kitchen door. 'I wouldn't want to give your family any more of a reason to be worried about you.'

'Leave the girl be, she's not even finished her breakfast yet,' Rina scolded, glaring at her husband. 'At least let her eat first before you think about throwing her out; the poor little mite's barely touched her food.' She turned to give Terri a gentle smile. 'Don't mind him.' She winked, lowering her voice to a playful whisper. 'His bark is far worse than his bite. Now come on, eat up.'

Stifling a groan, Archie swallowed down a large gulp of his tea before giving the clock on the wall a surreptitious glance. He wanted the girl gone, preferably before he opened up the pub. The last thing he needed was for anyone to actually see her, especially the gossip mongers who'd have a field day, and already he could imagine the rumours that were bound to circulate. After draining his drink, he scraped back his chair and got to his feet, his broad frame appearing far too large for the kitchen. 'We open in an hour,' he reminded his wife with a jerk of his head towards the hallway, the hidden meaning behind his words not lost on either of the women. 'So maybe it would be best if she got off home before the Murphys send out a search party.'

Rina flapped her hand dismissively. 'That's right,' she called out to his retreating back. 'We open in an hour and those barrels won't change themselves, will they.'

It took everything in Archie to bite back a retort. He knew Rina's game; he'd been married to the woman for long enough to know what went on in that head of hers. She was the human equivalent of a mother hen clucking around her chick, only Terri wasn't their child, wasn't their responsibility and never would be. By circumstances out of their control, he and Rina were childless and always would be. If he'd had his way they would have had a house full of children, perhaps even as many as to make up a football team. Over the years he'd seen the longing in his wife's eyes each and every time one of their siblings had welcomed a new child or grandchild into the world, and he'd stood by feeling helpless, knowing there was nothing he could do to ease her pain. No matter how much they may have wanted a family of their own, it wasn't meant to be, and they had been left with no other choice but to make the most out of the life they'd been so cruelly dealt. A familiar wave of sadness washed over him, and just as quickly, Archie pushed it away again. Their longing for a child had almost ripped apart their marriage, and as each month that passed had turned into years, their hope of having a family of their own had faded too, leaving in its place nothing but disappointment and bitterness. Somehow, although to this day Archie wasn't sure how, their marriage had survived. When it came down to it, all he had was Rina, she was the only woman he had ever wanted, and in their own way they made their marriage work, they were a partnership and he would even go as far as to say that Rina was his best friend, although at times he could happily throttle the life out of her, such as now for example.

Still grumbling to himself, he made his way behind the bar and began straightening out the glasses, more so out of habit than for any other reason. Satisfied that everything was as it should be, he unlocked the cellar door, yanked on the cord for the light, then ducked his head in order to descend the concrete steps that led down to the cellar. A loud pounding on the pub door made Archie stop dead in his tracks, his heartbeat picking up pace as he looked over his shoulder. For a brief moment he closed his eyes, irritation sweeping through him. He was in half a mind to ignore the knocking; they weren't due to open for another hour, not that it would do him any good in the grand scheme of things. Frankie Gammon was a persistent bugger and he'd proven that fact time and time again.

'All right, I'm coming,' he shouted out as he climbed back up the steps and slammed the cellar door shut behind him.

Within seconds, he was across the pub and unlocking the door, the scowl across his face more than enough to alert anyone with half a brain cell that he wasn't in the mood to be messed with.

'Archie.' Frankie Gammon breezed across the threshold with his henchman swiftly following close behind. 'I was beginning to think that you were ignoring me,' he said with a wide, calculated smile spread across his round face. 'That you'd forgotten our arrangement.'

Archie's lips curled into a snarl. They had no arrangement, at least nothing they had actually agreed on. Gammon had barked out his orders and expected Archie to follow through whether he wanted to or not.

'You owe me.' Frankie continued to look around him, his fox-like, sly eyes taking in the pub's fixtures and fittings as though he were calculating how much everything was worth. 'And you wouldn't want to make me angry, would you?'

'I owe you fu—' Before Archie could finish the sentence, Frankie flicked his head towards the bar, indicating for his henchmen to swipe the optics, glasses, and anything of any value to the floor.

A combination of both helplessness and anger flowed though Archie's veins. He was no walkover and yet the knowledge that his Rina was upstairs and potentially in danger made acrid bile rise up in his throat. It was no secret that Gammon was unhinged, that he got a kick out of intimidating those he believed to be weaker than himself. Without even thinking the consequences through, Archie flung his hand out, grasped Frankie around his throat then proceeded to slam him heavily against the wall. The scent of cheese and onion crisps permeating from Frankie's breath invaded Archie's nostrils. 'Get out of my pub,' he growled, his voice low and menacing. 'You're not welcome in here.'

Despite the fact Frankie's plump cheeks turned a darker shade of red as he grappled for air, a cruel smirk tugged at the corners of his lips, his gaze focusing on something or rather someone over Archie's shoulder.

The hairs on the back of Archie's neck prickled and as he turned his head, the sight of his Rina and Terri standing in the doorway that separated the pub from their home made his heart sink to his boots. The fear across Rina's face was enough to break him and dropping his hand, he took a reluctant step away from Frankie.

'I thought as much.' Frankie smirked. Straightening out his jacket, he looked Rina up and down, his tongue snaking out across his top lip in a provocative gesture.

Beside him, Archie clenched his fists into tight balls. All it would take was one punch and Frankie would drop to the floor like a sack of potatoes. Contemplating doing just that, Archie glanced towards the henchmen. It didn't take a genius to tell him that he was severely outnumbered, that his actions would have consequences, that he would end up putting Rina even further at risk.

'So this is how things are going to pan out Archie my old son.' Frankie grinned as he prised open the till and began pocketing handfuls of notes and coins. 'Every week, you and your good lady wife,' he said, nodding towards Rina, 'are going to hand over 500 nicker to ensure that this lovely establishment of yours doesn't burn down to the ground.'

Archie's heart sank. They didn't have 500 pounds to spare each week, not once they'd paid out the brewery and any other overheads that they might have. Not that he actually had any intentions of willingly handing over his hard-earned cash, and if Frankie thought otherwise, then he was severely lacking when it came to brain cells.

As if sensing the turmoil running through Archie's mind, Frankie spread open his arms and gestured around him. 'It's a small price to pay.' He shrugged. 'I mean, I can't be any more generous than I'm already being. I could just as equally up the price to say, I don't know...' He shrugged again, the same sickening smirk filtering back across his face. 'Maybe we could make it a grand, how would that suit you?'

'We'll pay the 500,' Rina piped up, her voice quivering as she silently beseeched her husband not to argue the case.

Frankie chuckled and stabbing his finger in Rina's direction, he gave a salacious wink. 'See, she knows the score, she's a clever woman your wife.' He clicked his finger towards his henchmen and beckoned for them to follow him out of the pub. 'This time next week Arch' – he slapped Archie on the back, his eyes hard – 'I'll be back to collect what's mine, so make sure you have my money ready for me, because' – he glanced towards where the optics had once stood – 'as you can see, I'm not a patient man and you really don't want to upset me. Oh, and one more thing...' He grinned. 'No running your mouth off to the old bill.' He made a slicing action across his throat, the threat hanging heavy in the air. 'I'm sure that I don't need to remind you of what happens to snitches.'

* * *

Once Frankie had left the pub, Terri physically jumped as Archie went on to slam the door closed then hastily slipped the locks back into place. Instinctively her hand reached out for Rina's, her breath catching in her throat. It wasn't so much Frankie who had scared her but rather one of his henchmen. She would have recognised him anywhere, and as much as his face had been covered by a makeshift balaclava, the hint of a pale pink scar that peeped out above the thin material was enough to tell her that it was her uncle Michael. And even more than that, his cold eyes that had raked her over were enough to alert her to the fact that he'd seen her, too. That he now knew where she'd hidden for the night to escape from his clutches.

'The bastard,' Archie seethed, his face almost purple with rage. 'The no-good, fucking bastard.'

After giving Terri's hand a gentle squeeze Rina released her grip then rushed around the bar and flung herself into her husband's arms.

'We should go to the police,' she cried. 'We can't let him get away with this.'

'And how would that be of any to help us?' Archie roared back, prising his wife away from him. 'You all but agreed to his demands. Besides, you heard yourself what the bastard said, he'll come back and burn us down, nothing will be left, and that means no pub, and no livelihood. We'll be finished.'

Wringing her hands together, Rina stared up at her husband. 'But we can't just stand by and do nothing. This is our home. It's all we've got. Every penny we have to our names has been ploughed into this place.'

Still standing in the doorway, Terri bit down on her bottom lip. The despair in Rina's voice tugged at her heart strings. Rina had been good to her; she'd taken her in when most people would have turned her away. The tiny woman had even gone up against her husband on Terri's behalf, and although Terri hadn't been able to hear much of their conversation, she'd heard enough to know that Archie hadn't been happy about the situation, that he hadn't wanted her to stay the night. Not that she entirely blamed him; not only was she a stranger but she was also a Murphy, and considering her family's reputation, she didn't blame Archie for his reservations.

Her mind wandered to her uncle. Should she tell Rina and Archie that she had recognised Michael as being one of the henchmen? Perhaps she could even plead with her uncle, explain to him that Rina and Archie couldn't afford Frankie Gammon's demands. Would her pleas even help, and more to the point would Michael care. He detested her and was hellbent on seeing her harmed. Would her presence at the pub only antagonise him and bring Rina and Archie further ramifications? But if the police were informed then just maybe it would be enough to see Michael sent back to prison, perhaps this time for life? Clearing her throat, she took a step forward. 'My uncle Michael,' she said, her voice barely louder than a whisper. She glanced down to where the optics had been smashed to smithereens, the spilt alcohol creating a sticky puddle on the wooden floor. 'He was one of the men. I recognised him...'

Archie's eyes hardened, and his lips curled into a snarl. Before Terri knew what was happening, he'd charged around the bar, gripped her by the shoulders and begun to roughly shake her. 'Is that why you turned up here?' he demanded as spittle gathered at the corners of his lips, bringing further testament to just how angry he was. 'Did they send you here to be their mole, to gather information on us?'

Tears slipped down Terri's cheeks, her heart beating so hard and fast that she could scarcely breathe. 'No,' she cried out in fear. 'No, I would never do something like that.'

'Archie!' The alarm in Rina's voice was evident as she desperately pulled on her husband's arm. 'Stop,' she begged him. 'She's nothing but a child; of course she had no part in this.'

It was on the tip of Terri's tongue to remind them that she wasn't a child, that she was almost twenty-one, an adult. But on seeing the anger still resonating across Archie's face, she forced her lips to stay firmly clamped together.

'She's no child,' Archie seethed. 'She's a Murphy. You know as well as I do what they're like; they're scum, the whole bloody lot of them. What makes this one here any different?'

Terri blushed a deep shade of red, shame coursing through her veins. Archie was right, her family were scum. Why should he expect her not to be cut from the same cloth?

'I swear to you.' A lone tear slipped down her cheek and she hastily swiped it away. 'I'm not like my family. I had no idea that Michael would turn up here, that he could be involved in something like this.'

His face still a mask of anger, Archie shoved Terri away from him. 'I want her gone,' he reiterated to his wife. 'And the sooner the better. And as for that family of hers, they're barred for life, have you got that?' he yelled, stabbing his finger forward. 'I don't want to see hide nor hair of them anywhere near here again.'

As they watched Archie storm out of view, Terri's shoulders heaved. 'It's okay,' she sniffed as Rina made to wrap her arms around her. 'I'll... I'll leave.' Fresh tears filled her eyes and she allowed them to slip freely down her cheeks. Where would she even go? She couldn't go home, she knew that much. Perhaps if Rina was to lend her a coat she could wander the streets, maybe even find a secluded spot to sleep the night. 'Archie is right,' she cried. 'And the last thing I would ever want to do is bring you even more trouble.'

'Oh no you will not,' Rina huffed. 'It might be Archie's name above that door,' she said, jerking her thumb in the direction of the entrance door. 'But I've got as much right to have who I want in my home as he does.'

'I will not send you back to your family, at least not until I know that you'll be safe.' She gave a gentle smile and lifted a lock of hair away from Terri's face. 'Everything is going to be okay my darling. Archie will soon calm down and see that you had no part in this. He may act like a caveman at times,' she said, laughing, 'but he isn't completely blind as to what's going on around him. He'll soon come to realise that you're innocent, you just wait and see.'

Despite the warmth in Rina's voice, Terri couldn't help but hear the anguish there too. With Frankie Gammon barking the odds, demanding protection money, and her uncle Michael hellbent on seeing her harmed, possibly even dead, it wasn't going to be okay and Terri knew that as well as she knew her own name.

5

Michael Murphy was in his element. It felt good to be back in the game, to be a part of something big, and it couldn't get any bigger than working for Frankie Gammon. He'd been handpicked by Gammon himself, headhunted you could even say. The very thought was enough to make Michael smile even wider. And as for spotting his niece hiding out at the boozer, the sight of her terrified face when she'd recognised him was almost enough to make Michael want to piss himself from excitement. He rubbed his hands together with glee, imagining all the ways he was going to bring the little bitch to her knees. She thought she was so much better than him. Oh, she might not have said it to his face, but he'd seen it in her eyes. It was that Tempest blood she had running through her veins; her old man had been exactly the same, and as for her half-brothers, they were two jumped up pricks if ever he'd seen them. It was almost as though they believed that their own shit didn't stink. Well Michael had news for Ricky and Jamie Tempest, they stunk just the same as everyone else.

Lounging on a chair in Frankie's flat in Dagenham, Essex,

Michael grinned. 'We showed him who's boss, all right. And if he knows what's good for him, Archie Taylor will pay up.'

Frankie didn't answer and as he absentmindedly chewed on his thumbnail, staring into the distance, his shoulders were hunched.

Michael narrowed his eyes, his hard gaze scrutinising Frankie's demeanour. He'd fully expected him to be celebrating Taylor's downfall, and Michael was in the mood for a party. For the past ten minutes he'd been eyeing up two rucksacks that had been slung into the corner of the lounge. They were filled to the brim with narcotics and he'd give anything to lay his hands on the pills Frankie dished out at the school gates. He could do with a buzz and by all accounts the gear Frankie sold was top notch. But instead of the euphoric atmosphere Michael had been anticipating, there was a hint of nervousness in the air – why that was exactly, Michael couldn't quite tell. If he hadn't known any better, he would have sworn that Frankie looked as though he had the world and its troubles weighing him down, as though he were the one who was being hounded for protection money, not Archie Taylor.

'What's with you?' Michael barked out. 'We're on the up; it's time to party.' He reached into a carrier bag and took out a can of lager, snapped open the pull ring, then guzzled down half the contents before belching loudly.

The sound of the pull ring snapping open broke Frankie's reverie and turning his head, he glared. 'This ain't the time for you to be getting pissed out of your nut,' he spat.

'What do you mean?' Michael's eyebrows knotted together, his spine snapping a little straighter. 'We've got that old fucker Archie running scared; we're gonna be rolling in dough. We should be celebrating.'

A sneer creased Frankie's face and turning to look back at the door, he tilted his head to the side as though he were listening out for someone approaching.

His back instantly up, Michael followed Frankie's gaze. 'What's going on?' he asked as he gripped on to the arms of the chair, his knuckles turning white. Was this some kind of set up? Had Frankie double crossed him? Paranoia engulfed Michael and he was in half a mind to jump out of his seat, clench his fists into tight balls and start throwing punches. Whilst he'd been in prison, he'd had his fair share of run-ins with those he'd considered to be an ally but who had eventually betrayed his trust and stabbed him in the back. Was history about to repeat itself? Was he about to find himself on the receiving end of some vendetta? It was only the fact that Frankie looked anxious, as though he were actually fearful, that stopped Michael from pummelling the life out of him.

The sound of loud knocking on the front door was enough to fill Michael with dread, and as the apprehension around him intensified, his body involuntarily stiffened.

'Keep your mouths shut,' Frankie barked out in a warning, his hard eyes looking at each of his men in turn. 'And remember, let me do the talking.'

The colour that was rapidly draining from Frankie's face didn't bode well. Could it be the old bill coming for them? Had that old fucker Archie got on the blower to the filth? Or could his earlier intuition have been correct and Frankie had actually been the one to have tucked them all up. What if the whole situation had been an elaborate set-up from the off, a sure way to put him back behind bars once and for all? And considering he'd been caught bang to rights, all thanks to the pills nestled inside the rucksacks, he was bound to have the book thrown at him. As for the filth, he'd put nothing past them; they were well known to use underhand tactics and it was common knowledge that they relied on snouts for their information. Only, in the short time Michael had known him, he'd never suspected Frankie to be in the old bill's pocket. And the fact he made a living selling speed and ecstasy to kids was hardly something the police would turn a blind eye to, was it?

The front door swung open and Michael's heart pounded inside his chest. Panic was beginning to get the better of him and as every instinct inside of Michael told him to make a run for it, he braced himself to have it away on his toes, not that he was likely to get very far he conceded. He'd be lucky if he made it more than ten feet away from the front door before finding himself face down on the concrete, his arms wrenched behind his back and handcuffs snapped on his wrists.

Beads of perspiration coated Michael's top lip and forehead and the feeling of dread engulfed him. Instinctively he knew the game was up. He'd been in an all too familiar situation before and just like then, he could almost feel the anticipation spreading through his veins, as though he were a tightly coiled spring ready and waiting to be released. More than anything Michael didn't want to go back to prison. He'd rather die than serve out another lengthy sentence and the mere thought of losing his freedom all over again was enough to make him want to scream out loud at the injustice of it all. He couldn't go back to being locked up for twenty-three hours of the day and being treated no better than a caged animal, and as for sharing a cell again, and having no other choice but to breathe in another man's body odour, excrement and piss for the remainder of his life was enough to make his stomach sink down to his boots.

Much to Michael's relief, instead of the old bill that he'd been fully expecting, a man stood in the doorway and he was big too, possibly one of the biggest men Michael had ever seen. Not only was he tall but from where Michael was sitting he could see that his body was formed of solid muscle.

For the briefest of moments Michael could do nothing but stare. He gave a shake of his head, snapped his slack jaw closed and rubbed at his eyes, certain that they were playing tricks on him. No.

A bubble of hysteria began to rise within him. No, it couldn't be true. He looked around him, his eyes almost bulging out of his head. The man was supposed to be dead; he knew that for a fact because Bianca had made a big song and dance about it at the time. There had even been a funeral, not that he'd actually attended, but Bianca had and if anything had been amiss, or if she'd had her suspicions that the funeral wasn't kosher then she would have told him. And even more than that, there was no way in hell that Bianca would have been able to keep something so colossal to herself; even on a good day her mouth was bigger than Blackwall tunnel.

Still too stunned to speak, Michael jumped out of the chair and took a step backwards, almost colliding with the men behind him in the process. 'What the fuck is going on?' he finally hissed, his breath coming out in short sharp, ragged bursts. 'How is...' He swallowed deeply, not taking his eyes away from the man before him. How could this be possible? How could he not have aged in all the years since he'd last seen him? He'd been pushing fifty back then and had in actual fact been murdered on his fiftieth birthday and yet almost twenty years later his face was still free from wrinkles, and his hair still dark without a single grey hair peppering his head. 'How the fuck is Terry Tempest still alive?'

Frankie swung his head around to look at Michael, his furrowed forehead accentuating his beady eyes that at that precise moment in time were shooting Michael a glare sharp enough to cut glass. 'What are you talking about?' he snapped. 'This is Raymond Cole you stupid fucker, not Terry Tempest.' He swallowed deeply then turned back to look at the man in question, his lips twitching nervously. 'I've been expecting you. Come on in.'

Raymond gave a chilling laugh and his voice when he spoke was low and menacing. 'As if you'd be able to stop me from doing otherwise.'

Frankie bowed his head, and with a sudden clarity Michael

understood exactly what was going on. For all his talk, Frankie wasn't the boss, he never had been. It was this man in front of them who they were working for, he was the one who held all of the power, and more importantly was the one they should be wary of.

With an air of arrogance Raymond stepped further into the house, his strides long and purposeful and his muscular frame appearing even more defined, as though he spent hours working out at the gym or rather, as Michael highly suspected, he shoved steroids down his throat by the bucketload. 'Well,' he demanded in a gruff voice. 'Bring me up to speed?'

'I...' A tremble racked Frankie's body and as his lips continued to quiver, he cleared his throat. 'I mean, we.'

'Today,' Raymond barked out with a glance at his watch. 'I haven't got all day to listen to you muttering and stuttering.'

His voice ever so slightly faltering, Frankie took a deep breath. 'We've done what you said, we've thrown our weight around.' He shot a glance towards his firm as though silently willing them to confirm that everything he said was true. 'We've been noticed.'

Raymond laughed even harder, the sound coming across as almost eerie in the small lounge. 'You've got their attention you mean?'

Frankie nodded, his teeth biting into his bottom lip so hard that Michael wouldn't be surprised if he drew blood.

'About fucking time,' Raymond answered with a curt nod. 'Have they made contact yet?'

Frankie shook his head, his eyes downcast, reminding Michael of a naughty school boy standing outside the headteacher's office. The scene before him was so surreal that he felt the urge to laugh, a huge belly laugh that would have him doubled over with tears streaming down his cheeks. Never had he imagined that he would see the day when Frankie Gammon was afraid, and he wasn't talking about the man being a little apprehensive, he looked absolutely terrified. It was so palpable that Michael could almost taste it.

As he continued to watch the exchange that took place before him, Michael's heart leapt. He still wasn't entirely sure what was going on, but putting two and two together, one thing he did know was that this, whatever this actually was, was so much bigger than he could have ever hoped for and he knew for a fact that he wanted in, that he wanted to be a part of the action. 'Who?' he piped up, excitedly. 'Whose attention have we got?'

All heads turned to look at him, and in that instant Michael wanted to kick himself. Him and his big mouth. It had always been his downfall, and just like Bianca, he never knew when to keep it closed. And not for the first time in his life had he made himself look like a first-class fool; not only that, but it was more than apparent that Frankie had purposely kept him in the dark, that despite being headhunted, Frankie obviously didn't trust him as far as he could throw him.

It was Raymond who finally answered. 'My father's sons.' He lifted his hand to his face, his fingertips lightly caressing the thick, faded, gnarled scar that ran from his temple to his jaw. A permanent reminder of his last encounter with his brothers. 'Ricky and Jamie Tempest,' he spat.

The words were like music to Michael's ears. Now everything made sense. No wonder he'd mistaken him to be Terry Tempest; he was Tempest's son, he could see it for himself now, and although they may have been subtle there were noticeable differences between the two men. Raymond was slightly taller for a start, not to mention his shoulders were broader. But other than that, the dark hair, blue eyes, and facial expressions were almost identical, and he knew for a fact that the Tempest genes were strong and he should know since he'd been forced to look at his niece on a daily basis for the past four years.

Stepping forward, he shoved out his hand. 'Any enemy of the Tempests is a friend of mine,' he said, grinning. 'It's because of those bastards that I served a lump, the best part of my life locked up like a caged animal. I was in my prime,' he continued. 'And I had a good future ahead of me. I could have been someone, I—'

'Shut the fuck up,' Frankie hissed between clenched teeth, his eyes silently warning Michael to take heed of his words.

Michael swallowed deeply. He looked down at his still outstretched hand then quickly dropped it to his side, the blatant snub causing his cheeks to redden. As much as he tried to avert his gaze, he couldn't help but stare at Cole or in particular the scar that ran down the length of his face. Intrigue gnawed away at Michael. How had he come by it, he wondered. Perhaps a blade, or some other tool. Whatever the method, it was pretty obvious that it would have been brutal. His fingers reached up to touch his own pale pink scar. In comparison it was nothing, a mere scratch and he felt almost foolish in thinking that it had given him an edge, that it had made him look all the more menacing.

Not taking his hard gaze away from Frankie and Raymond, Michael continued to watch the men from afar, the earlier excitement he'd felt once again flowing back through his veins. Despite Cole's indifference towards him, the day just got better and better. Not only did he have his niece running scared, but the fact Cole had an obvious beef with the Tempest brothers was enough to make him want to punch the air in delight.

Craftily, he cocked his head to one side. Seeing as Cole was Terry Tempest's son, did he know that he also had a younger half-sister, and even more than that, did he know that Michael was the said sister's uncle? Puffing out his chest with a measure of self-importance, Michael bit back a laugh. In a roundabout way he and Cole were family. Okay, so they may not have shared the same blood, but they did have a mutual family member in common, one who Michael was now determined to get on side, at least for appearances' sake anyway. He still despised the little bitch, still wanted to see her strung up, but if she was the means of an in with her half-brother then just maybe he would thaw towards her a little, or at least enough to become Cole's right-hand man, a position that he deserved and was more than capable of. After all, he was the head of the Murphy family. It went without saying that by rights he should have been at the very top of the pecking order. In fact, he would go as far as to say that Frankie Gammon should have been well and truly below him. When all was said and done, he was small time, a runt, and had little to no experience of how to run a firm, unlike Michael, who had a copious amount of experience.

Happier now that he had a plan of action in place, Michael retrieved another lager from the carrier bag. He felt like celebrating and he had a sneaky suspicion that from now on, life was on the up. If he was really lucky, he may even be able to kill two birds with one stone and with a little help from Raymond he might even be in the position of getting rid of the Tempest brothers along with his niece in one fell swoop.

6

Terri's ears were pricked and her back ram rod straight as she paced the small hallway at the bottom of the stairs that led up to the pub's accommodation. For more than thirty minutes Rina and Archie had been closeted away in their flat. And even though it was more than clear that they were arguing – or at least this was what Terri presumed if the harsh, clipped tones that wafted down the stairs were anything to go by – there had been no telltale thumps or screams to indicate that Archie had physically lashed out at his wife. And that was what usually happened following an argument, wasn't it? Or at least this was what happened within her own family. Violence was an everyday occurrence for the Murphys; it was the only way they knew how to communicate with one another. She'd actually lost count of how many times she'd woken up to see her grandmother with a split lip or blackened eye after she and Terri's grandfather had quarrelled. And as for her mother and uncles, they hit and kicked out at one another so often that Terri wouldn't be surprised if one day they actually murdered each other.

Moments later, Rina made her way down the stairs and on spotting Terri anxiously chewing on her thumbnail, she gave a smile.

'He can be stubborn bugger,' she proclaimed with an exaggerated sigh. 'But he never has been, nor will he ever be, a match for me.'

Terri's heart began to pound inside her chest. Did this mean Archie had agreed that she could stay a little longer, that he wouldn't be throwing her out on to the street after all?

'Don't look so scared,' Rina laughed as she slipped her arm through Terri's and guided her through to the bar area. 'I told you that his bark is far worse than his bite.' She leaned in closer and lowered her voice until it was a whisper. 'Beneath that hard exterior of his he's like a big fluffy teddy bear once you get to know him.'

Terri's eyes ever so slightly widened. From what she knew of him, Archie Taylor and teddy bear were words that didn't belong in the same sentence. He was more like a grizzly bear: imposing, gruff, and more importantly someone she wouldn't want to get on the wrong side of.

'So...' Placing her hands on her hips, Rina cocked an eyebrow. 'His lordship has agreed,' she said with a jerk of her head towards the ceiling, 'that you can stay here for as long as you need to.'

Relief surged through Terri's veins, and she felt an overwhelming need to burst into tears. The prospect of sleeping on a park bench exposed to the elements, not to mention any other horrors she may have come across, had all but terrified her. 'Really...?' Terri gulped down the hard lump in her throat, and her voice when she spoke came out as a strangled sob. 'And Archie is okay with me staying, he doesn't mind?'

Rina flapped her hand. 'Let me tell you a little something about my husband.' She gestured towards the thin gold wedding band on her ring finger. 'Do you see this?'

Narrowing her eyes, Terri nodded, unsure of where Rina was going with the conversation.

'Now just because we're married that doesn't mean that Archie rules the roost, nor does it mean that when he says jump, I ask how high. We're a partnership, always have been and that, my darling,' she giggled, 'means that my husband had better well remember that if he knows what's good for him. Besides.' She pouted. 'A little bit of womanly charm every now and then doesn't hurt anyone and seeing as it's me who cleans his shirts and puts the dinner on the table,' she said, leaning in closer and giving a wink, 'means that I will always have the upper hand where Archie Taylor is concerned.'

A burst of laughter escaped from Terri's lips and on hearing heavy footsteps descend the stairs, she clamped her hand over her mouth just in time as Archie rounded the bar.

Rina smiled brightly up at her husband. 'I was just telling Terri the good news.' She reached out and squeezed Terri's hand in a comforting gesture. 'That she's welcome to stay here for as long as she needs to.'

As she took in Archie's red cheeks, Terri held her breath, awaiting his response. To her dismay he didn't look quite as enamoured with the situation as his wife did. She cleared her throat to speak when Archie held up his hand, cutting her off.

'Just maybe,' he said with a glance towards Rina, 'you and me got off on the wrong foot. It was wrong of me to judge you by your family's association. And...' He gave Rina another glance, his cheeks turning even redder. Whether that was to bite his tongue to stop himself from blurting out his true thoughts or because he really did feel remorse Terri wasn't so sure, although she would put money on it being the former. No matter what Rina said, Terri knew that her presence wasn't entirely welcome, at least not where Archie was concerned, and she had a feeling in the pit of her stomach that until she proved him otherwise, he would continue to view her with a measure of distrust. 'I'm happy for you to stay here for as long as you need, provided that family of yours stays out of my way.'

Terri nodded, her heart lifting. 'I'll pay my way,' she said, looking between the couple. 'I could work behind the bar.' She looked across to the pumps and chewed on her bottom lip. She'd had several jobs since leaving school: a receptionist in a rundown hotel, an assistant in a nursery school, and she had even tried her hand at hairdressing, not that she'd lasted very long in that job as she hadn't been able to stomach the stench of perming lotion. So how hard could it be to pull a pint? 'Or I could collect the glasses and wipe down the tables. I'd even scrub out the toilets if you need me to.'

For the first time since laying his eyes on Terri, Archie's expression softened. 'We'll see.' He cast a glance at the empty spaces where the optics had once stood before Gammon's henchmen had swiped them to the floor. 'We won't be in a position to pay you much though,' he added with a measure of bitterness.

'I don't need paying,' Terri was quick to answer. 'I'll do it for free. All I need is a roof over my head, somewhere safe to stay.'

'Well, you've already got that sweetheart,' Rina chipped in. 'You'll be as safe as houses here. And don't you worry about food either. I'm sure that an extra couple of potatoes won't break the bank.'

The grin across Terri's face was so wide that her cheeks ached. She'd never had anyone want to do something nice for her before; come to think of it, she hadn't even had anyone care for her, not really. Her grandparents may have done their best in raising her, but they certainly wouldn't have won any parenting awards. It had been the child benefit money they had had their sights set on, not their granddaughter. And when it came to her mum, Bianca had never really showed much of an interest. The bond between mother and daughter was virtually non-existent. There had barely even been any physical contact between them, and Terri could count on one hand how many times Bianca had pulled her in for a hug, and even then it had only been because she'd wanted to get one over on

Michael, knowing just how much her daughter's existence grated on him.

As an image of her mother sprang to Terri's mind, the smile slipped from her face. Bianca was bound to kick off once she found out that Rina and Archie had taken her in. After the anger, and the screaming and the shouting, she was bound to put on the tears, and crocodile ones at that. No doubt she would claim that Terri had abandoned her family. It was laughable really; just the day before, the very same said family had tried to harm her, and other than shout at Michael, Bianca had stood by and done little else. She may as well have given Michael the green light to unleash his anger upon her for all she'd done to actually stop him lashing out at her only child.

'Well then.' Rina clapped her hands together, breaking Terri's reverie. 'Standing around chatting the day away won't get us anywhere, will it.' She tossed a damp cloth in Terri's direction. 'We'd best open this pub and you, young lady, can make a start by wiping down the tables.'

Terri grinned; she'd do more than just wipe down the tables. She was prepared to do anything and everything in her power to prove to Rina and Archie that she could be trusted, and more importantly that they hadn't made the biggest mistake of their lives by taking her in and giving her a home.

* * *

By the time the bell had been rung for last orders, Terri was exhausted. Her feet and back ached, not to mention her cheeks from how much she'd smiled throughout the day. Despite how hard she'd worked, she could honestly say that she'd found the whole experience exhilarating. No wonder Rina and Archie loved their jobs, and they were naturals too, often greeting the customers and not just the regulars as though they were old friends. But it was the atmosphere Terri loved the most, that and the sense of belonging.

No one had questioned why a Murphy was working at the pub, or at least as far as she was aware of. In fact, the customers had seemed to embrace her as one of their own, something that had taken her aback at first. She hadn't expected to be welcomed quite so easily. Some of the customers had even been downright cheeky and complimented her looks, telling both Rina and Archie that she was far too beautiful to be wiping down tables and that they should put her behind the bar. She'd laughed at that and glancing down at the jeans and sweatshirt Rina had loaned her, both of which were far too small considering there was at least a four-inch height difference between the two women, she couldn't quite see where the customers were coming from. Fair enough, she thought she was pretty in her own way, but she wasn't what she considered to be stunning, not like the models and influencers she'd seen on social media. Although she did have a nice figure she supposed, she wasn't too thin, had curves in all the right places, and had long, dark hair that was both thick and glossy.

At one point even Archie had complimented her. He'd told her that she was doing a good job and on hearing those words Terri had thought that her heart would burst with pride. More than anything she wanted to make them proud and wanted to prove to herself that she was worthy of their kindness, that she wasn't just another Murphy whose sole purpose in life was to look out for herself and not care one iota about anybody else.

As the last straggling customers left the pub, Rina locked the door then slipped off her high heels, her body sagging. 'My feet are bleeding killing me,' she complained as she lifted her knee and massaged the ball of her foot.

Terri smiled. She understood where Rina was coming from; her feet ached too and she hadn't even been wearing heels.

As Rina switched off the main lights, the strategically placed lighting above the optics encased the bar area in a soft glow. 'We'll clean this lot in the morning,' she said, casting her gaze over the tables still littered with used glasses. 'You did well today, you're a proper little natural. And as for that lot' – she jerked her thumb towards the door that the customers had exited through – 'they bloody loved you.'

'Does that mean I can work again tomorrow?'

'Too bloody right you can,' Rina laughed. Patting Terri's hand she cocked her head to the side, a playful expression filtering across her face. 'I'll tell you what,' she said, opening the fridge and plucking out a bottle of wine. 'We should have a little drink, celebrate your first day in your new job.'

Terri's eyes widened. Considering the family she came from, she'd never really been much of a drinker. It wasn't so much that she didn't like the taste of alcohol, but more so because she didn't want to follow in her mother's footsteps. At the best of times her mum was a disaster waiting to happen, but with a drink inside of her she became a downright nightmare and would think nothing of lashing out at her only daughter or anyone else within her vicinity come to that. Her nan had often stated that Bianca could cause a fight in an empty room, and it was true. Bianca thrived on creating animosity and more often than not wasn't happy until she'd riled her family up, especially her brother Kevin, who she'd often goad to the point that he saw red and would chase her around the house armed with one of his knives.

'Come on,' Rina coaxed. With the bottle of wine tucked underneath her arm, she reached out to collect two wine glasses. 'A glass or two won't kill you. Oh, and do me a favour darling, and grab a couple of bottles of beer for Archie.' A sad expression replaced her smile as she glanced to where the optics had stood. 'He needs a little something to help him unwind,' she sighed. 'Something to forget his troubles.'

Doing as she was asked, Terri collected the bottles then followed Rina up to the flat. As she entered the lounge, her shoulders instantly relaxed. Compared to her grandparents' house, the Taylors' home was cosy and welcoming and although the furniture may have been mismatched it just seemed to fit Rina and Archie's personalities to a tee.

Once they were settled on the sofa, Terri tucked her legs underneath her and sank back into the cushions. Taking a sip of her wine, she swallowed the liquid down and gave a satisfied sigh. 'I could get used to this,' she giggled.

From her position on the sofa, Rina leaned back on her elbow and studied Terri, a wide smile plastered across her face.

'What?' Terri asked, her cheeks flushing pink.

'Oh, it's nothing.' Still smiling, Rina waved her hand dismissively.

'No go on,' Terri coaxed. 'You were going to say something.'

'It's just... well...' Taking a sip of her wine, Rina shifted her position to look Terri in the eyes. 'How on earth did you turn out to be such a nice girl?' Realising what she'd just said, Rina slammed her hand over her mouth. 'Oh my God,' she cried. 'I can't believe I just said that out loud. I am so sorry darling. No matter what I or anyone else thinks of them they are still your family and I had no right to say something like that.'

'It's okay.' Terri's face fell and giving a shrug, she stared down at her wine glass and rubbed her thumb up and down the tiny beads of condensation, smearing them into obliteration. It wasn't the first time she'd been asked the exact same question and the truth was she didn't know how to answer. She'd always assumed that she had taken after her father but ever since Michael had dropped the bombshell that her dad had been the instigator behind the human trafficking scandal, she wasn't so sure any more. 'Can I ask you something?'

Rina nodded. 'Of course you can darling, fire away.'

Clearing her throat, Terri looked up. 'Did you ever meet my dad?' As she asked the question, she searched Rina's face. For what reason she wasn't so sure, the only thing she knew was that she had to know the truth. Could Michael have been lying, could her dad have been innocent of any wrongdoings? She better than anyone knew just how wicked his tongue could be and it was in his nature to be vindictive.

Rina sighed and as her husband walked into the room, she glanced up at him. 'Everyone knew your dad or at least they had heard of him. He was well known around here. I wouldn't say that I knew him well though,' she said as Archie made himself comfortable in the armchair opposite her. 'But from what I remember of him, Terry Tempest was a handsome bugger, a charmer too.' She grinned. 'Dark hair, bright blue eyes and the kind of smile that made women fall at his feet – and believe me, they did. He would have women queueing up to get his attention, not that I ever saw him complain,' she laughed. 'He was a hot-blooded man after all.' She lifted her eyebrows to look at her husband and stuck out her tongue. 'Like someone else I know, not mentioning any names.'

Rolling his eyes, Archie gave a disgruntled shake of his head. 'It's my job to talk to the customers. And you're a fine one to talk; every time I look at you, you're chewing someone's ear off.'

'Anyway,' Rina continued with a flap of her hand. 'I can only imagine that all of this attention must have stroked his ego. And you and your brothers all look like him too, same blue eyes, same smile, all three of you are his double. He would never have been able to deny he was your father I know that much. But...' She paused and took a deep breath, her expression becoming serious. 'He also had an edge about him, and the truth is despite the looks and the charm there was something about Terry that scared me.' She gave a little shudder and rubbed at the gooseflesh covering her arms. 'I'm not saying he would have ever harmed me, but he did have this vibe about him. Maybe it was my gut telling me I should steer clear of him. I don't know.' She waved her hand in the air, tilted her head to the side then looked into the distance as though she were reminiscing about her younger years. 'Whatever it was,' she said with a shake of her head, 'it made me feel uneasy around him.'

'So you didn't actually know him on a personal level?' Terri's heart sank.

'No, not exactly.' Rina looked across to Archie. 'We'd only had this place for a few months when he was murdered, six at the most, and prior to that whenever he came in, I did everything in my power to stay out of his way. I was young and naïve back then, and probably a little bit too timid to be running a pub on the outskirts of East London,' she laughed. 'I used to ask Archie or one of the barmaids to serve him, but you got on well with him, didn't you?' she added, turning her head to look back at her husband.

Terri's heart lifted. 'So you knew my dad then?' she asked, sitting forward on the sofa, her eyes flashing with excitement.

'I did.' Archie nodded. 'Or at least I knew the person he portrayed himself to be. And let me just say this, despite what Rina says, he wasn't as bad as some made him out to be, at least not on the surface anyway. He could be a gentleman when he wanted to be; it was how he fooled all of us into thinking he was a nice, decent bloke I suppose.'

'What do you mean he wasn't that bad?' Rina's mouth dropped open and she narrowed her eyes. 'What about that night when he threw that poor fella through the window? It was chaos,' she said, turning her attention back to Terri. 'There was glass everywhere, people screaming, and as for your dad.' She shook her head at the memory. 'I thought he was going to kill the poor man.'

Screwing up his face, Archie shook his head. 'The geezer deserved everything he'd had coming to him. Tempest had given him ample warning to back off and it was his choice to carry on goading him.'

'It was awful,' Rina mouthed to Terri. 'It took me hours to clean the blood out of the carpet.'

Terri's eyes widened at the mental image Rina had projected. She had always guessed that her father was no angel, but she had never imagined he could be so violent or dangerous.

'Terry may have had a rep,' Archie continued, 'and you certainly wouldn't have wanted to cross him, but he never looked for trouble per se, although it would be fair to say that trouble often found him. It went with the territory I suppose.' Archie shrugged then, lifting the bottle to his lips, he took a deep swig. 'He was involved with some pretty heavy people; the Carter family from over Barking way, Paul Mooney and his boys before they were murdered in cold blood just up the road from here, Moray Garner and Danny McKay. Men you really wouldn't want to make an enemy of but from what I could tell, your dad was well liked and respected. In the short time I knew him, he never gave me any reason to bar him, and other than that one time it kicked off and he hurled that geezer through the window he was usually on his best behaviour. It was that side kick of his that used to cause the most trouble. The atmosphere would change the moment he walked through the door, it was like walking on bleedin' eggshells.' Archie screwed up his face at the memory. 'Right from the get-go I knew there was something off about him; he would swan about as if he owned the place, it used to grate on my nerves I remember that much.'

'I'd forgotten all about him,' Rina piped up. 'Kenny Kempton,' she added, tipping her wine glass in Terri's direction. 'That was his name. He was your dad's business partner and a nasty piece of work to boot. It wouldn't surprise me if he was the one to have led your dad astray.'

'Leave it out,' Archie groaned. 'Terry Tempest wasn't the kind of man to be easily led. He wasn't coerced into forcing those women on the game; that was all his doing so don't be putting ideas into the girl's head. She needs to know the truth about her old man, that he could be a nasty bastard when the mood took him. If anything, it was the drugs that changed him; he lost all sense of decency once that shit was flowing through his veins.'

'Drugs?' Terri's eyes widened.

'Coke, pills, weed.' Archie answered. 'You name it, and he was on it. Besides, it was no secret that he was more often than not coked out of his nut.'

Terri swallowed deeply, shame coursing through her veins. It had been bad enough to learn that her father hadn't been the man she'd always believed him to be, but adding drugs to the mix was enough to leave her feeling horrified. Just how much of a monster had he been? 'I think...' She cleared her throat and shook her head. 'That deep down I always knew what he was like, I just didn't want to believe it. I mean' – she shrugged, not feeling an ounce of loyalty towards the woman she had the misfortune to call mother – 'you only have to take one look at my mum to know that my dad wasn't a good man. No decent man would ever want to get involved with her, would they?'

Archie gave a sad smile. 'You've got that much right,' he said, taking another sip of his beer. 'Despite his faults though, I was actually sorry to hear that Terry had been murdered, but then...' Archie sighed. 'Well, let's just say one or two things came to light, and the things that were being said weren't so nice; in fact, it was downright shocking. It changed my perspective on him I can tell you that much. At first, I didn't want to believe any of it was true, I'd waved it off as gossip; the man had been in my pub, I'd served him, spoke to him, and despite who he was I'd actually liked him. I'd even go as far as to say that I'd had a lot of respect for Terry Tempest.'

Her heart breaking that little bit more, Terri swallowed down the hard lump in her throat. 'But it was all true wasn't it,' she croaked out. 'My dad really did do those terrible things they accused him of.'

'He did,' Archie sighed again. 'From my understanding, there was more than enough evidence to suggest he'd been involved. It was your brothers Ricky and Jamie who I felt sorry for. They were only young at the time, not much older than you are now and I know that Terry's deceit had left them feeling devastated. It's understandable; they were close to their dad, used to follow him around like lost puppies. Terry would often make a joke out of it and call them his shadows.'

'And don't forget Tracey, Terry's wife,' Rina said, shaking her head. 'That poor woman had no idea what her husband had been getting up to behind her back. Night after night she shared a bed with that monster and all the while he'd been pimping out those poor girls and screwing just about anything with a pulse. It doesn't even bear thinking about does it. Talk about living a double life; the man had no morals,' she said, screwing up her face.

Terri's cheeks flamed red. Until now she had never questioned how her existence had come about. Had her dad been married whilst she'd been conceived? Had he and her mum had an illicit affair, and was she the result of said affair?

'At the end of the day,' Archie continued. 'It was Terry's family who I felt sorry for, they were the ones left behind to bear the consequences. It couldn't have been easy for them being looked down upon by all and sundry and viewed with suspicion,' he added, pointing the bottle forward. 'The crimes Terry was involved in were unforgiveable and sadly his wife and sons were the ones to pay the price for his greed and depravation.'

At the mention of her brothers, Terri's heart began to beat faster. What was the betting that Ricky and Jamie had been involved in the prostitution racket too? Nothing would surprise her where they were concerned. As the saying went, like father like sons, and how could they have not had any indication as to what Terry was like? Especially if they were as close as Archie had indicated. No, Terri decided, they must have known; it would have been impossible for them not to have. It didn't take a genius to tell her that her brothers were just as ruthless as their father, maybe even more so considering they'd got away with the crimes they and their father had been involved in. A shudder ripped through her. Could this mean that she too was depraved, that her genes and the blood that ran through her veins meant she was as warped and as capable of evil as her father and brothers? The mere thought made her stomach turn somersaults.

As the conversation moved to other interests, Terri remained quiet, her thoughts plagued by the despicable crimes her family had committed. Why did she have to be born into the Murphy family and even more than that, why did she have to come from a man who had hurt so many innocent people? She was ashamed of her background, ashamed of who she was and where she had come from. More than anything she wished that she could have been born into a normal family like her school friends had. She would have given anything for her parents to have been hard working and kind just like Rina and Archie were. Perhaps if she had parents like them then she would have had a decent chance at life; as it was, Bianca was always on at her. *Why didn't she have a boyfriend? It wasn't normal for a girl of her age not to go out with her mates pissing it up.* That was the thing with Bianca though, she expected everyone to live by her morals however fucked up they might be. Was it any wonder that Terri wanted to leave both the Murphy and Tempest surname behind her? All she wanted was a fresh start and to get on with her life. Momentarily, Terri closed her eyes, a sense of foreboding weighing heavy in the pit of her stomach. No matter how much she might want to get away from her family, her roots, she had a nasty feeling that it would be far easier said than done.

7

Ricky Tempest was fast on his way to losing his patience. After spending the past few days staking out Frankie Gammon's usual haunts, he and Jamie had come away empty handed. More's the pity. He'd been looking forward to driving his fist into Gammon's smug face. Repeatedly. Not only had Gammon been keeping a low profile but to put a finer point on things he'd pretty much dropped off the face of the earth, taking his so-called firm with him.

'Come on,' Ricky urged the man sitting opposite him. 'Help me out here. You and your brothers make it your business to keep tabs on everything that goes on in the manor. And I know for a fact that you know exactly where I can find him, or at least you've got a pretty good idea where he could be hiding out.'

Jonny Carter lounged back on a chair, his shoulders lifting up into a carefree shrug. After hanging up his boxing gloves and throwing away a promising career as a professional boxer, Jonny had spent the majority of his adult life working alongside his elder brothers from their scrapyard in Barking. Not that dealing with scrap metal was how the Carter brothers really earned their living. No, the scrapyard was simply a cover for their day job, debt collecting. And even then, collecting debts wasn't how they'd managed to accumulate a vast amount of wealth over the years.

Amongst the criminal underworld, the Carters were commonly known as lucky thieves, although it would be fair to say that luck had played no part in the fact they had never so much as had their collars felt, let alone been charged with a crime and sent down for any considerable length of time. And considering armed robberies were what the Carter family excelled in, that was saying something. They would often joke that there was nothing they wouldn't attempt to lift and if it had their name on it then as far as they were concerned it was theirs for the taking; well, other than diamonds that was. They'd never seemed to have much luck when it came to that particular gem and had all but given up trying to get one into their possession, although it hadn't been for want of trying.

'No can do,' Jonny answered with a shake of his head. 'It would be more than my life is worth to divulge information about our mutual acquaintances, and believe me, when it comes to Gammon, I'd more than happily wipe the scum bag out myself. Let me put it this way, the quicker Gammon draws his last breath the better it will be for everyone concerned. And it would make my day all the more sweeter if he was to have a bloody ending, preferably something brutal, torture perhaps,' he added with a grin. 'Or maybe a bullet to the back of his nut; I'd even make him dig his own grave first. Although if you want my opinion that would be too quick. He's a fucking weasel, a lowlife and the no-good bastard deserves to suffer. I take it you've heard that he's been dealing at the school gates, selling shit to innocent kids? I heard that one of the poor little sods ended up being hospitalised, that the poison Gammon sold him was potent enough to kill a horse or was that horses,' he pondered. 'Either way' – he shrugged – 'Gammon is bang out of order.'

'Yeah, I heard.' Ricky ground his teeth together, the muscles in his jaw tightening even further. Drugs had never been his scene, or at least the hard stuff anyway. Cannabis on the other hand was something that did interest him and was more or less socially acceptable nowadays, not that he intended to start dealing any time soon. 'All the more reason to get rid of the ponce then,' he stated with a wink. 'All I need from you is an address for him, so do us both a favour and hand it over.'

Sitting forward in the chair, Jonny rested his forearms on the desk, his expression becoming serious. 'I can't,' he answered. 'You know as well as I do what my brothers are like or should I say one brother in particular,' he sighed. 'Sonny and Mitchel, I can handle, but when it comes to our Jimmy' – he gave a shake of his head and blew out his cheeks – 'I'm not in a position to go up against him. He's a law unto himself and even worse than Tommy was and I never thought I'd say that. I'd always assumed that Jimmy was the weakest link in our family, Gary aside of course.' He grinned, referring to his middle brother who had been killed in a gas explosion not long after Jonny's eldest brother Tommy had been found murdered. 'Like everyone else, I thought Jimmy was a follower, a sheep, and that he was only in this game because he copied everything Tommy did. But I was wrong; he rules our family with an iron fist. You've met my old man and know exactly how much of a cantankerous old bastard he can be, but even he has the sense to keep schtum whenever Jimmy is around. Trust me, my brother would skin me alive if I was to bring any unwanted attention to the family and believe it or not, I'm quite fond of the body I just so happened to be blessed with.'

Ricky's shoulders drooped. He should have known it would be pointless coming to the youngest Carter brother for help. In a way he reminded him of his own brother. Like Jamie, Jonny wasn't only reckless, but he was also in the habit of taking far too many risks, risks that would more than likely get him killed one day. He also treated life as though it was one long standing joke, as though everything he did was for his sole amusement and the fact he was a Carter was the equivalent of having a green light hanging over his head. He could literally commit murder and his brothers would still bail him out. So the fact he was acting so cagey when it came to Gammon didn't sit right. Why was he holding back? Could he have a hidden agenda, a reason why he didn't want to go up against his brothers, Jimmy in particular. 'This isn't the time for making wisecracks,' Ricky barked out.

'Who said anything about wisecracks?' Jonny shot back. He gestured towards himself. 'This body is like a fucking temple mate.'

'Yeah, if you say so.' Ricky rolled his eyes, barely able to keep the irritation out of his voice. If Jonny Carter's head was to get any bigger, he'd have trouble getting through the door and that was an understatement. 'Do me a favour and stop pissing me about. We're not strangers, our families go way back, so spare me the bullshit. Are you going to help me out or not?'

Jonny raised his eyebrows and before he could open his mouth to answer Ricky shifted his position and shook his head.

'Don't say it,' he sighed. 'It's been a long time since my dad... well you know... Since he did what he did. And I know a lot of people turned their backs on us, but me and Jamie have proved ourselves time and time again. We had nothing to do with the prostitution racket and it's about time people got that through their thick skulls.' He swallowed then rubbed his hand over his face, his cheeks turning red. All these years later and he still felt ashamed of the heinous acts his father had committed and a tiny part of him didn't blame those who had distanced themselves from them or pointed fingers.

As much as he hated to admit it, he and Jamie were as good as guilty too. Fair enough they hadn't been involved in the business of pimping out women, but still, how could they not have known what their dad was involved in? They had pretty much lived in Terry's pocket; not only had they worked for him, but they had also socialised with him. They should have seen the signs, should have known that the money Terry was flashing about had to have come from somewhere. Instead, they had blindly believed everything Terry had told them, that the debt collecting business was booming and, in their defence, why would they have ever questioned their father, why would they have suspected that things weren't adding up?

'I know a lot of people out there still don't trust us but I'm asking you as a mate for a favour. Forget what my dad did, that was all on him not me or Jamie, you know we had no part in any of that. That isn't what we're about and you know it.'

'Look.' Jonny held up his hands. 'You don't need to explain yourself to me. Like you just said, I know you from old and I know you and Jamie well enough to know that you weren't involved in any of the shit your dad had been getting up to. I'd like to help you out, really I would, but as I've already stated I can't and you know exactly why. Come on mate.' He gave an exaggerated sigh. 'You all of people should understand what it's like. You've been there, done it, lived the life. And you've seen my brothers in action enough times to know that they're the real deal and I'm already skating on thin ice as it is where they're concerned. One more fuck up on my part and it'll be curtains.' He made a slicing action across his throat before collapsing back in the chair. 'They'd more than likely disown me; either that or kill me stone dead. Fuck me, Jimmy would more than likely parade my head on a spike out there,' he said, gesturing to the forecourt. 'As a warning to the others not to piss him off. There's only so far I can push them and I've already used up every get-out-of-jail-free card available to man.'

A snort of laughter escaped from Ricky's mouth. Despite what Jonny said, the Carters were a close-knit family; fair enough, they may have had their fall outs over the years, it was only natural after all for siblings to have disagreements, but once all was said and done they were loyal to one another just like he and his own brother were. 'Stop with the dramatics,' he laughed. 'That would never happen and you know it. Come on, there must be something you can give me.' He lifted his eyebrows then tapped the side of his nose. 'Off the record of course, just between the two of us.'

Jonny chuckled and shook his head. 'That's the thing though. As soon as I open my trap it won't stay off the record, will it? No doubt you'll tear out of here, go after Gammon, and before you know it my name will have been brought into the equation. And that,' he said, stabbing his finger forward, 'means that my brothers will get wind of my involvement and the last thing I need is to have them breathing down my neck. I only just made it out alive the last time they went to town on me.'

Chewing on the inside of his cheek, Ricky sighed. Considering both families were in the enforcing game he was surprised that Gammon hadn't targeted the Carters. It wasn't as though their reputations were any different from his and Jamie's. Although it would be fair to say that there were more of them; perhaps that was what gave them the edge, a reason for Gammon to stay as far away from them as possible. He crossed his arms over his chest and cocked his head to the side, a steely glint clearly visible in his blue eyes. 'And there was me thinking that you wanted to come into your own. That you were just biding your time before taking over the family business now that Jimmy wants to cut ties and make a permanent move over to Spain.'

The nerve in Jonny's jaw pulsated, his expression hardening. 'How the fuck do you know about any of that?' he hissed.

Ricky laughed. 'Because I hear things,' he said, motioning to his ear. 'And because I know what you're like. You're ambitious and you've got your eye on the crown. And don't even bother trying to deny it; like I've already said, I know you well enough to know that you're astute, that you've got a good head on your shoulders. Once Jimmy is out of the picture you want to take over the reins. I also know' – he glanced around the portable cabin that served as the Carter brothers' office and took note of the rickety filing cabinet that had had the same pile of paperwork stacked on top of it for as long as he could remember – 'that you're more than prepared for when that time comes, that you'll do everything in your power to steal the rug from under your brothers' feet, even if that means going up against Sonny and Mitchel in the process. You want to be the one they all look up to, and more to the point you want to be the one they take orders from.'

Jonny ran his tongue across his teeth. 'And,' he said, mirroring Ricky's stance, 'so what if I do want all of that? Once Jimmy fucks off to Spain, the family is going to need someone to take charge. And I'm the only one with a bit of savvy, the only one who knows how the business runs, and I'm not talking about this place or even the debts,' he said, glancing around him and lowering his voice. 'I'm talking about the real business, the bank jobs. Sonny and Mitchel haven't got a clue, they're about as much use as a priest in a brothel. And as for my nephews, other than Tommy's boys or even Cameron,' he spat, 'who, might I add, takes after his father Gary a little bit too much for my liking and doesn't have the nous to take over, the rest of them are still kids. What the fuck do they know about acquiring shotguns or even staking a place out? We would more than likely be carted off in handcuffs if the planning was left to them and that's one risk I'm not prepared to take.'

It was exactly the response Ricky was hoping for. He gave a knowing smile, sat forward, then rested his forearms on his thighs. 'Then in that case we can help each other out. When the time comes for you to take over, you're going to need allies, and you'll have that from me and Jamie, I give you my word on that. As long as you play ball, I can guarantee that you'll have our backing. It doesn't take a genius to work out that having us on side will help your cause or' – he let out a dramatic sigh and spread open his arms – 'we could always switch our loyalty over to... oh I don't know,' he said with a wave of his hand. 'Say Sonny and Mitchel for example. I'm pretty sure your brothers would snap our hands off to form an allegiance with us.'

'That's blackmail,' Jonny pointed out.

Ricky shook his head. 'It's business,' he corrected. 'Now are you in or are you out?'

For all of two seconds Jonny pondered the question over. 'You drive a hard bargain, Tempest,' he said, holding out his hand.

Ricky took the proffered hand into his and shook on the deal, all the while noting that the handshake was firm, not that he should have expected anything different. Jonny Carter may have been significantly younger than him, twelve years younger to be precise, but even so he was by no means weak. 'Likewise Carter.' Ricky grinned before popping a piece of nicotine gum into his mouth and chewing. 'Now if you don't mind, I need that address and pronto, so do us both a favour and send it over,' he said, motioning to his mobile phone.

'Leave it out,' Jonny chuckled as he pulled open the desk drawer and rummaged around for a pen and a scrap of paper. 'I'm not that daft. I'm old school mate. Do you honestly think I'd be stupid enough to leave an electronic trail behind me?' Scribbling down the address, he glanced up. 'Our Tommy,' he said, grinning. 'Say what you want about him but he was a fucking good teacher. Taught me everything I needed to know.'

As he took the sheet of paper and studied the address, Ricky nodded. He hadn't known Tommy Carter well seeing as Tommy had been a few years older than him but from what he could remember, the eldest Carter brother had been considered a legend amongst his peers and was still talked about with a measure of respect, even years after his death. 'I don't doubt that for a single second,' Ricky said, returning the smile.

With an address for Frankie Gammon firmly tucked into his jacket pocket, Ricky started the ignition and drove out of the Carter brothers' scrap yard. The fact he'd had to resort to blackmail just as Jonny Carter had correctly stated was at the forefront of his mind. Despite the fact he and Jamie were now on friendly terms with the Carters, in the beginning, just after Terry had posthumously been formally named as being the instigator behind the human trafficking scheme, the Carters, just like the majority of his father's business associates, had done their best to steer clear of them. It was only their father's childhood friend Max Hardcastle who had actually stood by them, not that Ricky would have blamed him if he too had decided to have it away on his toes. As it turned out, Max had had other ideas; not only had he taken himself and Jamie under his wing and given them employment, but he had also gone on to marry their mother, Tracey.

As he drove towards Dagenham, Ricky's thoughts wandered to his dad. It wasn't often that Terry sprang to his mind these days; after all, he'd caused so much heartache that it was far easier and a lot less troublesome to push any memories of him far away. And on the odd occasion that Jamie or even his mum brought him up, Ricky would hastily change the subject. In a way he supposed he just didn't want to deal with the turbulent thoughts Terry's memory conjured up. He'd once idolised his dad, just as his own son, Mason looked up to him. It was how it was supposed to be: fathers were meant to be their children's heroes. Only in Terry's case, nothing could be further from the truth. And as much as Ricky still might love him, any respect Ricky had once held for his dad was long gone. He'd seen his mum suffer far too much for what Terry had done and for that reason alone he could never forgive his father for his wrongdoings. Not only had he seen his mother's tears, and witnessed her heartache, but he'd also seen the evidence of his father's womanising with his own eyes. Two children his dad had fathered out of wedlock, the first being Raymond Cole, a bonafide nutcase in the making if ever he'd seen one, and then the daughter he had created with Bianca Murphy.

Once he reached the turning that led to the Murphy family home, Ricky was unable to stop himself from taking a look, his hard gaze scoping out the road. He'd done it so often over the years that it had pretty much become a habit. He couldn't even explain to himself why he would want to seek out his father's daughter, let alone explain his reasons to anyone else. Maybe it was only natural that he should be curious; at the end of the day, Terri was his sister, albeit a half-sister. Despite his curiosity, he didn't actually want to form any kind of relationship with his youngest sibling. In fact, from the very moment he'd learned about Bianca Murphy's pregnancy, he'd decided that he wanted nothing to do with Terry and Bianca's offspring. He felt as though he were betraying his mother even considering forming a relationship with the girl, especially as Terri's conception had all but irrevocably broken Tracey's heart.

Yet despite his reticence to form a relationship with her, that didn't mean he hadn't subconsciously looked out for her over the years, because he had, even if he wasn't entirely sure why. Perhaps somewhere deep down inside of him he'd wanted to know what she was like. Did she take after his father or was she a mirror image of her mother? Not that he'd seen Terri often, mind, just glimpses of her every now and then and usually from afar. Although he had spoken to her once; she must have only been about five or six at the time, and he'd spotted her entering the local newsagent's alone, her grandparents nowhere in sight. Jumping out of the car, he'd entered the shop and finally found her in the magazine section. Her tongue poking out in concentration as she counted out the loose change in her tiny hand, every so often her gaze would flick up to the brightly coloured comics before her, her eyes lighting up in wonder as she studied the covers. He'd ended up paying for the comics, and even going as far as to throw in a bag of sweets and a bottle of pop too. From a safe distance he'd then followed her through the streets just to make sure she reached the Murphy home safely. With each step he'd taken, rage had torn through his veins; just what kind of upbringing was she being given if the Murphys deemed it appropriate to allow such a young child to wander the streets all by herself? She could have been abducted, knocked over by a car, or even wandered off and found herself lost. As much as he hadn't wanted to admit it, he couldn't help but see himself and Jamie in her. She had their eyes and dark hair, she even had the same button nose his own son had had at the same age.

Ten minutes later, Ricky stepped his foot on the brake and brought the car to a grinding halt outside the taxi office.

'Well?' Jamie asked as he yanked open the car door and took a seat beside him. 'Did Carter hand over an address?'

'What do you think?' Ricky replied as he watched his son climb on to the back seat. 'Carter might act like a prick at times but believe me, he isn't stupid.' Digging his hand into his pocket, he passed across the scrap of paper with Frankie Gammon's address scrawled across it.

'Dagenham?' Jamie exclaimed. 'You mean to tell me that little scrote has been on our doorstep, in our manor this whole time, and we didn't know?'

'Looks that way.' Ricky nodded as he flicked the indicator and pulled out on to the road.

'The fucker,' Mason chided from the back seat. He slipped his hand into his pocket and pulled out a ten-inch screwdriver, then turned the makeshift weapon over in his hand. 'Let me have a go at him first.' He grinned. 'I'll stab the wanker in the eye, and give it a good twist,' he said, mimicking the actions. 'It'd be one way to teach him a lesson he won't forget in a hurry.'

From his position behind the wheel, Ricky looked up and caught his son's eyes in the rearview mirror. 'There's something seriously wrong with you,' he declared with a shake of his head. 'If I didn't know better, I'd swear you were dropped on your head as a kid.'

Beside him, Jamie laughed and turning in his seat, he gave his nephew a wink. 'He might be a loose cannon, not to mention sick in the head,' he said, glancing towards his brother, 'but just you remember he's our loose cannon. Ain't that right Mase?'

As his son's laughter filled the car, Ricky groaned. His wife Kayla would have a hissy fit of epic proportions if she was to ever find out just how dangerous her only son actually was. As it was, Kayla fully believed her son to be the equivalent of a saint. How she'd even come up with the idea that Mason wasn't capable of causing harm was beyond him. Mason was a Tempest through and through and came from a long line of men who were both violent and downright dangerous and there was only one path he'd ever been destined to take and that was to follow on in his father's, uncle's, and late grandfather's footsteps.

Moments later, Ricky switched off the ignition outside a row of rundown houses, half of which looked as though they had been deserted for years if not decades if the boarded-up windows, overgrown front gardens, and missing roof tiles were anything to go by.

'Is this it?' Mason screwed up his face as he peered out of the window. 'You've got to be kidding me. Is this where Gammon actually lives?'

Taking back the scrap of paper, Ricky studied the address before looking over at the house. Mason was right, this had to be a mistake. The place was a shit hole and that was putting it nicely. He unclipped the seat belt, all the while keeping his gaze firmly fixed on the property. 'There's only one way to find out for sure, isn't there?' he finally answered as he pushed open the door and stepped out of the car.

'If Carter has sent us on a wild goose chase, I'll string him up by his bollocks,' Jamie grumbled as they walked down the pathway that was littered with crumpled beer cans and cigarette butts.

'You'll have to get there before me then,' Ricky replied as he looked up at the house. Banging his fist on the wooden front door, he took in the chipped and peeling paintwork, his forehead furrowing. This had to be a sick joke on Jonny Carter's part. There was no way in hell anyone actually lived at the property, not when the entire street looked as though it were fit for demolition. He'd been about to voice his opinion when the sound of muffled footsteps coming from somewhere inside the house reached his ears. Snapping his head towards his brother, Ricky widened his eyes slightly. 'Did you hear that?' he asked, his voice low.

Before Jamie had the chance to open his mouth and answer, Mason barged forward.

'Fuck this shit,' he growled. 'What are we waiting around for?' With that, he kicked out at the door. Within a matter of seconds the wooden frame almost came off its hinges as the door crashed against the wall with a loud clatter.

Glaring at his son, Ricky shook his head. 'Cheers for that,' he groaned, clipping Mason around the back of the head. 'You've more than likely alerted half of Dagenham that we've just kicked down Gammon's door.'

'And?' Mason shrugged as he stepped over the threshold, the screwdriver firmly clenched in his fist. 'Do I look like I give a flying fuck?'

Ricky was in half a mind to batter some sense into his son. Instead, he glanced across to Jamie and shook his head again. Mason had a lot to learn and that was an understatement.

The bare wooden floorboards beneath their feet creaked as they walked along the narrow downstairs hallway and if Ricky had thought the outside of the house was bad then the inside was considerably worse. Graffiti was spray painted across the walls, the once pale pink flowery wallpaper tobacco stained, peeling and speckled with what looked suspiciously like fungus.

'Carter was definitely winding us up,' Ricky stated as he peered into what he assumed to be the lounge. 'No way on earth does Gammon live here; it's not even habitable.'

'Could be a meet-up place,' Jamie answered, poking his head into the kitchen and wrinkling his nose at the sight of obvious drug paraphernalia that littered a rusty draining board beside an equally rusty sink filled with even more crumpled beer cans. 'You're right about one thing though, no one would willingly live in this place; I wouldn't even let my dog live here.'

'I think you could be right.' Mason placed his hand on the banister rail and looked upwards. 'But then again, Gammon is hardly big time is he. This' – he gestured around him – 'is about all he's good for if you want my—' Before he could finish the sentence, from out of nowhere, a figure bolted down the stairs and hurled himself into Mason, causing them to both tumble heavily to the floor.

In the scuffle that followed, a glimpse of steel in the assailant's fist caused the hairs on the back of Ricky's neck to stand upright. He opened his mouth to scream out for his son to watch his back when the man let out a blood curdling scream before slumping to the floor, his face pointing upwards and his eyes staring into nothingness. Sticking out from the side of his head was the screwdriver Mason was so fond of.

'Fuck me.' Clambering to his feet, Mason patted himself down before yanking out the screwdriver. Oblivious to the wet plopping sound as he jerked the weapon through muscle and brain matter,

Mason held the tool above his head, inspecting the bright red residue left behind. 'Where did he come from?' Lowering the screwdriver to his side, he gave the staircase a cautious glance. 'You don't reckon there's anyone else up there, do you?'

Ricky's nostrils flared and he clenched his fists, his earlier fear all but forgotten about as he bounded forward, grabbed his son by the throat and slammed him into the wall. 'What is wrong with you?' he roared, stabbing a stiff finger into the side of Mason's head. 'Is this a case of the lights are on but no one is at home?'

Mason's jaw dropped. 'What?' he stuttered, his face turning almost purple.

'What do you mean by "what"?' Giving an incredulous laugh, Ricky turned to look at his brother. 'Please tell me this is some kind of wind-up?' He snapped his gaze back to his son, barely able to comprehend how something he had produced could have turned out to be so dense. 'All thanks to you, the geezer is brown bread. You've killed him.'

'Yeah, and?' Mason shrugged. 'It's no big deal. If he's one of Gammon's henchmen then he's a scumbag. We've done society a favour by getting rid of the ponce.'

Ricky's jaw tightened. He'd always had a sinking feeling that his son was severely lacking common sense but surely he wasn't this stupid; no one could be this thick. 'He's hardly going to talk now is he, and unless it's escaped your notice, we're still none the wiser when it comes to Frankie Gammon's whereabouts.'

'Oh.' As Mason looked down at the corpse, the penny finally dropped. 'I didn't think of that.'

'Of course you didn't,' Ricky shouted as spittle gathered at the corners of his lips, bringing further testament to just how angry he was. 'You never think; that's your fucking trouble. All you ever do is dive in feet first and fuck the consequences. Thanks to you' – he continued to stab his finger into his son's head as if the action would somehow knock some sense into Mason – 'our only lead is now as stiff as a board; he's about as much use to us as a glass hammer.'

'Bruv.' Pulling on his brother's arm, Jamie gave a small shake of his head. 'He didn't have any other choice.' He kicked the carving knife the man had been brandishing a safe distance away from them. 'He had a blade on him and from where I was standing it didn't look like he was afraid to use it.'

As the enormity of the situation sank in, Ricky pinched the bridge of his nose. Jamie was right; the tables could so easily have been reversed. It could have been his only son lying on the floor, his blood seeping into the dusty floorboards as he took his last, ragged breaths. How on earth would he have found the words to tell Kayla that her only child was dead, how would he have lived with himself knowing that he had openly welcomed his son into the family business? 'I'm sorry,' he said, pulling Mason into a bear hug. 'I was out of order. You're my boy, and—'

'Leave it out, Dad.' As he disentangled himself from his father's embrace, Mason's cheeks flamed red. 'Despite what you may think of me, I'm not a little kid any more and it'll take a lot more than this prick,' he said, kicking out at the body, 'to take me out.'

Ricky nodded. He should have guessed as much. In many ways, Mason took after him; not only was he a lump but he also knew how to handle himself. As they trailed back out of the house, Ricky's expression was hard. Frankie Gammon had just made the situation personal and like fuck was Ricky going to forgive and forget in a hurry. If Gammon wanted a war, then that was exactly what he was going to get.

8

Michael Murphy was sick to the back teeth of looking at his sister's miserable boat race. It wasn't even as though she and the little bitch, as he still thought of his niece, were that close. Bianca may have birthed the brat but that was as far as it went; she hadn't been around to see the girl grow up, nor had she lifted a finger to actually take care of her. Even after her release from prison, Bianca hadn't seemed interested in forming a bond with her daughter. No, the only priorities Bianca had had were to get paralytic drunk, cause aggravation, and then shag as many men as she possibly could and not in that particular order either.

'I blame you for this,' Bianca huffed as she slumped on the sofa, a can of lager in one hand and an ever-present cigarette in the other. 'My baby would still be here if you hadn't gone garrity on her.'

Michael rolled his eyes. Was she taking the piss? Even when Terri had been at home Bianca had barely spoken to her other than to bark out orders which more often than not consisted of using the girl as her personal skivvy. 'Give it a rest B,' he sighed. 'You're hardly mother of the year material. Besides, she's not a kid any more; it's about time she learned how to stand on her own two feet.'

Bianca continued to sulk. 'She's still my child, my baby,' she grumbled before taking a long slurp of her drink. 'And I'll tell you something else for nothing,' she said with a crafty glint in her eyes. 'She's still got a right to her father's fortune. My Terry would have wanted his only daughter to be taken care of, I know he would have; I can feel it in here,' she said, pointing to her chest.

'So now you're saying you're psychic,' Michael laughed. 'That Tempest is communicating with you from beyond the grave?'

'I knew you'd take the piss,' Bianca screeched as she threw the empty can in Michael's direction, narrowly missing his head by a hair's breadth. 'You just don't get it, do you? Terry was the love of my life.'

'You were an easy shag,' Michael retorted. 'Nothing more than that. It was hardly a love story.'

Bianca screwed up her face. 'Think what you want,' she spat. 'But my baby was the result of our union. She's special and she deserves her due and that bitch wife of his is sitting on a tidy sum of my daughter's money.'

Michael couldn't help but laugh out loud. It was typical of Bianca. She wasn't interested in Terri, she never had been. No, the only thing she was interested in was Tempest's money, or more to the point, getting her hands on it. Right from the off, he could have told her that she didn't stand a chance of getting a penny out of Tracey Tempest, and he'd been right all along.

'You can laugh,' Bianca snapped as she took out a fresh cigarette and began the process of lighting it from the previous butt. 'But I'm going to make sure my girl gets what she deserves.'

'And how are you going to do that?' Lounging back on the sofa, Michael smirked. 'Come on B,' he said, spreading open his arms. 'I'm all ears. How exactly are you planning to get Tempest's wife to hand over the cash? That's if there is even any money left. We're talking almost twenty years later; she's probably spunked it all by now.'

Sinking her teeth into her bottom lip, Bianca pondered the question. 'Of course she's still got the cash,' she finally answered, taking a deep drag on the cigarette. 'She's married to what's his face... That's it, Max Hardcastle,' she said, pointing the cigarette forward. 'And you can't tell me that he's short of a bob or two.'

Michael laughed even harder. 'Good luck with that.'

As she continued to smoke her cigarette, Bianca stared out of the lounge window. 'I just need to find my girl.' She gave a bright smile. 'Once she knows she's entitled to her dad's money she'll soon want to come running back home, I know she will. She takes after me; she's a fighter and won't let anyone walk all over her, especially not Tracey fucking Tempest. As it is, I've got a bone to pick with that bitch; Terry was my man, and I know for a fact he was planning to leave her for me, he told me so enough times, he loved me.'

'Yeah you keep telling yourself that.' Getting to his feet, Michael walked to the door. Bianca was deluded. Terry Tempest had never had any intention of leaving his wife. Right from the off all his sister had ever been was Tempest's bit on the side. She was an easy lay and would spread her legs for just about anyone and had proven that fact time and time again.

'Where do you think she could have gone?' Bianca asked, looking up at her brother, breaking his reverie.

It was on the tip of Michael's tongue to put his sister out of her misery and blurt out that he knew exactly where the little bitch was hiding out. Thinking better of it, he gave a shrug. 'No idea, sis.' As for Terri taking after her mother, from what Michael knew of the girl, nothing could be further from the truth. In his mind, his niece was severely lacking a back bone and if he didn't know any better, he would have sworn that she had no Murphy, or come to think of it, any Tempest blood running through her veins.

He glanced towards the window, taking note of the snow that had fallen over night. 'If she stayed out in this weather, you'll more than likely find her frozen to death.'

The worried expression that creased Bianca's face as she snapped her head back to look out of the window was priceless. Under any other circumstances, Michael would have fully believed that his sister was worried about her only child's welfare. Only, he knew Bianca even better than she knew herself and the demise of her daughter wouldn't hurt as much as the thought of losing her only link to Terry Tempest's money.

Still smirking to himself, Michael left the house. He needed to have a word with Frankie Gammon, needed him to put his actions where his mouth was and actually get rid of the Tempest brothers once and for all. Or better still, he could give the job to Michael; God only knew he needed to do something, anything, to be able to get into Raymond Cole's good books and what better way to form an allegiance with the man than to wipe out the bane of his existence, the one thing that he despised more than anything else, his half-brothers.

* * *

Armed with a carrier bag filled with booze, Michael had a spring in his step as he made his way towards the house Frankie Gammon used as a meeting place. By the time he'd reached the rickety garden gate that led to the house, his eyebrows were scrunched together. The front door sat ajar, which wouldn't have been unusual if Gammon or any or the other firm members' had been loitering outside, but as it was, there was no one else around.

'Hello,' he tentatively called out as he gingerly pushed the front door open wider. The scene before Michael was enough to make a sliver of white cold fear shoot up the length of his spine. Sprawled out in the hallway was a body, or at least, Michael took a wild guess that it was a body, if the amount of blood that had pooled beside the man's head was anything to go by.

'Fuck,' Michael hissed. 'Fuck, fuck, fuck.' He looked around him, unsure what he should do next. Should he enter the house, or should he leave as quietly as he'd arrived? No one even need know that he'd been here; it wasn't as though he'd told anyone he was planning to turn up.

He was about to retrace his steps when Michael paused. He wanted to get into Raymond Cole's good books and proving himself to be a coward wasn't going to bode well; not only that but he also didn't want to miss out on the action once the body was discovered.

Taking a deep breath, he tiptoed into the house and after giving the corpse the once over, just to make sure that the man, whose name for the life of him he couldn't remember had indeed ceased breathing. He made his way into the kitchen and rummaged around the cupboards and drawers, on the lookout for any drugs that hadn't yet been shipped out. With a handful of pills stuffed into his trouser pockets, he took one final look around him then pulled out his mobile phone.

'Frankie,' he screamed down the phone. 'You'd better get over here now. We've been done over.' Satisfied with his performance, Michael pulled out a can of beer from the carrier bag, dug his hand into his pocket and pulled out two pills. Popping the tablets onto his tongue, he snapped open the ring pull and took a deep swig, almost downing half the contents in one go. Once he'd finished his drink, he crumpled the can in his fist, tossed it into the sink then made his way back out into the hallway. Standing beside the corpse, he waited until he heard the sound of cars screeching to a halt outside the house before dropping to his knees and pretending to resuscitate the dead man. Of course, it would be pointless; he didn't need a genius to tell him that any attempts to bring the man back to life would be futile. The man was brown bread, probably had been for hours, and the only foreseeable future ahead of him was a date with a wooden box and a six-feet-deep hole.

By the time Frankie Gammon and Raymond Cole appeared at the front door, Michael was out of breath from his efforts. 'The dirty bastards did him over,' he cried, his own face pale and his hands covered in blood. 'And I can tell you now, I'll have them over this. I'll kill every last one of them with my bare hands for what they've caused. No one and that means no one,' he snarled as his eyes locked with those of Raymond Cole's, 'takes the piss out of us and gets away with it.'

As Raymond nodded, somewhat impressed, Michael made a mental note to pat himself on the back for a job well done. He had Cole's attention now and as he staggered to his feet, it took all of his effort to stop a smirk from filtering across his face. Being the gambling man that he was, he'd bet everything he had that by the end of the week he would become Cole's right-hand man, a role that he was determined would be his even if that meant he had to use dirty tactics to get what he wanted. After all, Michael was a Murphy; playing fair had never been a part of his vocabulary, and if Frankie Gammon wasn't careful, he was going to learn the hard way not to mess with him.

9

For three weeks, Terri had been staying with the Taylors in relative bliss. And during that time, she had never felt so at home. She and Rina had become firm friends and even Archie had seemed to thaw towards her. One time he'd even slung his arm around her shoulders and hugged her to him, and had even gone as far as to take her aside and personally thank her for making his Rina so happy. Terri had thought that her heart would burst with love for the couple. In such a short space of time, she had come to view Rina and Archie as the family she had always wanted, and she loved and respected them far more than she ever could her own family.

The only fly in the ointment was Frankie Gammon. His visits to the pub were becoming more and more frequent and his demands for protection money all the more extortionate. As if that wasn't bad enough, there was also her uncle Michael to contend with. No matter how much she'd tried to keep out of his way, she knew he'd seen her. The all too familiar sickening smirk he gave every time he turned up at the pub with Frankie Gammon was enough to tell Terri that he was plotting a payback of some sorts. It had even got to the point that each and every time the door swung open Terri would hold her breath, a part of her half expecting Bianca to storm through the pub and drag her out by her hair. Nothing would surprise her where her mother was concerned. Knowing Bianca, she would more than likely put on a big show, perhaps even claim to be the victim; after all, she thrived on being the centre of attention, got a kick out of it, in fact.

'I'm bloody beat,' Rina cried, throwing a damp cloth in a messy heap on top of the bar and kicking off her heels. 'And as for my poor feet, I think I lost all feeling in them hours back.'

A wide smile spread across Terri's face. Despite her complaints, Rina adored working at the pub. 'You say that every night,' she giggled. 'You love it, just admit it.'

Rina flapped her hand. 'Tell that to my feet,' she groaned, giving a playful wink. 'Here, I tell you what I could do with right now: a nice bubble bath then to curl up on the sofa with a cup of tea and maybe a couple of those bourbon biscuits I've been hiding in the back of the cupboard.'

'You and your sweet tooth.' Terri laughed even harder. 'I don't know who loves them more, you or Archie. I've got an idea: why don't you run yourself a bath and I'll make you a cup of tea and dig out the biscuits?'

'Deal.' Switching off the bar lights, Rina hugged Terri's slim frame to her. 'What would I do without you, eh? You're a bloody godsend to me and Archie, that's what you are. And he may not have said it out loud but my Archie is fond of you I can tell.'

Terri's heart swelled. She was fond of Archie too. He may come across as imposing but Rina had been right when she'd said that underneath his hard exterior, he was like a big, fluffy teddy bear.

They had barely made it out into the hallway when the sound of glass smashing made both women jump out of their skin.

'What the bloody hell was that?' Rina shrieked as her husband bounded down the stairs, his face a mask of both confusion and worry.

'Rina.' Holding his wife at arm's length, Archie cast a critical gaze over her body as if he were inspecting her for any injuries. 'What happened? Have you been hurt?'

'No... I'm okay.' Shaking her head, Rina looked over her shoulder to where the source of the glass smashing had come from. 'Just a little shook up, that's all.'

Satisfied that his wife hadn't been harmed, Archie made his way through to the pub. Careful of where he trod, he manoeuvred around the broken glass. 'The bastards,' he hissed.

After Rina had slipped her heels back on, Terri followed her through to the bar, her mouth dropping open as she took in the damage. Not only did shards of glass cover the tables, chairs and surrounding carpet, but there was also a gaping hole in the window where there should have been a pane of glass.

'Who would do something like this?' Rina gasped.

Archie bent down and retrieving a household brick, he pulled away a scrap of paper that had been crudely fastened to it. As he read the note, his lips curled into a snarl. 'I'll give you two fucking guesses,' he barked back as he passed the note across, unlocked the door, then stormed outside.

Rina scoured the note, her eyes growing wider with every passing second. 'Gammon,' she said in a low voice. 'But why... why would he do this to us?'

'Why do you think?' Returning back inside the pub, Archie ran his hand through his hair, the muscles across his shoulder blades turning rigid. 'It's a warning,' he declared. 'A reminder of what will happen if we don't pay up.'

Despair flooded through Rina and as tears sprang to her eyes, she clasped the note tightly in her fist. 'Enough is enough,' she cried. 'We have to go to the police. They would help us; they would put a stop to Gammon's demands.'

'No police,' Archie growled as he snatched the note back out of his wife's hand and tucked it into his pocket. 'You should know me better than that; I've never been a grass and don't intend to become one now. Running to the police is not how things work around here and you know that. It would only make the situation ten times worse. We'd be classed as snakes; is that what you want?' he continued to shout. 'For this lot around here to have a reason not trust us? A reason for them to take their custom elsewhere?'

'I know that you're an old fool,' Rina retorted, throwing her arms up into the air. 'That you think you can win against Gammon. Why can't you see that he is already winning, that he has already won,' she corrected. 'He's destroying everything we've worked so hard for, our dream. We're barely surviving as it is and now this.' She turned to look at the broken window, tears flooding her eyes and blurring her vision. 'More money that we'll have to pay out, money that we don't have,' she reminded her husband.

Archie sighed, and as he helplessly looked around him, his shoulder blades that moments earlier had been taut were now sagging. His gaze landed on Terri. 'There is one way,' he said, cocking his head to one side before hastily blowing out his cheeks and averting his gaze. 'It may not work, and I don't even know if they would be willing to help us but what do we have to lose? It's either them or Gammon and between the two I know who I'd rather deal with.'

The words hung heavy in the air and the hairs on the back of Terri's neck prickled. Without Archie even needing to say their names aloud she knew instinctively who he was referring to and a familiar sense of panic engulfed her. 'No,' she wanted to scream out loud. 'Please, please no. Seek out someone else, anyone but them.'

Other than her uncle Michael, there were only two other people who were able to scare the living daylights out of her. Two men who she would do everything in her power to avoid at all costs and God only knew how much she'd tried over the years to stay out of their way, to make herself as invisible as possible whenever they were within close proximity. Her half-brothers. Ricky and Jamie Tempest.

* * *

The next afternoon, Jonny Carter pulled into the car park of The Merry Fiddlers pub, or the Fiddlers as it was more commonly known by the locals. Stepping out of the car, he locked up, then strolled towards the entrance.

As was typical of a Saturday lunchtime, the pub was a hive of activity and weaving his way through the patrons, he greeted those he recognised with a wide smile, stopping here and there for a quick chat.

'Jonny,' Archie Taylor announced once Jonny had finally reached the bar. 'Just the man I was hoping to see.'

'Yeah and why's that?' Placing his hands upon the bar, Jonny glanced towards the pumps. 'If it's something to do with one of my nephews,' he groaned, 'then talk to Jimmy about it. I've just about had it up to here with their crap,' he said, pointing to his temple. 'And as I just told what's his face back there' – he jerked his thumb behind him and scowled – 'what they get up to outside of work is none of my business. And believe it or not, I'm not their keeper and never have been.'

Archie shook his head. 'Nah,' he answered with a half laugh. 'It's nothing like that. The little toe rags have actually been behaving themselves of late. Your young Tommy even helped me to evict some tosser hell bent on causing aggro a few nights ago.'

'Really?' Jonny lifted his eyebrows. He knew for a fact that his nephews were a rowdy bunch, young Tommy being one of the worst. It came with the territory, he supposed. They were Carters after all and had certainly never claimed to be choir boys. Considering the family they came from, it would be more laughable if they were to actually start toeing the line. Not that he entirely blamed his nephews for acting out; he'd been exactly the same at their age, if not even worse, much to his elder brothers' chagrin. As a youngster, he'd often thought of himself as untouchable and as a result had been nearly uncontrollable, with an attitude to match. It was only by some miracle that he'd actually made it to adulthood and even then it had been by the skin of his teeth. As for the younger generation of Carters, they had an image to live up to, a legacy to behold that had been passed down from father to son and he knew from experience that there was always someone, somewhere, who wanted to cause aggravation. 'So what is it you want to have a word about then?'

A sigh escaped from Archie's lips and as he looked around him, he gestured towards the hallway that led up to his flat. 'Maybe it would be for the best if we speak in private, away from any prying eyes,' he said, lowering his voice.

Jonny's forehead furrowed and as he followed Archie's gaze, his back was instantly up. It was unlike Archie to be so cagey, and for the briefest of moments a sense of foreboding rippled through him. Could someone be waiting in the wings, hidden out of sight, ready to jump him? It wasn't as though it would be the first time that someone had tried to catch him unawares, and he still carried a gnarled scar on his forearm where someone had once attempted to kill him outside his eldest brother's club in Soho. He gave a slight shake of his head, reminding himself that he'd known Archie for years and had in fact been coming to the boozer long before he'd even legally been old enough to buy alcohol, not that Archie would have ever been in a position to turn him away. It was one of the perks of being born into the Carter family. As he continued to look around him, Jonny's gaze fell upon the boarded-up window. 'Looks like you've had some trouble in here,' he stated with a nod of his head.

'Yeah you could say that.' Archie cleared his throat. 'Shall we?' He put out his hand, indicating for Jonny to follow him.

Taking one final glance around him, Jonny made his way behind the bar. He'd barely just made it into the hallway when he took note of Rina trotting down the stairs towards him. As always, she flashed him a wide smile, although it would be fair to say that she looked tired, weary even, making the fine lines around her eyes appear more prominent.

'Hello Jonny, my darling. It's nice to see you,' she said, coming forward and standing on her tiptoes to kiss his cheek. 'I was only saying to Archie the other day that you haven't shown your face in here for a while.'

A smile filtered across Jonny's face and as his shoulders relaxed, he pulled the woman into a hug. 'Hello Rina.' Despite just how feisty she was it was no secret that Archie adored the tiny woman and that he would never willingly put her in danger. 'So what's with all the secrecy?' he asked, looking between the couple.

Archie and Rina shared a glance and after patting her husband's arm, she made her way behind the bar, her high heels clip clopping as she went.

'Well?' Leaning casually against the wall, Jonny crossed his ankles and dug his hands into his pockets. 'What's going on?'

Archie sighed and rubbing at the back of his neck, he shook his head. 'You saw the window for yourself,' he said, jerking his head towards the pub.

'Yeah,' Jonny answered with a shrug. 'It would have been pretty hard not to miss it.'

'I need to have a chat with the Tempest brothers,' Archie

blurted out. 'And seeing as you're both in the same game, well I was hoping that you'd be able to have a word with them and set up a meeting. I would do it myself but...' He glanced away. 'You know what they're like; at the best of times it can be hard to pin them down.'

Jonny narrowed his eyes, his gaze going from Archie to the window and then back to Archie again. He'd always been under the impression that Ricky and Jamie were fairly easy to find; they certainly never hid themselves away, and more often than not at least one of them if not both could be found at the taxi firm they owned. 'Why? What does the window have to do with the Tempests?'

As he bowed his head, Archie's shoulders were slumped and considering he was a large man, he suddenly seemed so much smaller, as though his age had finally caught up with him.

'Archie,' Jonny reiterated. 'Seriously pal, I don't have the time to be playing games. Are you in some sort of trouble? Was it the Tempests who caved the window in?' Even as he asked the question Jonny knew the answer would be no. The Tempest brothers may have been a lot of things, but they weren't amateurs when it came to demanding protection money, especially seeing as their preferred method of intimidation was kneecapping those who didn't repay their debts on time. They wouldn't have wasted precious time on smashing windows to get their point across.

Archie snapped his head up. 'Of course not. It's nothing to do with the Tempests, at least not in the way you're thinking. And if it wasn't for the fact that this is their manor so to speak, I would be coming to you and your family for help.'

'Okay.' Jonny nodded. 'So do you mind telling me what's going on then?'

'Frankie Gammon,' Archie answered through gritted teeth.

'What about the bastard?' Jonny hissed. Pushing himself away from the wall, his fists involuntarily curled at his sides. 'Where does that lowlife come into any of this?'

'It was him who put the window through. You could say it was a warning of what will happen if we don't pay up on time.' He slipped his hand into his pocket and pulled out the crumpled note that had been attached to the brick and passed it across.

As he read the note, confusion was etched across Jonny's face. 'I don't understand.' He shook his head as though trying to work out exactly what Archie was trying to tell him. 'What do you mean by "pay up"? Why would you even need to pay up?'

'Exactly what I said.' Archie gave a helpless shrug. 'He's been demanding protection money from us. If it was down to me then I'd deal with this myself. I might be getting on in years, but I've still got some pride left inside me and believe me when I say this, I'm not afraid of the man and never will be. I still know how to handle myself; I wouldn't have lasted two minutes in this game if I couldn't,' he added. 'But...' He looked towards where his wife was standing behind the bar, his expression instantly softening. 'I can't put my Rina in danger, and you know yourself what Gammon is like. The sly bastard is unhinged, he would use her to get to me; he's already more than hinted at that fact.'

'Yeah.' Jonny nodded thoughtfully. He knew exactly what Frankie Gammon was like, hence why he'd finally given in to Ricky Tempest's demands and handed over an address for the no-good ponce. 'Look.' Jonny gave a reassuring smile. 'I can set up a meeting, no big deal. But are you really sure that you want to be in Ricky and Jamie's pocket? What's to say they would be any easier to deal with? The demands they put forward may be far worse than anything Gammon would put on you.'

After giving the question a moment's thought, Archie leant back against the wall. 'I don't have any other choice,' he sighed. 'And deep down, Ricky and Jamie are good lads; I've known them since they were kids. They might have reputations and I don't doubt for a single second that they can handle themselves, but at least they've got morals, unlike Frankie Gammon. They would never harm my Rina, or any other woman come to think of it; it wouldn't even enter their heads to use her as a way of retaliation, nor would they ever be unreasonable when it comes to paying protection money.'

'Fair point,' Jonny agreed. Despite their father's crimes, to his knowledge neither Ricky nor Jamie had never so much as raised their voices to a woman let alone used one as leverage. 'Leave it with me and I'll see what I can do.'

'Cheers Jonny.' Archie thrust out his hand. 'I knew I'd be able to count on you.'

As they shook on the deal, Jonny chewed on the inside of his cheek. Returning to the bar he ordered himself a beer, then took a seat on a bar stool. Between mouthfuls, he couldn't help but glance up at the boarded-up window. He would never have said it out loud, but the fact Gammon even had the audacity to demand protection money on what was commonly considered to be the Tempest brothers' territory didn't sit right with him. Just what exactly was Gammon trying to prove? And how had he gone from pushing pills to extorting money in such a short space of time?

Downing his drink, Jonny slipped off the stool, said his goodbyes, then left the pub. By the time he'd reached his car, he was already scrolling through his contact list. He needed to get in touch with Ricky and Jamie and fast. He had a nasty feeling that there was more than met the eye where Gammon was concerned, and if he hadn't known any better, he would have sworn that Gammon had a personal vendetta against the brothers. The question was: why? Unless Gammon had been living underneath a rock for the past twenty years, he was bound to know that Ricky and Jamie were no pushovers; everyone knew it, hence why anyone with half a brain cell gave them a wide berth.

Moments later, after switching off his phone, Jonny jumped into the car, turned the ignition, then, pushing his foot down on the accelerator, screeched out of the car park and headed towards the Tempest brothers' taxi firm just a short five-minute drive away. By the time he'd reached his destination, just one glance towards the taxi office was enough to tell him that all hell was about to break loose, and he had more than just an inkling that Frankie Gammon was about to feel the full force of the Tempest brothers' wrath.

* * *

Within a matter of hours, Ricky and Jamie had set up a meeting with Archie Taylor. Breezing through the pub door with a swagger that bordered on arrogance, they took a moment to look around them. The hushed silence that fell over the pub was enough to alert them to the fact that their presence had been duly noted, which in their eyes was a bonus. They wanted word to get out that they'd been seen entering the boozer, and even more than that, they wanted the news of their arrival to reach Frankie Gammon's ears. With a bit of luck, he may even turn up and if he did then Ricky and Jamie were more than prepared for him.

Taking their cue from Archie, the brothers made their way through the throng of patrons, their expressions hard and their lips set into thin lines. Coming to a table on the far side of the premises, they pulled out a seat, sat down, then lounged back on the chairs as though they didn't have a single care in the world.

'Thank you for coming at such short notice.' Archie placed a bottle of brandy on the table before them then set about pouring their drinks. 'But as I'm sure Jonny told you, I'm at my wit's end. I don't know where else to turn.'

'I take it that's Gammon's handiwork?' Sitting forward and

resting his forearms on the table, Jamie jerked his thumb behind him, gesturing towards the boarded-up window.

'Yeah.' Slamming the note down on the middle of the table, Archie's cheeks turned red as he lifted a glass to his lips and swallowed the liquid down in one large gulp before refilling his glass a second time and doing the same again. 'Amongst other things, he threatened to burn us down if we don't pay up.'

Narrowing his eyes, Ricky shot Jamie a look. Their half-brother Raymond had had a penchant for playing with fire and had actually succeeded in burning down the car showroom that had belonged to Max Hardcastle.

'And, well as you can imagine,' Archie continued, oblivious to the sudden tension that came from the two brothers. 'My Rina is terrified that we'll end up being burnt alive while we're sleep. I had to go out and buy extra smoke alarms just to put her mind at rest.'

Jamie sighed. He gave the note a customary glance before looking across at his brother and giving a shake of his head. He and Ricky had always had a lot of time for Archie Taylor and his wife Rina. As far as landlords went, Archie was a good bloke; he could be fair when he needed to be and had a no-nonsense attitude about him which went a long way in Jamie's book when it came to running a boozer. Archie was also no pushover and the fact Frankie Gammon was demanding protection money from him was a piss take of the highest order, especially when the pub was on their manor.

'As of today, Gammon is finished.' Ricky's lips curled up into a snarl. 'I give you my word on that.'

Archie nodded. 'And how much is all of this going to cost me?' He glanced towards his wife, watching as she busied herself around the bar. 'We're just about making ends meet as it is and my Rina—'

Jamie held up his hand, cutting Archie off. 'I've been coming in here since I was... I don't know, eight or nine, maybe even younger than that.' He leaned back in the chair and smiled. 'I used to sneak mouthfuls of my old man's beer when he wasn't looking. I think he knew what I was up to,' he laughed. 'He would have seen it as a rite of passage. I mean, all kids try it on, don't they and being the little scallywag I was I tried it on more than most. I've got nothing but good memories of this place,' he said, looking around him. 'We used to come here for all the big celebrations, birthdays, Christmas, New Year's Eve. I can still remember my mum and dad having a dance; more often than not, my mum would be holding my dad up because he was so pissed, but that was what it was all about, having a good time. And so to be told that that parasite Gammon is making demands on what was my dad's turf, on what is now our fucking turf,' he growled, motioning towards Ricky, his expression becoming suddenly menacing. 'Well, you can just imagine how much that has riled me up.'

Archie swallowed deeply and lowering his head, he cleared his throat. 'You still haven't answered my question. How much is this going to cost me?'

Ricky took a sip of his drink. 'How much was Gammon demanding from you?'

'It started off at 500 nicker per week,' Archie answered, glancing at the note. 'But now he's more than doubled that amount. He's already smashed the optics, glasses and rifled through the till. Then there's the window to contend with; getting that fixed is going to cost me some considerable dough, money that I don't have might I add, not when I'm replacing the damage he's causing on a weekly basis. It all mounts up; I can't run a boozer if I don't have any glasses or booze to serve.'

'Fuck me, it's even worse than I thought.' Slumping back in the chair, Jamie gave a half laugh. 'The prick hasn't got a scooby has he?'

Ricky shook his head. 'Doesn't look like it.' Folding his arms over his chest, he cocked his head to one side as he studied Archie. 'Luckily for you, we already have a personal beef with Gammon, and that,' he said, pointing his finger forward. 'Means that long before Carter,' he said, nodding towards the man in question as Jonny entered the pub and made his way towards them, 'set up this meeting, the no-good bastard was on our radar.'

Archie looked up, a spark of hope flickering in his eyes. 'So what does that mean for us, for me and my Rina?'

'It means' – Jamie grinned – 'we could sort out your little problem. We won't want payment as such, just a percentage of this place. I've always fancied owning a boozer and as I've already stated, I have fond memories of coming here as a kid.'

Archie shook his head, his eyebrow rising. 'I don't understand,' he began.

Jamie's grin widened. 'Say me and Ricky were to pump 50 per cent into this place, from my calculations, on today's market, that would be roughly three hundred and fifty grand give or take a few quid. Now that,' he said, sitting forward, 'would make us your business associates and as co-owners we would have a say in how this place is run. Not only that but it would also mean any protection money Gammon has the front to try and demand is now null and void and with a bit of luck it would also draw him out. He clearly has some kind of an issue with us and once he knows we're involved with this place he'll more than likely come crawling out of the woodwork. And what's more, our association with the pub would give us a legitimate reason to wipe the sly bastard off the face of the earth without any aggro coming back on us.'

Steepling his fingers in front of him, Archie thought the proposition over. 'And you think this could work? That it would get Gammon off our back?'

Both Ricky and Jamie nodded.

'And it would be kosher and above board?'

'Straight down the middle mate, fifty, fifty,' Ricky answered. 'We could get the contracts written up within a matter of days or at the latest a week or two and once you've signed along the dotted line, the cash would hit your bank account as quick as that,' Ricky said with a click of his fingers.

'Three hundred and fifty grand,' Jamie added with a raise of his eyebrows. 'That's a lot of dough. No more money worries. You and Rina could even take a holiday, somewhere exotic. Think of it as taking a well-deserved rest, all the while knowing that this place would be left in safe hands.'

Archie chewed on the inside of his cheek. 'It's been years since me and Rina had a holiday,' he admitted.

'Then this would be your chance,' Jamie coaxed. 'Just imagine it, sun, sea, and as much sangria as you could possibly drink.'

'I don't know.' Archie hesitated. 'Rina...'

'Rina isn't stupid,' Ricky butted in. He motioned towards the broken window. 'This is just the beginning. What do you think will happen when you can't pay up? Do you really think Gammon will let that slide? No.' He leaned in closer. 'After he's smashed this place up, he'll move on to breaking bones. The question is, will they be yours or Rina's?'

The colour drained from Archie's face. 'What do I have to do to keep my wife safe?' he asked.

Jamie stuck out his hand. 'Shake on the deal and we'll take it from there.'

Momentarily closing his eyes, Archie groaned. 'She's going to bloody kill me,' he said, thrusting out his hand to shake on the deal. 'Trust me, Gammon won't get a look in once my Rina finds out that I've as good as signed away half the business.'

* * *

Hiding in the shadows, Terri watched as Archie pulled out a chair and took a seat at a table. From her position she couldn't hear what was being said, but from the way Archie and her brothers' heads were bent towards each other, she could tell that they were in deep conversation.

'Excuse me darling.'

As a figure gently pushed past her, Terri looked up, the scent of his expensive aftershave assaulting her nostrils. She'd never seen the man before and as he headed for Archie's table, she moved closer to the bar, intrigued.

'Who's that man?' she asked as she sidled up beside Rina just in time to watch the newcomer take a seat at the table opposite her brothers and Archie.

'That, my darling,' Rina said, resting her forearms on the bar, 'is Jonny Carter.' She gave him a wistful look, a soft smile creasing her face. 'If only I was ten years younger.'

Terri giggled and as Rina turned to face her, Terri squashed her lips together, hiding her laughter.

'Okay,' Rina sighed with a flap of her hand. 'Point taken. If only I was twenty years younger. God, the things I'd like to do to him.' She wiggled her eyebrows seductively. 'Not forgetting the things I'd like him to do to me.'

Terri's jaw dropped, a shocked expression filtering across her face as she motioned towards the man she had come to love as a father. 'And what about poor Archie? I thought you only had eyes for him. You said that he was the love of your life.'

Rina flapped her hand. 'You know I love the bones of that man.' She straightened up and began wiping down the bar. 'Even Jonny over there wouldn't be able to tempt me away from him. Although' – she winked – 'I'd enjoy every second of him trying to steal me away.'

'So who is he?' As she joined Rina and placed her elbows on the bar, Terri rested her chin in her hands. She could see for herself that he was handsome and had a certain charisma about him. Was it any wonder that Rina had broken out in a hot flush over the man?

'He's one of the Carter brothers,' Rina sighed, lowering her voice. 'And a bloody good armed robber too. He used to be a boxer years ago, they all were, the brothers I mean, and they're a big family, six boys in total. Me and Archie used to go and watch them fight at the Circus Tavern and they were good, better than good actually, they had a natural talent, especially Tommy, the eldest, God rest his soul,' she said, looking up at the ceiling and making the sign of the cross across her chest.

'Armed robber,' Terri gasped.

Laughing out loud, Rina tossed the damp cloth onto the bar and draped her arm loosely around Terri's shoulders. 'Nothing for you to worry your pretty little head about. He's quite harmless, unless you get on the wrong side of him of course.'

Terri snapped her lips closed. She had no intentions of getting on the wrong side of the man, and seeing as he was sitting with her brothers, she had a feeling that he wasn't quite as harmless as Rina made him out to be, proving to her once and for all that looks could be deceptive.

Twenty minutes later, after shaking the men's hands, Archie made his way back to the bar, his expression closed off.

'Well?' Rina asked, concern clouding her face.

'It's done.' Glancing behind him, Archie indicated to the now-empty table. 'As of today, Gammon is finished; he won't be causing us any further problems.'

'And...?' Biting down on her bottom lip, Rina looked up into her husband's face. 'I'm guessing they aren't going to help us out of the kindness of their heart. So how much do they want?'

Archie sighed. 'They put forward a deal that we would be fools not to take them up on.'

'What kind of a deal?' Rina probed.

'Let me worry about that,' Archie answered, averting his gaze. 'The main thing is that Gammon will be dealt with. The plan the Tempests have come up with will soon have the little weasel running for the hills. Even Jonny Carter is gunning for the bastard, that's got to tell you something.' He kissed the top of his wife's head and even as Rina hugged Archie to her ample chest, Terri couldn't help but notice the worry in the older woman's eyes, nor the look of guilt that flashed across Archie's face.

Terri's gaze snapped towards the entrance; she could understand Rina's concern. What would become of them if Frankie Gammon decided to retaliate? Would Ricky and Jamie Tempest view both the Taylors and herself as collateral damage, mere casualties in the war they had become embroiled in? It was a stark reminder that despite the fact they shared the same blood, she and her half-brothers were strangers and always would be.

10

Raymond Cole was feeling restless. He'd never been one to have much patience and the fact he'd waited near on twenty years to exact his revenge on his brothers was beginning to take its toll. Instinctively, his fingers reached up to touch the thick, gnarled scar on his cheek. He wasn't even sure which one of his brothers had marked him. At the time he'd been hovering between life and death, all thanks to the brutal, relentless beating they'd dished out, but if he was to point fingers, he'd take a wild guess at Jamie being the culprit. Out of the two brothers, it was no secret that Jamie was the mouthy one, he was hot tempered too, unlike his elder brother Ricky who was more of a thinker and who thought through his actions.

'So what do we do now?'

As all eyes turned to look at him, Raymond looked up, a snarl creasing his face.

'We can't let the bastards get away with this.'

Raymond narrowed his eyes. The hostility he felt towards the man questioning his tactics radiated off him in waves. He'd detested the little weasel on sight; he had a slyness about him that grated heavily on Raymond's nerves, and he didn't trust him as far as he could throw him, not that he could say he'd ever had a trusting nature to begin with. From an early age, Raymond had soon figured out that those who were meant to love him unconditionally had never wanted him in their lives. Time and time again his mother had told him that she'd wished she'd aborted him and as for his father Terry, the only times he'd made the effort to contact him were when he finally remembered that he'd sired a third son. Yet despite this, Raymond had loved his father, he'd looked up to Terry and had wanted to be just like him when he grew up. He'd wanted to make him proud and even more than that, he'd wanted Terry to freely spend time with him.

'What do you mean by we?' He got to his feet, his muscular frame becoming all the more menacing as he stalked across the room. 'Since when did my business become something for you to poke your nose into?'

Michael Murphy attempted to smile. 'You know... this.' He gestured around him, his gaze lingering on the hallway where he'd discovered the bloody body before Frankie's henchmen had disposed of him in an unmarked grave in a quiet, secluded corner of Epping Forest. 'They've taken the piss out of us.'

'No, I don't know,' Raymond growled. 'So, I'll ask you again,' he said, his voice rising with each and every word he spat out. 'What do you mean by us?'

Michael opened his mouth to answer before hastily closing it again.

'Let's get one thing straight,' Raymond continued to snarl, the nerve at the side of his eye convulsing. 'There is no us, we, or whatever the fuck else you want to call it.'

'Yeah but...' Undeterred, Michael looked around him. 'They killed one of our own. We can't let them get away with that.'

'And who the fuck are they?'

The slyness in Michael's eyes intensified. 'The Tempests,' he was quick to answer. 'It had to be them; who else would dare take one of us out? You have to remember, I know these fuckers.' He sat forward in the chair and stabbed a stiff finger into his chest, his expression contorting with rage. 'I know exactly what they are capable of. It's because of them I served a stretch. Sixteen years of my life spent banged up no better than a caged animal and all the while they were on the outside living the life of fucking Riley, doing well for themselves.' A crafty grin etched its way across Michael's face. 'They've never even given two fucks about their sister, or rather your sister, seeing as you all share the same father.' He rubbed his hand across his chin as though contemplating the situation. 'Terri, my niece,' he was quick to point out. 'They kicked the poor little cow to the kerb, never so much as gave her the time of day. I mean' – he spread open his arms, the lies easily tripping off his tongue – 'I've tried to do my bit over the years, I stepped up, was there for her, even provided for her whenever I could. But it's just not the same, is it? I'm her uncle not her brothers, not her direct flesh and blood so to speak.'

Raymond looked up. He could vaguely recall Bianca Murphy claiming she was pregnant with his father's kid. Not that he'd given two fucks at the time, nor had they crossed his mind since then, why would they, they meant nothing to him. 'What's she like?' he asked.

Michael opened his mouth before hastily closing it again, wondering how best to answer. He could hardly blurt out that he thought Terri was a little bitch, that he wished she'd never been born. 'She's a Tempest through and through,' he finally answered, forcing himself to smile in an attempt to hide the loathing he felt for his niece. 'She's a nice kid, got a temper on her though, doesn't take fools gladly.'

Raymond burst out laughing. 'And I bet that went down like a lead balloon with those two cunts,' he said, referring to Ricky and Jamie. 'No wonder they want nothing to do with her; they're more than likely worried she'll be able to claim some of the dough they inherited from my old man.'

Glad to be back on neutral territory, Michael grinned. This was more like it; this he could deal with. 'Yeah, the no-good tossers.'

From across the room, Frankie Gammon nervously cleared his throat. 'He's got a point,' he begrudgingly said, tipping his chin towards Michael. 'I reckon they're on to us. It wouldn't surprise me if Archie Taylor went running to them for protection.'

A smile tugged at the corners of Raymond's lips. He'd been banking on the guvnor of The Merry Fiddlers to turn to his brothers for help; it was their so-called manor after all, and one of the reasons why he'd ordered Frankie to demand protection money from the landlord in the first place. It wasn't as though he actually needed the cash; why would he when he had his minions selling pills, cannabis, cocaine, heroin, and any other drug he could lay his hands on by the bucket load. Narcotics was where the real money came from and it was a lucrative business, one that had served him well over the years. The measly 1,000 pounds that was to come from Archie Taylor was the equivalent of a drop in the ocean as far as Raymond was concerned, nothing more than mere pocket money. He could easily flutter away the same amount of cash in the casinos on a nightly basis without so much as blinking an eye. Poker was a particular favourite of his, not that he was averse to trying his luck on the slot machines. Win or lose, it was the buzz, the thrill of the chase that Raymond enjoyed the most.

Rubbing his thumb across his bottom lip, Raymond was deep in thought. 'Maybe it's time to up the ante,' he finally announced. 'Time to really rile those bastards up. They've been a bit too quiet for my liking.' He shot Frankie a pointed look as if daring him to argue the case. Despite Gammon's so-called hard man reputation,

Raymond had found him to be lacking when it came to asserting his power. Perhaps he should have known better, seeing as Gammon had neither the intelligence nor the muscle to ever become anything more than a glorified joey. In fact, he wouldn't be surprised if Gammon was to actually shit himself if he were to ever come face to face with Ricky and Jamie Tempest.

Beside him, Michael rubbed his hands together with glee. 'Now we're starting to get somewhere.' He grinned with excitement. 'It's about time we fucked them over.'

Raymond returned the grin, although it would be fair to say that it was somewhat forced. 'So what are you useless fuckers waiting for? Get out there and do something proactive for once in your miserable lives.'

As the men scrambled up from their seats and headed for the door, Raymond watched them go. 'Oh, and Michael,' he said as he popped a cigarette between his lips and took his time in lighting up, 'seeing as we're family now, don't let me down.'

Michael puffed out his chest. 'I won't,' he answered, flashing a wide toothy grin. 'You can count on me to shake things up.'

Raymond nodded and as two thick plumes of cigarette smoke lazily drifted down from each of his nostrils, he waved his hand dismissively. At times, Michael Murphy reminded him of an over eager puppy, and he was in half a mind to put him in his place or better still, to kick him to the kerb. It was only for the fact that he may very well come in useful one day that Raymond hadn't already given him his marching orders. In fact, regardless of the circumstances, namely that he was his half-sister's uncle, as soon as Michael had served his purpose, which he inevitably would, then Raymond was determined to enjoy every second of tearing him down.

* * *

From her position behind the bar, Rina Taylor's forehead was furrowed. For the past ten minutes she'd been keeping a close eye on her husband and the Tempest brothers as they sat at a table far away from any prying eyes.

'Here.' Beckoning for Terri to join her, Rina cocked her head to the side. 'What do you reckon they're up to over there?'

Taking a quick peek from behind her hiding place, Terri shrugged. 'Having a chat from the look of things.'

Rina rolled her eyes. 'I'd already gathered that much. And I don't know what you're skulking in the shadows for; they haven't so much as looked in your direction,' she said, shaking her head. 'And even if they did, what does it matter? I thought you said they have no idea you're their sister.'

The colour drained from Terri's face. 'Half-sister,' she whispered, shooting another glance towards Archie's table.

'Oh darling.' Rina's expression softened. 'Sister or half-sister, at the end of the day it makes no difference; you're still family, you still share the same blood.'

Terri shook her head. 'But we're not family though, are we? Not really. We're nothing but strangers.'

Rina sighed. 'And it's a downright shame if you ask me. No matter the circumstances, you still share the same father; you're all Tempests and there's no getting away from that fact.' Straightening up, she eyed Archie with a level of suspicion as he made his way behind the bar. 'What was all that about?' she demanded to know.

'Nothing. Just a chat, that's all. They wanted to see how things were going, you know, what with Gammon and everything. Wanted to make sure there'd been no comebacks.' He lifted his eyebrows and grinned. 'They offered to get the window fixed for us too,' he said, nodding towards the sheet of plywood tacked to the window frame.

Rina's mouth dropped open. 'Why on earth would they do something like that?'

Averting his gaze, Archie shrugged. 'Because they're good lads, that's why.'

As she placed her hands on her hips, Rina frowned. 'I don't understand.' She glanced towards Terri as if she would have the answers she so desperately craved. 'Why would they do that? Or more to the point, what are Ricky and Jamie getting out of this?'

'Like I already said,' Archie answered as he attempted to slip past his wife. 'They're good lads and just want to help us out, nothing more than that. Besides, they have their own issues with Frankie Gammon to contend with; they want to see him brought down as much as we do.'

'Is that so?' she probed, nodding down at the large brown envelope her husband was desperately trying to hide from her. 'I expect you want me to believe that that's nothing too.'

As he shrugged his shoulders, Archie gave a lopsided grin. 'I told you I'd take care of things and I have. Maybe one day you'll even thank me, and I'll tell you something else,' he said, leaning in closer. 'First thing tomorrow morning, you can get yourself down to the travel agent's and pick up a couple of brochures. It's about time we had a little holiday, just the two of us, somewhere nice and hot.'

'Yeah, if you say so.' Rina rolled her eyes before flicking the bar towel at her husband's retreating backside. 'And pigs might fly Archie Taylor,' she called out to him. 'Unless it's escaped your notice, we're not exactly rolling in money.'

Once her husband was out of sight, Rina narrowed her eyes. 'What on earth was all that about?'

Leaning against the bar, Terri pulled her shoulders up into a shrug. 'Maybe Archie just wants to take you away for a while, to have a little rest and recharge your batteries. I think it would do you both the world of good.' She smiled. 'You never get to have a day off, at least not a full one anyway. There's always something that needs to be done; if it's not the accounts, then it's checking stock levels, washing the bar towels, cleaning. Last week you spent the entire morning trying to get through to the brewery. The list is endless.'

Rina sighed. It was true; there was always a never-ending list of jobs that needed doing, but even so, as nice as it would be to take a well-deserved rest, they didn't have the money for holidays. It was hard enough finding the money to live day to day, how could they spend hundreds of pounds, if not thousands, on a holiday that they couldn't afford let alone justify. And even if they did have the cash, who was going to run the pub while they were away? They couldn't just abandon the business for a week or two; the customers would be in uproar. Even so, that still didn't answer why Ricky and Jamie wanted to help them out. They may have been good lads as Archie had so rightly pointed out, but it still made no sense to her why they would be willing to fork out money from their own pocket to fix the window, not unless they were getting something out of it.

As she went back to pulling pints, Rina's mind was elsewhere. It was unlike her Archie to be so secretive. She'd been married to the man long enough to know when he was keeping something from her. As it was, he'd never been a very good liar and she'd always been able to see right through him. He may as well be made from a pane of glass; she could read him that easily. Her mind wandered back to the envelope and as she glanced towards the table where Archie and the Tempest brothers had been sitting, her stomach churned with worry. Could Ricky and Jamie have persuaded Archie to take part in something illegal? Perhaps paying for the window to be fixed was their way of ensuring that Archie did their bidding. As soon as the thought popped into her mind, Rina shook her head. Archie was as straight as a die, he always had been. He may turn a blind eye where the customers were concerned but he himself would never become embroiled in criminal activity. He'd always prided himself on being an honest, hardworking man, just as his father and grandfathers had been before him.

'I think you're worrying over nothing,' Terri announced, breaking Rina's thoughts. 'Archie isn't stupid; he would never do anything to jeopardise what the two of you have together.'

'Yeah, you're right.' Rina smiled. 'He might be an old fool but he's my old fool and let's face it, he may have his moments but deep down he's a good man, or at least he is most of the time, anyway,' she laughed good naturedly.

* * *

Later that evening, Terri wrapped her fingers around a thick length of cord, her gaze firmly fixed upon the clock on the wall. Archie was a stickler for ringing the bell for last orders dead on time, not a minute before and not a minute after.

As soon as the clock turned eleven Terri tugged on the cord. She was dead beat and couldn't wait for the customers to leave. All she wanted to do was sink onto the sofa and close her eyes with her legs curled underneath her.

'Come on you lot,' Rina shouted out. 'Don't you have homes to go to?'

Amid the customers' groans, she and Rina poured out their last drinks. The sound of the till ringing as they hastily made their way through the throng of queueing patrons was enough to put a wide smile upon Terri's face. Over the past week, business had been booming, much to Archie and Rina's relief and today was no exception. A part of her wondered if Archie was right and that the only reason they were so busy was because her brothers had been seen frequenting the pub. 'This lot are scared they'll miss something,' Archie had said, thumbing the table he, Ricky, and Jamie had been sitting at. 'And if it kicks off in here, they all want to be able to say that they'd witnessed the trouble first-hand.' Terri wasn't so sure; did her brothers really wield that much power?

They had just finished taking the orders of the last straggling customers when the pub door banged wide open with such ferocity that the glass panels rattled.

'We're closed...' Rina called out, the words dying in her throat as she took note of Frankie Gammon and his firm stepping inside the pub.

The fine hairs on the back of Terri's neck stood upright and as she snapped her head towards Archie, a shiver of fear ran down the length of her spine. As much as Frankie Gammon scared her, it was her uncle Michael who she was more terrified of. Would he force her to leave the Taylors and return home? Perhaps this time he would call for her mother, and the last thing Terri wanted was for Bianca to turn up and cause a scene.

'Get out,' Archie snarled, his arms crossed over his wide chest. 'I've already told you multiple times you're not welcome in here.'

A wide grin spread across Frankie's face, causing his heavy jowls to wobble with the action. 'That's where you're wrong,' Frankie said in carefree manner. 'We had a deal.' He turned his head to look at Rina, his pink tongue darting out as he licked along his top lip. 'And you owe me. So unless you want my boys to tear this place down brick by brick, you'd best pay up.'

As several of the customers made to rise from their seats in an attempt to come to Archie's aid, Archie waved them back down. 'There's been a change of plan.' He gave a smile, his voice sounding almost jovial. 'We no longer need your protection. In fact,' he said, taking a step closer, his fists clenched at his sides, 'my new business partners are more than capable of taking care of any problems that may arise.'

Terri jerked her head around to look at Rina. The fact the older woman's jaw had almost dropped to the floor and that her hand had fluttered up to clutch at her throat was enough to tell her that Rina was just as stunned by the revelation as she was.

'You see, this place,' Archie continued as he gestured around him, 'is now co-owned by the Tempest brothers. And as I'm sure you're more than aware, they can take care of their own business.'

A stunned silence fell across the pub and if it wasn't for the sound of blood whooshing in her ears, Terri would have presumed that she'd lost her hearing, that the shock of what Archie had just announced had somehow rendered her deaf.

'No,' Rina gasped, breaking the silence. 'How could you?' Tears welled in her eyes and as Terri made to grab for her hand, Rina threw her away from her. 'What do you mean the Tempest brothers are now our business partners?' she cried as she ran around the bar. 'You had no right to do that. And how...' She stumbled over the words, her eyebrows scrunching together. 'How could you have done something like this without speaking to me first? We're more than man and wife, we're a partnership.'

Archie cast his gaze downward, a slight shrug pulling at his shoulders. 'I had no other choice,' he admitted. 'It's because of this bastard,' he said, glaring across to Frankie. 'It's the only way to get this fucker off our backs.'

Rina's mouth opened and closed in rapid succession, reminding Terri of a fish out of water. 'How could you?' she screamed, slapping whichever part of her husband's body she could lay her hands on. 'And to the Tempests of all people. We're finished now, can't you see that? Finished.'

Terri's heart beat so hard and so fast that she thought she would collapse. Rina was right; what would it mean for them, for all of them, now that her brothers were co-owners of the pub? Were they planning to sell the pub from under Archie and Rina's feet? Could the couple very well end up homeless, and their business in tatters? A lone tear spilled down Terri's cheek; she was so preoccupied with the predicament Archie and Rina had found themselves in that she'd forgotten her uncle Michael was in the room. It wasn't until his hard laugh resonated through the air that she whipped her head around to look at him.

'As entertaining as all of this is,' Michael continued to laugh. 'You're boring me now.' Bringing himself up to his full height, he slipped his hand inside his jacket. 'Tempests or no Tempests, you still owe us and we're not leaving here without the cash.'

Tightly grasping his wife's wrists in an attempt to stop her from lashing out at him, Archie shook his head. 'You're getting fuck all from me,' he growled, addressing Frankie Gammon. 'So do yourselves a favour and get the fuck out of my pub before I have you thrown out.'

Frozen to the spot, Terri could only look on helplessly. The event that followed happened so fast that she could barely catch her breath let alone force her feet to move. Within a matter of moments, Archie staggered forwards before dropping to his knees, his hand clutching at his chest.

Terri screwed her eyes shut tight, too afraid to watch. *Please be a nightmare*, she begged. *Please let me wake up*. Only the blood curdling screams that came from Rina told her that this was no nightmare, this was real, this was happening, Archie had been stabbed.

Rina dropped to her knees and desperately tried to stem the bleeding. The bloodied knife that was still gripped firmly in Michael's hand glinted underneath the light.

'Help him,' Rina screamed, her eyes wild with panic. 'Please, please someone help him.'

The desperation in Rina's voice shook Terri to the core. She snapped her head around to look back at Michael, and the sickening smirk across his face filled her with hatred. Finally she found the strength to move forward and raced around the bar. From somewhere behind her she could hear someone shouting out to call for an ambulance, their screams as frantic as Rina's had been and as Terri sank to the floor, deep down in her heart she knew that it was too late, Archie was already gone. No matter how quick the ambulance arrived or how many chest compressions the paramedics gave him, it wouldn't be enough to bring him back. And as much as she didn't want to see them, the signs were all there, the stillness of his body, his lips that had turned blue from lack of oxygen, the bright red blood that covered the front of his shirt and then his chest that failed to move up and down.

Dread filled Terri's heart. She pulled Rina into her arms and held on for dear life as they both sobbed. Instinct told her that from this moment on both her and Rina's lives would never be the same again.

11

Tears threatened to spill from Terri's eyes. The grief she felt was still so raw. In the short time she'd known him, she had grown to love Archie and he had been the only father figure she had ever known, much more so than her own father or even grandfather had ever been.

Anger spurred her on and as she charged into the taxi office her brothers owned, she was all but ready to see blood spilled, preferably Ricky's and Jamie's. After all, in her mind they were responsible for Archie's death. Instead of protecting him they had done the total opposite and sacrificed him like a lamb to the slaughter.

'You bastards,' she spat through clenched teeth. The fear she'd once felt for her brothers had long evaporated; now, the only thing on her mind was revenge. 'You as good as killed him,' she shrieked, her hand flying out to deliver a sickening blow to Jamie's cheek.

'Woah.' Jumping to his feet, Mason raced around the desk, his arms encircling Terri's waist as he pulled her off his uncle.

'What the fuck do you think you're doing?' Ricky shouted as he too got to his feet, his expression hard.

Clawing at Mason's hands, Terri's gaze flew towards Ricky. The shock resonating across both his, Jamie's, and Mason's faces wasn't enough to satisfy the fury that flowed through her veins. She wanted to hurt them, to tear them apart with her bare hands, and more than anything she wanted them to feel the same indescribable pain that both she and Rina felt.

'You killed him,' she continued to scream. 'You killed Archie.'

With a flick of his head, Jamie indicated for Mason to release his grip. 'Let's get one thing straight,' he said, his voice a mere growl as he rubbed at the stark red hand print clearly visible upon his cheek. 'We had fuck all to do with Archie's murder.'

The high-pitched cackle that escaped from Terri's lips bordered on hysteria. 'You used him. You used him as bait,' she spat. 'You were meant to protect him. He trusted you.'

Her hands shot out again, only for Jamie to have already anticipated the action and as he rose to his feet, he swatted Terri away from him as though she was nothing but a mere fly. 'Back off,' he warned. 'And calm the fuck down.'

The tears Terri had tried so desperately to keep at bay spilled down her cheeks. 'Don't,' she cried. 'Don't you dare tell me to calm down. Archie is gone.' Holding her head in her hands, she sank onto a chair. She felt drained, the pain in her heart consuming every ounce of her being. 'It's because of you that he's gone.'

Jamie and Ricky shared a surreptitious glance.

'That wasn't our intention,' Jamie offered in the way of an apology. He gave an exasperated sigh. 'Archie was in the wrong place at the wrong time. It was us Gammon was after.'

Terri looked up, the anger in her eyes so palpable that she could almost taste her fury. 'So I was right all along. It was because of you that Archie was killed.' She balled her fists, her sharp talons digging into the flesh of her palms. 'And as if that wasn't bad enough, you took advantage of Archie, you used his trouble with Frankie Gammon as a way of getting your hands on his business.

What about Rina, eh? Are you going to force her to sell up, to leave her home?'

'No.' Ricky shook his head. 'Unless Rina plans to sell Archie's percentage of the pub then she can stay for as long as she wants.'

A snort of laughter escaped from Terri's lips. 'Well, that's very noble of you,' she sneered, clapping her hands together. 'But it still won't bring Archie back, will it? Rina will still be a widow. She's heartbroken; the life has been sucked out of her.'

'We know,' Ricky sighed. 'Archie's death is bound to leave a gaping hole.'

Nausea rose in Terri's throat. They just didn't get it. To them, death was nothing, not that she could say she was surprised. They had swinging bricks where their hearts were supposed to be. They were nothing but monsters, just as their father had been before them. Springing to her feet, she took a moment of satisfaction to see them flinch away from her, more than likely expecting her to lash out at them again; it was exactly what they deserved, after all. More than anything, she needed air, needed to get away from them; they were toxic, their very presence tainting everything around them. She'd said her piece, had let it be known that she blamed them for Archie's death. With one last glare, she ran from the office, her hand clasped tightly across her mouth. She wasn't prepared to completely break down, not in front of them; they had already seen enough of her tears and she wouldn't give them the gratification of knowing that their actions or rather their lack of actions had irrevocably broken her heart in two.

* * *

'Put your tongue back in Mase.' Jamie flicked his head towards the door that Terri had exited. 'She's off limits.'

'What?' Spinning around to look at his uncle, Mason narrowed his eyes. 'Why the fuck would she be off limits? She's a bit of me she is, and I bet she's a right goer. She's got some fight in her I know that much. For a moment there I thought she was going to scratch your eyes out.' He gave Jamie a wink. 'You can't tell me that you wouldn't go there, that you'd kick her out of bed. As for me,' he said, thumbing his chest, a wide grin spread across his face, 'she can scratch me as much as she wants and I'd happily live with the scars; fuck me, I'd even show them off.'

Jamie's expression hardened. 'I said that she's off limits,' he roared. 'So do us both a favour and shut the fuck up before I end up putting you on your arse and shutting you up once and for all, and believe me, you won't want that.'

Mason's jaw dropped. 'What's going on?' he asked his gaze going from his uncle to his father, then to the door. 'Don't tell me that you've already been there?' he asked, screwing up his face. 'That you've already had a piece of her?'

Jamie jumped out of his seat so fast that the chair he'd been sitting on toppled to the floor. 'What did I just fucking say?' he yelled, gripping onto the desk so hard that his knuckles turned white. 'Shut the fuck up.'

'Hey,' Ricky hissed, silently warning his brother to back off. 'Enough. You can't blame him for voicing his opinion,' he sighed then looked away. 'He doesn't know the truth, does he.'

Blinking rapidly, Mason stared at his uncle. 'Know what?' he said, stuffing his hands into his pockets, somewhat wary of Jamie after his outburst. 'It was a joke, that's all. I mean... I know you wouldn't go there, that you wouldn't play around on Georgiana,' he said, referring to Jamie's wife. 'You idolise her, worship the ground she walks on, everyone knows that.'

Satisfied with Mason's answer, Jamie yanked the chair upright and took a seat, debating within himself just how much information he should divulge to Mason. After a few moments of silence, he took a deep breath. 'I'm sorry,' he said, holding up his hands. 'I wouldn't have, you know,' he said, referring to the fact he had just threatened his only nephew with violence, 'but you need to stay away from her. She's—'

'Jamie,' Ricky interrupted with a shake of his head, his eyes flashing dangerously. 'Enough.'

'He needs to know the truth,' Jamie protested. 'He was drooling all over her and you and me both know that that can't happen. Ever.' He turned to look at Mason and lifted his eyebrows. 'She's our sister, half-sister actually. And that, sunshine, makes her your aunt. So whether you like it or not she's off limits.'

Screwing up his face again, Mason paled. 'Leave it out.' He gave an incredulous laugh and shook his head. 'Nah, you're lying. How could she be your sister? She doesn't look anything like us.' He reached up to touch his dark hair and as much as he hated to admit it, he could see the resemblance between them; if nothing else, their eyes were identical, the exact same shade of blue. 'Shit,' he mumbled as he slumped back onto a chair and kicked his legs out in front of him, his expression resembling that of a sulky teenager. 'I can't believe this. Cheers for the heads-up Dad. What if I'd met her on a night out?' He pressed his fist to his lips, swallowing down his repulsion. 'I wouldn't have given it a second's thought.'

'Yeah, you've got that much right,' Ricky conceded. 'It is shit; the whole situation is from start to finish.'

'Are there any more aunts out there I should know about?' he asked with a hint of sarcasm. 'You know, just in case I end up in a club one night and pull one of them.'

Jamie shook his. 'Not that I'm aware of, although, knowing what my old man was like, nothing would surprise me. He could have had a dozen kids and we'd be none the wiser.'

'I'm going to question every bird I look at now,' Mason complained, thumping his fist on the arm of the chair. 'This is going to fuck me up,' he spat, tapping his temple. 'Make me paranoid. And that's another thing: I still don't get it.' He shrugged, looking between his dad and uncle. 'I mean, how can she be your sister?'

'How do you think?' Ricky groaned. 'You're a bit too old for the birds and the bees talk don't you think.'

Mason rolled his eyes. 'I know how Dad; fuck me, I'm not that stupid.' He shook his head again, his face contorting with confusion. 'Did Nan give her up for adoption or something?'

Ricky puffed out an agitated breath. 'What do you think? Can you honestly imagine your nan ever willingly putting her own child into care?'

'No,' Mason was quick to reply. 'She would never do something like that.'

'Well then, there's your answer. She's my dad's daughter,' Ricky sighed. 'Being the unscrupulous bastard he was, he had an affair with Bianca Murphy and she,' he said, nodding towards the door, 'is the outcome.'

'So what are we going to do now then? About her I mean,' Mason asked as he looked between his father and uncle. 'She didn't look like she was going to let this drop.'

'Nothing.' Jamie shrugged. 'Other than us having a stake in the boozer, it's not our problem.'

'Yeah, but Frankie Gammon is our problem,' Mason pointed out. 'And you said that you liked Archie, that you'd respected him.' He turned to look at his dad. 'You were gutted when you heard he'd been topped. You even threatened to slice the culprit's throat from ear to ear when you get your hands on him.'

Running his tongue across his teeth, Jamie averted his gaze. As much as he might have wanted to hunt down Archie's murderer, if he was being honest with himself, the only reason he didn't want to get involved was because he didn't want to admit that being within Terri's vicinity rattled him far more than he was ever prepared to let on. Like Ricky, he may have caught glimpses of her from afar over the years, but he'd never actually come face to face with her before. He hadn't wanted to; even the mere thought of doing so felt as though he was betraying his mum somehow, not that she wouldn't have understood if he or Ricky had wanted to forge a relationship with their sister. His mum, Tracey, was a diamond and as much as she might despise his and Ricky's father, she would never have held a grudge against his offspring. Not only that, but she had since moved on with her life, with Max, and she was happy too, probably the happiest he'd ever seen her.

'He's right,' Ricky sighed. 'You know he is. We're involved in this whether we want to be or not. We signed a contract, knowing full well that becoming Archie's business partner would have ramifications, that Gammon wouldn't take the situation lying down. And now we have to deal with the consequences. The very least we can do is make sure that Rina is okay.'

'So, we'll send her some flowers then.' Jamie shrugged.

Ricky raised his eyebrows. 'That's not going to cut it and you know it.' Digging out his car keys, he pointed the key fob at his brother. 'We sort this out, now, today.'

Reluctantly, Jamie rose to his feet. Coming face to face with Terri twice in one day was a lot for him to get his head around, especially when his cheek was still smarting from her slap.

12

So many bouquets of flowers had been propped up against the outside wall of the pub that every time the door opened, the scent of roses, freesias, and lilies would waft inside. Not that Rina could stomach stepping outside to look at them. The well-wishers meant well, she knew that, but she wanted to grieve alone and couldn't bear to see the pity on people's faces.

When all was said and done, Archie had been a private man; he may have laughed and joked with the customers, but he'd never crossed the line and mixed business with pleasure, preferring to keep the two separate.

Wrapping her dressing gown tighter around her, Rina rubbed at her eyes. She hadn't even been able to find the strength to get dressed this morning. She couldn't, and more than anything, she didn't want to deal with the reality that Archie was really gone.

From her position at the kitchen table, Rina looked down at her mug of tea. It had long since turned cold, not that she'd even taken a sip; how could she when her heart ached so much that her entire body felt numb?

'Would you like me to make you a fresh cup?'

Without looking up, Rina shook her head. Terri meant well, and she knew the girl was worried for her, Rina could see it in her eyes, but making endless cups of tea that would sit untouched and eventually turn cold wasn't helping, nothing was going to help, how could it. No amount of crying was ever going to bring Archie back to her. He should have been preparing to open the pub, no doubt grumbling about the day's work ahead of them. Instead, his lifeless body lay in the morgue. Fresh tears spilled down Rina's cheeks. Why? She wanted to scream at the top of her lungs. Why did Archie have to leave her?

'The police left this for you...' Terri's voice trailed off as she pointed to the contact details for the police officer who had taken their witness statements. Rina couldn't even remember his name; she'd barely been listening when he'd introduced himself; everything was such a blur, and she hadn't slept in over thirty-eight hours. Was it any wonder that she couldn't think straight? 'Maybe when you're ready you can give them a call,' Terri added.

Rina nodded. In her mind there was nothing more to say. She'd already given her statement, had already told the police who had been responsible for Archie's death, so why weren't they out there looking for the murdering bastard?

'I'll get that.' Terri motioned towards the hallway and moments later Rina could hear her padding down the stairs to open the front door. Whoever it was, they hadn't knocked on the main pub door, more than likely guessing that they wouldn't be opening up, not today, tomorrow, nor the day after if Rina had her way. The only thing she wanted to do was crawl into bed, pull the covers up over her head and be left alone in peace to have a good cry.

'Rina.'

Rina looked up, her eyes and cheeks still wet.

'I wasn't sure whether I should come or not... or if you'd rather be left alone?' Standing awkwardly in the doorway to the kitchen,

Jonny Carter gave a small smile. He looked down at his hands, then remembering the roses he was holding, he stepped forward and placed them on the table. 'If there's anything that I can do for you, and I mean anything,' he emphasised, 'then just say the word and I'll do it.'

As she swallowed down the hard lump in her throat, Rina's voice cracked with emotion. 'Find him,' she croaked out. 'Find Gammon and make him pay for what he's done.'

* * *

Terri snapped her head around to look at Jonny Carter in an attempt to gauge his reaction to Rina's request. Before he could open his mouth to answer, she instinctively knew that he'd pledge his allegiance to find Archie's murderer, that at that precise moment in time he would have promised Rina the earth if it would help put an end to her tears. Only, Terri knew that despite what she'd told the police, it wasn't Gammon who had taken Archie's life. She'd merely agreed with everything Rina had said, needing to get her own head around the fact that amongst other things, her uncle was also a murderer. That wasn't to say Frankie Gammon hadn't been a willing participant, because he had been. If it hadn't been for him demanding protection money, then Archie would still be alive, but it had been Michael who'd committed the heinous deed. She'd seen the bloodied blade in her uncle's hand, had seen his wicked smirk as he'd thrust his fist forward and twisted the knife in an upward movement. Archie hadn't stood a chance; the damage Michael had inflicted had been too severe for him to ever walk away unscathed.

'I promise you.' Crouching down beside Rina, Jonny grasped her tiny hand in his. 'That I will find the bastard and that I will deal with him.'

As Rina's sobs turned to hiccups, Jonny pulled her closer and whispered words of comfort. Moments later, he straightened up, his expression becoming closed off as he turned to look at Terri. 'Will you be staying with Rina?'

Terri nodded.

'Good.' He flashed a sad smile, his face instantly softening as he reached down to pat Terri's shoulder. 'Take care of her.'

'I will do,' she answered, her gaze following him as he left the kitchen and made his way down the stairs. She heard him open the front door, his voice and then the voices of two other men suddenly filtering back up to the kitchen.

The blood drained from Terri's face and as she shot a look towards Rina, her eyes widened to their utmost. Of course she would recognise their voices; it would have been hard to mistake them seeing as she'd stormed into their office just hours earlier to have it out with them. Had they come to do their worst, to prove to her once and for all that they were monsters? Were they planning to throw Rina out of her home, or perhaps they had come in retaliation for the slap she'd delivered to Jamie's cheek? Goose flesh covered Terri's arms and she was in half a mind to make a dash for it and lock herself away in the bathroom, not that the flimsy lock would be enough to keep her brothers out for long.

'Is that Ricky and Jamie I can hear?' Rina asked, dabbing at her cheeks.

Rina broke her reverie and as her brothers' heavy footsteps could be heard climbing the stairs, Terri nodded and took several steps back, almost colliding with the kitchen cabinets in her haste to make herself as invisible as possible.

It was Ricky who entered the kitchen first and like Jonny, he carried a small bouquet of flowers wrapped in clear cellophane. 'I am so, so sorry Rina. Archie was a good man and will be sorely missed.'

Terri's forehead furrowed, confusion etching across her

features. This wasn't what she'd been expecting at all. Was her brother actually being nice? If anything, she'd expected to hear arrogance in his voice or for him to immediately begin throwing his weight around, shouting the odds, demanding that Rina leave her home.

'These are from my mum,' he said, placing the bouquet beside the roses. 'She said if there's anything you need then to let her know.'

Rina sniffed back her tears. 'Thank you,' she said, dabbing once more at her watery eyes. 'If anyone knows how it feels to lose someone close to you then it would be your mum. I can still remember how much it affected her when your dad died.'

At the reference to Terry Tempest, an awkward silence fell across the kitchen, and as Ricky and Jamie gave Terri a surreptitious glance, she averted her gaze. Still, she could see the faint red mark her palm had left upon Jamie's cheek, not that he hadn't deserved the slap she conceded, because he had. In her mind he and Ricky were as much responsible for Archie's death as Michael and Frankie Gammon had been, if not even more; they were supposed to have protected him.

'Terri darling,' Rina said. 'Would you mind putting the flowers into a vase for me?'

Not trusting herself to speak for fear that her voice would come out as a terrified squeak, Terri nodded, and as she gathered the flowers and walked across to the sink, her hands ever so slightly trembled. Cutting away the cellophane, she could feel the weight of her brothers' stares boring into the back of her head. She wanted to kick herself; why had she thought it a good idea to confront them? What if her outburst had made the situation ten times worse? Perhaps she'd planted a seed into their minds; maybe the notion of kicking Rina out of the pub had never even entered their heads until she'd brought it up. Guilt tore away at Terri. What had she done? She'd always had a quick temper, and as much as she tried to reel it in, she wasn't able to stop herself from erupting with fury once the switch had been flicked, hence why she had lashed out at Ricky and Jamie in the first place. As for Rina, she would never forgive her if she was to ever find out that she had only been kicked out of her home because of her and her big mouth.

'Is there any truth to the rumour that Gammon was responsible, that he was the bastard who stabbed Archie?' As Jamie asked the question, Terri turned her head slightly to look at him. To her surprise he sounded genuine, as though he actually cared about Rina and Archie's downfall.

Rina's voice broke as she answered. 'It was him all right,' she spat, her face contorting with anger. 'You know yourself that he'd been demanding protection money from us, that he'd broken the window, the optics, the glasses. He even threatened to burn us down if we didn't pay up.' She gave a shuddering intake of breath. 'It was him; he killed my Archie. I was there, I saw everything as plain as day.' Her eyes suddenly widened. 'What if he comes back? What if the police don't find him in time? Oh God, what if he tries to kill us too?' she cried, her hand clutching her chest. 'We were there, we saw everything, we're witnesses.'

'Trust me, that's not going to happen.' Jamie shook his head. 'Gammon might be a lot of things, but he isn't stupid. He's bound to know the old bill will be looking for him. He would have already had it away on his toes.'

Gripping on to the draining board, Terri closed her eyes tightly. It was on the tip of her tongue to blurt out the truth that Frankie Gammon wasn't the real threat, the one they should be afraid of. It had been Michael who'd murdered Archie, he was the one they should fear. She opened her mouth to say something, then just as quickly clamped her lips closed again. Shame engulfed her, her own uncle had killed Archie, as much as she was a Tempest she was a Murphy too. Would Rina view her differently, perhaps even put some of the blame on to her shoulders?

'And as for the pair of you,' Rina scolded, her hard gaze going between Ricky and Jamie. 'If you think that you're going to turf me out of my home then you have another think coming. My Archie loved this pub and if I have to, I'll fight tooth and nail to keep it.'

Ricky held up his hand. 'Rina,' he said softly with a shake of his head. 'Come on, you've known us long enough to know that we would never do something like that. Do you really believe that we would be that spiteful, that we would throw you out onto the street at a time like this?'

Rina sniffed loudly. 'I don't know.' She started to sob again and held her head in her hands. 'I don't know anything any more other than that bastard Gammon killed my husband.'

'It wasn't him,' Terri blurted out, her breath catching in her throat. 'It was Michael.'

'What?' Shaking her head, Rina screwed up her face. 'What are you talking about? It was Frankie Gammon. I saw him; I watched him do it with my own two eyes.'

'No, you didn't.' Coming forward, Terri crouched in front of Rina and clasped her forearms. 'You and Archie were arguing at the time.' She shook her head as if to push the sickening images to the back of her mind, not that they ever went away. Archie's murder played out on a loop. Over and over again in her mind's eye, she saw him drop to the floor in a pool of blood. 'I mean, it all happened so fast it would be easy to make a mistake, but it wasn't Frankie... it was my uncle. It was him who thrust the blade forward, I saw him.'

The colour drained from Rina's face and as she reeled back in the chair, she pulled herself free from Terri's grip. 'Are you trying to tell me it was a Murphy who killed my Archie?' she gasped. 'And all this time you've said nothing. You led me to believe that Frankie Gammon was responsible for everything so that you could cover up for that uncle of yours. You even told the police it was Gammon; I was there when they took your statement, I heard you say his name.'

'It wasn't like that.' The hairs on the back of Terri's neck stood upright. 'I didn't lead you to believe anything,' she cried. 'You'd already made up your mind that Gammon was responsible, that you'd seen him...'

'You were still protecting him,' Rina spat, cutting Terri off. 'Oh my God, they say that blood is thicker than water but if I hadn't heard it with my own ears, I would never have believed you could be so deceitful, that you could purposely keep something like this to yourself. We took you in when you had nowhere else to go, we gave you a job, a home, put a roof over your head and all the while you were planning to betray us.'

Terri's heart began to pound inside her chest. She wasn't protecting Michael; she despised her uncle. He was a sadistic bully. Why on earth would she even want to protect him? She wanted him to go to prison for what he'd done, she wanted to make him pay. And the fact Ricky and Jamie were witnessing her humiliation was more than she could bear. Tears filled her eyes, and she hastily swiped them away. 'Rina,' she pleaded. 'It wasn't like that, I swear to you it wasn't. If I was trying to keep Michael's identity a secret, then I would never have told you he was responsible. If anything, I would have kept up the pretence that Frankie Gammon was the murderer even if he was innocent.'

Rina squashed her lips together and the sob lodged at the back of her throat came out as a shrill cry. 'You're right, it wouldn't make sense. I'm so sorry darling,' she cried, clasping hold of Terri's hand. 'I didn't mean to lash out. I don't know what came over me. The truth is, I don't know if I'm coming or going any more.'

'It's okay,' Terri tried to soothe Rina as she pulled her into her chest and stroked her hair. 'It's been a long day and you've had a big shock; it's bound to take its toll on you.'

'Tell me about it,' Jamie groaned, rubbing his hand across his cheek.

As Terri looked up, a pink blush spread across her face. She still couldn't believe she'd found the courage to slap Jamie, and even more than that, that she was still alive to tell the tale. She'd heard so many rumours about her brothers over the years and the despicable crimes they had committed that she had been too afraid to even look at them let alone actually speak to them. And that was another thing; seeing as they had never acknowledged her existence, did they even know they were her siblings?

'Maybe we should get off,' Ricky said as he began to move towards the door. 'I can see you've got a lot on your plate. Don't worry about this place.' He motioned around him. 'We'll work something out.'

Rina nodded her thanks, then tilting her head to one side, she studied them. 'Look at the three of you, all together in the same room. You look even more alike than I first thought.'

Terri froze and as she held her breath, awaiting her brothers' response, she gave them a sidelong glance. If Ricky and Jamie hadn't known before that she was their sister, then they certainly did now.

'Yeah well,' Jamie answered, breaking the silence. 'My dad's genes were strong. I'd be more surprised if we didn't look alike.'

As she exhaled a shaky breath, Terri pulled herself up to her full height and stared her brothers down. She wasn't sure whether to feel relief or anger that they had always known who she was. And if they knew then why had they never sought her out or tried to form any kind of relationship with her? They were her elder brothers; they were meant to protect her, not leave her to suffer alone at the hands of the Murphys. Surely, they must have known what kind of upbringing she would have with them, that her grandparents and even her mother had never cared for her. She'd been dragged up rather than brought up, and if anything, it was more of a surprise that she had morals and that she was able to feel empathy for others. If the Murphys had had their way she would have turned out as bad as they were: a thief, a liar, someone who cared for no one other than herself.

'You needed a gentle nudge in the right direction,' Rina announced once Ricky and Jamie had left. 'If I could I'd bang your heads together. You're family and I wish the three of you would stop being so stubborn. Archie was right: deep down they're good lads; you should give them a chance and get to know them, make amends before it's too late.'

Terri raised her eyebrows and as she returned to the task of arranging the flowers, she decided to keep her own counsel. Rina meant well but nothing she did or said could ever erase the hurt Terri felt. When all was said and done, her brothers had let her down. They hadn't wanted to get to know her; she had been a child, whilst they were grown men. They should have taken her under their wing, they should have protected her.

'Terri,' Rina urged. 'Get to know them and make up your own mind. You never know, you may be more alike than you think.'

Terri spun around. 'Why should I?' she snapped. 'They've clearly never wanted anything to do with me so why should I go out of my way to get to know them?'

For the first time since Archie's death, a small smile creased Rina's lips. 'And how about you?' she probed. 'You're not a child any more, you're a grown woman. What have you done to seek your brothers out?'

Turning back towards the sink, Terri thought over Rina's question. What had she done to get to know her brothers? Nothing, that was what. As much as they had known who she was, she had known who they were too and yet other than do everything in her power to avoid them, she had done nothing to actively approach them. It wasn't as though she hadn't known where to find them because she had.

'I don't think I can,' she whispered, the fear in her voice very much evident. 'They scare me.' She gave a helpless shrug, her shoulders slumping in defeat. 'I wish that I could say I wasn't a coward but when it comes to them I am. They only have to look at me and I want to run away and hide. I'm sorry Rina, but I just can't do it. I'm not strong like you, I'm weak.'

'Yes you can,' Rina implored. 'And you are a strong woman. Oh, you might not think you are, but in here' – she stabbed her forefinger into her chest, her eyes blazing – 'you are strong. You're a Tempest, sweetheart, and time and time again you've proved as much. You stood up to that family of yours. You left the only home you'd ever known without so much as a backward glance. You gave over Michael's name; that took courage my darling. Believe me, it took a lot of guts for you to do what you did.'

Terri's forehead furrowed. Could Rina be right? Could it be possible that she was a lot stronger than she'd ever believed herself to be? It was true, she had retaliated against Michael, and she had confronted her brothers. Not only had she stuck up for herself, but she'd also shown her family, Ricky and Jamie included, that she wouldn't be bullied, that she wouldn't allow them to walk all over her.

'Just think it over,' Rina continued. 'And seeing as they now own half of this place,' she said, looking around the kitchen and giving a sigh. 'Maybe this would be the perfect time to build some bridges.'

Terri nodded. Perhaps Rina was right. If nothing else, the talking to she'd given her was a wakeup call. At least one of them had to be the bigger person and make a move to put things right between them, and she had a sneaky suspicion it wasn't going to be her brothers.

* * *

Later that afternoon and with a bottle of brandy dangling from her fingers, Terri flung back her shoulders and pushed open the door to the taxi firm office. 'Enough of this bullshit,' she exclaimed, with a confidence she didn't feel, her gaze going between her brothers and Jonny Carter. 'We're having this out, here and now, the three of us and we're not leaving this room until the air has been cleared between us.'

Clearing his throat, Jonny looked between the siblings as he got to his feet. 'I take it that's my cue to leave,' he groaned.

Terri flashed him an apologetic smile and as he made for the door, she caught hold of his arm and gave it a gentle squeeze. 'Thank you for coming by to see Rina today; it might not have seemed like much, but it did help her.'

As he looked down at Terri's hand upon his arm, Jonny's gaze snapped across to the Tempest brothers before gently shrugging her off, their hard expressions enough to tell him they didn't appreciate the interaction between himself and their only sister. 'Is this a wise move?' he asked, making a point of gesturing towards Jamie's cheek. 'You don't want me to stick around and play referee do you? With five brothers of my own I have had some practice when it comes to things like this and if you're anything like my lot then before you know it the situation can quickly escalate. Punches could very well start flying, maybe a bloody nose or a bust lip, nothing would surprise me where this little firecracker is concerned,' he said, nodding towards Terri. 'And from the look of things she's got a good right hook on her.' He winked.

Terri gave a husky laugh. 'I think I can handle them.' It was a lie, not that she was about to tell Jonny or her brothers that. Not only did her insides feel like liquid, but it also took everything inside of her not to turn on her heels and run back out the door. Now that her anger had settled somewhat, she wasn't feeling so brave any more; if she was being truthful, she was downright terrified.

Once Jonny had left the office, Terri placed the bottle on the desk and cocked her head to one side. 'I wasn't sure if you would have glasses and so' – she unclipped her handbag, took out three plastic cups and placed them alongside the bottle – 'I thought I'd best bring some.'

Eyeing the bottle, Jamie lifted his eyebrows. 'This is a taxi firm,' he hissed. 'Hardly the environment to be drinking on the job is it.'

'Yeah, I thought you'd say that,' Terri said as she moved across to the door and slid the bolt across. 'So let's cut the crap. We all know that this place is a front for your real business, debt collecting, not forgetting protection money.' Her voice hardened and it took everything within her to stop the tears from flooding her eyes. 'You were supposed to have protected Archie; he reached out to you, but you failed him. You stood by and did nothing while he was brutally cut down.'

As the nerve in his jaw ticked, Ricky jerked his head towards the door. 'We weren't the only ones; what about Carter? He was as much involved in this as we are and yet he gets off scot-free.'

Terri swallowed down her annoyance. However much she hated to admit it, Ricky was right; Jonny had also pledged his allegiance to Archie, he'd even been the one to set up the meetings between them so shouldn't she have taken her anger out on him too?

Unscrewing the bottle and ignoring Ricky's remark, Terri poured a measure of brandy into each of the cups. Her heart beat so hard and fast that she was conscious of the fact her hand shook as she lifted the cup to her lips. 'To Archie,' she said, downing the alcohol in one go. 'The only dad I ever knew.'

Jamie blew out his cheeks and after giving his brother a sidelong glance, he lifted the cup. 'To Archie. May he rest in peace.'

As she refilled their cups, Terri forced her shoulders to relax. 'Now that the pleasantries are over and done with,' she said with a steely glint in her eyes. 'I want to know what you plan to do about this, because I can tell you now that I want my uncle's head delivered to me on a plate.'

A smile spread across Jamie's face. 'I think I could get used to having a sister around.'

Terri smiled as she looked between Ricky and Jamie.

'And you've got some balls, I'll give you that much,' Jamie laughed.

'I'm a Tempest,' Terri answered, her voice deadpan as she remembered Rina's pep talk. 'What else did you expect?'

13

Despite the cockiness in Michael's demeanour, the euphoria he'd felt directly after plunging the blade deep into Archie Taylor's chest had long since dissipated. He'd already done time for human trafficking and that had been bad enough, but when it came to murder, he was bound to have the book thrown at him and there wasn't a judge or jury in the country who would believe his excuses for taking a life; neither would they be willing to take his reasons into consideration. Not that Michael planned on telling anyone that he'd only committed the murder to get into Raymond Cole's good books. He'd never live it down.

'I can't believe this is happening,' Frankie Gammon bitterly complained, his flabby cheeks turning redder by the second as creamy white spittle flew out of the corners of his mouth, bringing further testament to just how enraged he was. 'They think it was me,' he hollered, pointing towards the lounge window. 'They're gonna be baying for my blood.' He turned his head to glare at Michael. 'It was you who stabbed him so why should I,' he said, stabbing his finger into his chest, 'take the rap for it?'

'Why don't you just try and calm down.' Lounging back on a

chair as if he didn't have a care in the world, Raymond Cole waved his hand through the air. 'If the old bill were on to you, they would be here by now. They'd have you banged up so fast that your feet wouldn't even touch the floor.'

'And who's to say they're not already on to me,' Frankie whined as he glanced out of the window for the tenth time in as many minutes. 'The street could be crawling with filth. They could be getting ready to pounce at any given moment.'

Raymond rolled his eyes. 'And are they?'

'Are they what?' Frankie all but shrieked.

'Are the filth outside the flat?'

Frankie's mouth dropped open and snapping his gaze back to the window he shook his head. 'I can't see anyone.'

'I don't know what you're getting yourself so worked up for.' Feeling a moment of bravery, Michael gave a nonchalant shrug. 'Like you said, it wasn't you who topped that old fucker Archie, it was me.' He grinned.

Raymond chuckled. 'There you go, problem solved. If anyone is going to end up doing time it'll be Murphy. You've got nothing to worry about.'

The smile slid from Michael's face and chewing on his thumbnail, he couldn't help but glance towards the front door. His nerves were beginning to get the better of him and Frankie was right, the old bill could very well be on to them; perhaps they were even under surveillance right now and they were standing around doing nothing. They may as well have been sitting ducks. Bianca had already been on to the phone to him that morning telling him that there was a price on Frankie's head, that it was only a matter of time until he'd be caught, if not by the police than by the locals who by all accounts wanted to string him up by his bollocks. And if that was to happen then there wasn't a chance in hell that Frankie would keep his mouth shut. No, at the first hint of trouble Frankie

Gammon would sing louder than a canary, he'd tell all and sundry that it had been him who'd stabbed Archie Taylor. All along he should have listened to his gut instinct. Right from the off he'd suspected that Gammon was a liability, that despite the tough man persona he might exhibit in front of his little firm he was fuck all, a no one, and even worse than that he had the capability to be a grass.

Jumping out of his seat, Michael rested his hands on the window sill and looked down at the pavement below to see for himself that the car park adjacent to the block of flats where Frankie lived was indeed deserted. It was no secret that Archie had been well loved; he'd been running the boozer for years and was considered to be a pillar of the community. Not only that but a lot of faces had frequented the pub during his reign as guvnor and he wasn't only talking about the Tempests, but also the Carter family, Max Hardcastle, the Fletcher family, Moray Garner, and Danny McKay to name but a few. The mere thought that he could be on their radar was enough to bring him out in a cold sweat. Oh, he could still have a tear up as and when he needed to, but he'd lost that edge he'd had as a young man, prison had seen to that. As soon as he'd stepped through the prison gates he'd more or less become a social pariah; turns out prisoners weren't so keen on men who trafficked women. And on a daily basis he'd paid the price for his crimes. He'd been bullied, beaten and tormented so much that it was a miracle he'd made it out in one piece.

'Yeah well.' Collapsing on to a chair, Frankie kicked out his legs, his expression sullen. 'Believe me when I say this, when the old bill comes knocking, I'll be sure to point them in the right direction,' he said, turning his hard stare on Michael.

Michael swallowed deeply; he didn't doubt Frankie in the slightest. If the tables were turned, he himself would have done the exact same thing, but in his defence, he didn't know the meaning of the word loyalty. The only person he'd ever thought about was himself. He'd thought about Bianca too once; they'd been close, had done everything together until she'd done the dirty on him and decided to keep Tempest's kid.

A familiar sense of anger flowed through Michael's veins. If it hadn't been for Terry Tempest he wouldn't have been in this position; he would have more than likely been running his own firm by now. He wouldn't have needed to impress anyone and certainly wouldn't have needed to top some pub landlord just to get into someone's good books. 'I was only doing what you told me to do,' he whined. 'You told me to shake things up, and I did that,' he said, pointing to himself. 'If it had been left to Gammon, we would still be tiptoeing around. We were starting to become a laughing stock; now they know we mean business, that we aren't afraid to get stuck in.'

'Talking of business.' Throwing a rucksack filled with narcotics onto Michael's lap, Raymond sneered. 'It's time to get back out there; the schools will be chucking out soon. Oh, and Michael,' he said, giving a smirk. 'Don't forget they're two for a tenner and don't let those little sods short change you either. I'm guessing that you do actually know how to count.'

Michael's jaw dropped and as he stared at Raymond, he shook his head in disbelief. Surely, he didn't expect him to show his face outside on the street. Not when there was a price on Frankie's head, and he was well known to be Frankie's right-hand man. He'd told just about anyone who would listen that he'd been personally head hunted by Gammon himself, and had made himself seem even more important than he actually was. 'What, now?' he gasped. 'You actually expect me to go out there?'

Raymond's smirk intensified. 'Well, Frankie here can't do it, can he, not when the filth could pounce on him at any given moment.

Besides, I've got something else in mind for Frankie, a little job that's going to need his undivided attention.'

Narrowing his eyes, Michael stared down at the bag. Head hunted or not, he was no lackey; he was Michael Murphy and his name alone deserved respect or at least it had before his imprisonment. 'Can't you get someone else to do it?'

'Yeah, I probably could,' Raymond growled, his cold eyes becoming hard flints and the muscles across his jaw clenching so tightly that Michael wouldn't be surprised if they cracked. 'But I'm telling you to do it.'

With the threat hanging heavy in the air, Michael swallowed deeply. It was this side of Raymond that made him feel uneasy. The man was unpredictable; he could be smiling and laughing one minute and then threatening to shove a blade into someone's neck the next. And Michael didn't doubt for one second that they were idle threats. Was it any wonder that Frankie was a bundle of nerves around him? It felt like they were walking on egg shells whenever Raymond was within their vicinity, each of them afraid of saying the wrong thing, knowing that it wouldn't take much to rile Raymond up, for him to unleash that formidable temper upon them. And as afraid as Michael was of getting a capture, he didn't want to lose face, didn't want to give Raymond an excuse to turn on him too. He had plans, big plans, and neither one involved him becoming known as a coward, someone who was afraid of his own shadow.

He got to his feet and reluctantly pulled the rucksack up on to his shoulder. If he was careful, maybe he wouldn't be spotted. He could use the back roads. It would take him a bit longer than usual to get to the school but it had to be better than walking the streets in plain view where just about anyone could see him, maybe even report his movements back to those searching for Frankie.

* * *

Regardless of the grey skies overhead and the threat of a heavy downpour, Bianca Murphy jutted out her hip, the short black lycra skirt and matching crop top she wore revealing a generous amount of skin. She hadn't even bothered to put on a coat; all she wanted to do was show off her curves, although describing the rolls of fat on display above the waistband of her skirt as curves may have been a slight exaggeration. She'd put on a lot of weight since her release from prison; the booze and endless supply of takeaways, cream cakes, crisps and chocolate bars were beginning to take their toll. Not only that but she'd never been one to take care of herself. She'd shower once or twice a week, preferring to have a quick wash down with a couple of wet wipes and only then if she remembered or could be bothered. As a result, Bianca's blonde hair was often greasy, the dark roots in desperate need of both a wash and colour. As for her skin, angry red spots littered her chin that no amount of concealer would be able to conceal, and ingrained along the creases of her nose, were a series of large blackheads. Not that Bianca cared either way; why should she when as far as she was concerned, she'd been blessed with a natural beauty just as her daughter had and although she may have plastered make-up all over her face in her youth, she no longer relied on cosmetics to enhance her looks.

Already, two passing cars had blasted their horns at her, making her smile until the passenger of the third car had shouted out asking how much she charged for a blow job, telling her they'd give no more than a fiver and that was if she was lucky. Cheeky bastards, she'd huffed. She'd never charged for sex in her life, had never needed to; she'd always had a queue of men waiting to ply her with alcohol before going back to their place for a night of fun. Not that any of them ever wanted her to stick around the next morning; she considered herself fortunate if they offered a hot drink before throwing her out on her ear.

Pacing back and forth across the pavement, Bianca dug her hand into her handbag and pulled out her cigarettes. Where the bloody hell was Michael? Twenty minutes she'd been waiting for him and she knew for a fact it didn't take this long to walk from Frankie Gammon's house to the secondary school.

After smoking her cigarette, Bianca dropped the butt to the floor and squashed it out underneath her heel. 'Come on,' she huffed, slipping her hand back into her handbag and fishing out her mobile phone. She was just about to dial Michael's number when she caught sight of him turning into the street.

'Where have you been?' she demanded, throwing her arms up into the air. 'I've been standing here for ages looking like a right lemon.'

Michael's face was red from the exertion of pounding the streets; he'd walked fast too, with the hood of his jumper pulled down low over his face just in case anyone should recognise him. By the time he reached Bianca the scowl he gave was enough to warn her that he wasn't in a good mood, not that he ever was of late. She couldn't remember the last time he'd flashed a smile, at least not a genuine one anyway.

'Well?' she asked again. 'What took you so long?'

Throwing back his hood, Michael took a cautious glance around him, avoiding the question. 'I've got work to do B,' he said, lowering the backpack, pulling across the zip to reveal the pills inside and then motioning towards the school that stood just feet away from them.

Bianca narrowed her eyes. Since when did Michael sell pills at the school gates? He wasn't some joey; the job was more suited to one of Frankie Gammon's minions. 'What's going on? Why has

Gammon sent you out to do his dirty work? I thought you said you were running his firm, that it was you they took orders from?'

'Why do you think?' Michael shot back. 'He can hardly be seen in public can he, not after what he did to Archie Taylor.' He lowered his voice, his gaze darting nervously up and down the street just in case a passerby should spot him. 'There's a price on his head and by association that means someone could come after me too.'

Bianca couldn't help but burst out laughing. 'I thought you were meant to be a tough man. That it would take a lot more than this lot around here to scare you?'

A hard glint flashed in Michael's eyes. 'You heard from that daughter of yours yet?' He smirked.

Bianca's face fell. 'You know I haven't.' She'd thoroughly believed that Terri would have come home by now, no doubt with her tail between her legs, professing how sorry she was for attacking Michael. She bit down on her bottom lip. Terri held the key to her father's fortune and without her, there was no way for Bianca to get her hands on Terry's cash. And she deserved that money. She'd brought up Terry's daughter and it was her girl's birthright to be given her inheritance. Fair enough, she may not have actually lifted a finger in raising Terri, but she'd still given birth to her. She'd sweated, panted, and felt as though her body was being torn in two just to bring the girl safely into the world. She'd done her bit, now she wanted what she was owed, her due.

Michael walked away, the smirk across his smug face intensifying.

'Hey,' Bianca called out as she tottered after him, her stilettos almost buckling under her weight. 'What's so funny?'

'Nothing.' Michael shrugged. He looked her up and down. 'You're starting to look like a prostitute. If I didn't know any better I'd think that you were on the game. Keep hanging around on street corners B and you'll soon earn a name for yourself; that's what you've always wanted though,' he goaded. 'To make a name for yourself.'

Bianca tugged her skirt down, not that it did much to cover the pasty white flesh on display. 'You can be a right nasty bastard when you want to be, do you know that, Michael?'

Michael turned away. 'I've never proclaimed to be nice, besides ,' he said changing the subject away from himself. 'I thought you were more interested in knowing where your kid is.' He flashed a knowing grin. 'You've been banging on about it ever since she upped and left.'

Bianca cocked her head to the side, her eyes narrowing until they were mere slits in her bloated face. 'You know where she is don't you?' she gasped.

'Maybe.' Michael shrugged.

As Bianca's mouth dropped open, Michael leaned in closer.

'She's been under your nose this whole time, hidden away in plain sight.'

Hope spread through Bianca's veins. And as her heartbeat picked up pace it took everything inside of her to stop herself from rubbing her hands together with glee. She was within touching distance of Terry's money; all she needed now was for her daughter to show her face at Tracey Tempest's door and the wheels would be set in motion. That money was theirs, or rather it was Terri's, but either way, Bianca would take the majority of it, if not all of it. In her mind she'd already spent most of it. She had her eye on a designer handbag, lovely it was, it cost the earth too but would be money well spent just to see the jealousy in everyone's eyes whenever she walked into the pub with it. 'Where is she?'

There was an all too familiar wicked gleam in Michael's eyes. He was enjoying himself, Bianca noted. He actually thought her predicament was funny, amusing, something he could have a good old laugh about.

'Where is she?' Bianca all but screamed, her patience getting the better of her as she lifted her fists, more than prepared to punch her brother if need be. She wanted answers and she wanted them now.

'All right, calm the fuck down.' With a chuckle, Michael lifted his hands in the air. 'She's been staying at the boozer. The Fiddlers. By all accounts she's made herself right at home with the Taylors.' He gave a crafty look. 'She's mugged you right off, made you look like a muppet.'

Anger creased Bianca's face, her annoyance with her brother temporarily forgotten about. 'Oh has she now?' she spat. 'Well it's about time I fetched her home then, isn't it?' Turning on her heel, Bianca flicked a lock of bleached blonde hair over her shoulder. 'Kicking and fucking screaming if needs be.'

14

From out of the corner of her eye, Terri watched Rina. Despite her insistence to open the pub, Terri still felt that it was far too soon. Archie had only been gone a few days and they hadn't even held a funeral for him yet; his body was still being held by the coroner until the authorities had finalised their enquiries. Not that Rina's supposed high spirits did anything to erase Terri's concern. Rina had gone from crying her heart out one moment and refusing to even climb out of bed to becoming businesslike the next. It wasn't natural, Terri decided and sooner or later Rina was bound to break.

'This place won't run itself,' she'd told Terri when she'd voiced her concerns. And in a roundabout way Terri supposed she was right, but waiting another day or two before opening up wouldn't have hurt either, especially as Ricky and Jamie had ploughed enough money into the business that Rina could afford to stay closed even if it was for just a few more days.

Wiping down the bar, Terri looked up in time to see Jonny Carter approach. He flashed her a wide smile and slipped onto a bar stool, his expensive aftershave assaulting her nostrils.

'I wasn't expecting to see the pub open so soon,' he remarked.

Terri sighed and as she shot a glance towards Rina, she lifted her eyebrows. 'Same here, but you know what it's like, Rina calls the shots, and she can be a stubborn bugger at times.'

'How is she doing?'

As Rina let out a high-pitched laugh, both Terri and Jonny turned their heads in her direction. Even to their untrained ears the laugh had sounded false, as though Rina was barely holding it together.

'She's putting on a brave face,' Terri exclaimed. 'But I wouldn't be surprised if she breaks down. She's bound to. She can't just pretend that everything is fine when it isn't, she's lost her husband for Christ's sake.'

Jonny nodded. 'Maybe it's the shock kicking in.'

'Yeah maybe,' Terri answered thoughtfully, worry flashing in her eyes. 'I just wish that there was something I could do to help her, something that would take the pain away.'

'I remember when my brother died,' Jonny continued. 'It took me a long time to get my head around the fact he was gone, that I'd never see him again. Every time I walked into the office, I expected to find him sitting behind the desk, still do sometimes.' He shrugged. 'And it's been years since he was murdered.'

'I suppose it's all part of the process,' Terri sighed. 'A way for the brain to cope with the trauma of losing someone close to you.'

'She'll get through it; she doesn't have any other choice, does she?' Resting his forearms on the bar, there was a twinkle in Jonny's eyes as he lifted himself up and looked Terri over.

'What?' Feeling self-conscious, Terri tucked a strand of dark hair behind her ear. 'Have I got something on my face?' She rubbed her hand over her cheeks, before patting herself down, checking that everything was as it should be.

'Nah, it's nothing,' he chuckled. 'I was just looking to see if there were any visible injuries. I was half expecting you and your brothers to have torn chunks out of each other after you kicked me out of the office.'

'I didn't kick you out, you chose to leave, big difference.' Terri rolled her eyes and as she flicked the bar towel towards him, she couldn't help but laugh. She could see for herself now why Rina was so taken with him. Not only was he a handsome devil but he could also charm the birds from the trees. He had a certain something about him, something she liked. He made her laugh too and that was always a bonus where men were concerned.

'Talking of your brothers, where are they?'

Terri shrugged. She hadn't heard from Ricky and Jamie since leaving the office the previous day even though they had promised to keep her updated if they had any news on Frankie Gammon or Michael's whereabouts. 'Have you tried the taxi office?'

'Yeah, the place was locked up.'

Terri frowned. From what she knew of her brothers, it was unusual for them to close the taxi firm early and digging her hand into her pocket, she pulled out her mobile phone, checking that they hadn't tried to call or had left her any messages. Could they have gone after Michael and Frankie and purposely not told her?

She'd been about to voice her concern when the pub door crashed open. Looking up, Terri's eyes widened, the colour draining from her face. She'd been dreading this day, had even feared it. Her mother on the war path didn't bode well for anyone, least of all herself. More than anything she wanted to make herself as invisible as possible, knowing that Bianca was about to cause a scene.

'So this is where you've been hiding, is it?' Bianca's shrill voice called out. 'While I've been going out of my nut with worry,' she screamed, pointing to her head, dramatic as ever, 'you've been here as happy as Larry working behind some poxy little bar.'

Rina bristled as she came to stand beside Terri. 'Who do you think you bleeding are calling my pub a poxy bar?'

Terri wrinkled her nose, the foul stench that radiated from Bianca filling the air. 'It's okay,' Terri said, holding out her hand to Rina. 'Let me deal with this.' Not that she actually believed her mother had been worried about her. Bianca's only concern in life was where she would be getting her next paycheque from so that she could buy her endless supply of alcohol, greasy takeaways, and cigarettes.

'Oh, will you now?' Placing her hands on her ample hips, Bianca scowled. 'A bit of cash in your back pocket and you suddenly think that you're Miss High and Mighty, that you're better than me. I wouldn't mind' – she made a point of looking around her and screwing up her face – 'but like I said, it's a poxy little pub in Dagenham, hardly the Ritz, is it? Come on, get yourself around here; we're leaving.'

'No, Mum.' As Terri shook her head, a newfound confidence washed over her. She had Rina and Archie to thank for that; they had shown her that there was so much more to life than being dragged down by her family's reputation. They had shown her kindness and had given her the fresh start she had so desperately craved. And when it came to Bianca, she had to stand her ground, otherwise her mother would walk all over her, just as she'd done ever since being released from prison. 'This is my home now, no matter what you say or how much you might threaten me, I'm going to stay here, with Rina.'

Anger flashed across Bianca's face. 'I don't think it's quite registering in that head of yours,' she spat. 'It's not your call to make. You're coming home with me even if I have to drag you there myself. We've got some things to take care of, things that will be of a great benefit to you and trust me, it's worth a lot more than this poxy place will ever be.' She raised her hand as if to pull Terri from around the bar when Jonny Carter intercepted the action, his strong grip on Bianca's arm stopping her from seeing her threat through.

'She's already told you once,' he growled as Bianca struggled to free herself from his grasp. 'She wants to stay here with Rina.'

Bianca's mouth dropped open. 'She's a kid,' she fumed. 'My kid, and if she knows what's good for her, she'll do as I say.'

Jonny shook his head. 'She doesn't look like a kid to me. In fact, I'd go as far as to say she looks old enough to make her own decisions.' He slipped off the bar stool, his tall, solid frame towering above Bianca. 'So why don't you do yourself a favour and leave quietly before I end up throwing you out.'

Bianca pulled herself up to her full height, her forehead furrowing. 'What the fuck is going on here?' she asked, looking between her daughter and Jonny. 'Don't tell me that you and him...' She gave an incredulous laugh, all the while shaking her head. 'You are, aren't you?' she said, wagging her finger between them. 'The pair of you are bloody at it. No wonder you don't want to come home, you're too busy spreading your legs for this one.'

Not for the first time, Terri wished that the floor would swallow her whole. Tears sprang to her eyes. She'd never felt so humiliated. She could barely look at Jonny, too afraid that she would see disgust written across his face.

'What did you just say?' Jonny tightened his grip and for the briefest of moments Terri thought he would lash out at Bianca, that he was so sickened by her remark he would shove her roughly away from him, perhaps even swing for her.

'You and her,' Bianca continued to laugh. 'It's about time she put it about. I was starting to think there was something wrong with her, that she was frigid because you sure as hell don't take after me in that department, do you darling.'

And there it was, the disgust Terri had so desperately prayed she wouldn't see upon Jonny's face.

'Get out,' he snarled, his handsome face contorting with rage.

'You can't chuck me out,' Bianca shrieked, her eyes flashing dangerously. 'Do you know who I am? I'm Bianca Murphy and no one tells me what to do.' She clenched her fist, ready to throw a punch.

'I know exactly who you are,' Jonny answered, his hand coming up to block any punches Bianca might throw at him. 'You're a disgrace. Who needs enemies when they've got a mother like you?' With those parting words, he proceeded to drag Bianca out of the pub while she continued to scream out obscenities, the majority of them aimed at her daughter.

Minutes later he returned, his face still a mask of anger and as he retook his position at the bar, he jerked his thumb behind him. 'She'll more than likely be back,' he declared, taking out his mobile phone and shooting off a text. 'Probably with the rest of the Murphy clan in tow. But for now, she's gone.'

Swallowing down her embarrassment, Terri averted her gaze. No one had ever put Bianca in her place before. More often than not most people were afraid of her, scared that Bianca would cause a scene and unleash her ferocious temper upon them, which she did often.

'Thank you,' she whispered, her voice so low that Jonny had to crane his neck to hear her.

'For what?' Jonny screwed up his face. 'For putting that psycho bitch in her place? It was about time someone threw her out. I know she's your mum and all that, but she was bang out of order. How the fuck you ever came out of her I'll never know. She's a state.'

Terri nodded, shame washing over her. He was right, Bianca had looked a mess and seemed to only get worse as the weeks and months went by. She had no care for personal hygiene, even her clothes were far too small for her, not to mention inappropriate. It made Terri question what her dad had seen in her. By all accounts, he'd been a handsome man and if he'd looked anything like her brothers then he could have had his pick of women, so what on earth would have made him want to have an affair with Bianca? Surely, he hadn't been that hard up, that desperate that he hadn't been able to choose someone better for himself?

'Look I'm sorry.' Jonny held up his hands, his expression contrite. 'I was out of line for saying what I did. At the end of the day, she's still your mum no matter what I or anyone else thinks of her. And it's not like we get to hand pick our families, is it? It's pot luck.'

'No, it's fine,' Terri reassured him. 'I didn't take offence, and you wouldn't be the first person to form the same opinion about her. I know better than anyone else what she's like, what they're all like,' she said, referring to the rest of her family.

A short while later Rina took Terri aside. 'Are you okay darling?'

Shaking her head, Terri brought her hands up to her face in an attempt to hide her humiliation. 'I can't believe she would say something like that,' she cried. 'My own mum, how could she? And in front of Jonny too.'

Rina sighed. 'I know sweetheart, the woman is a disgrace.'

'Why does she always have to be so vulgar?' Terri continued. 'It's bad enough that she walks around wearing nothing but skimpy outfits and then when she opens her mouth' – she gave a shake of her head, the shame she felt rushing to the fore – 'it's embarrassing.'

A twinkle glistened in Rina's eyes and tilting her head to the side, she flashed a smile. 'Not that I'd blame you if you and him were at it like rabbits.' She winked, glancing over her shoulder to Jonny. 'You have to admit, he's a looker. It's that Carter blood he has in him; they're all handsome devils. And if the rumours are anything to go by, he's got big feet too,' she laughed.

'Rina,' Terri gasped. 'I can't believe you just said that.'

Rina flapped her hand, her face the picture of innocence. 'Just a gentle little nudge in the right direction,' she whispered in Terri's ear. 'I've heard he's single too and just waiting for the right girl to come along. Don't think I haven't noticed the way you look at him; you get that dreamy look in your eyes whenever he's around. And take it from me my darling,' she said, her expression becoming sombre. 'You only live once; our time on earth is far too short so don't waste it by not grabbing what you want with both hands.'

Rina was right, Terri decided, Archie had still been relatively young when he'd been murdered, his life brutally cut down in the blink of an eye. She shot another glance towards Jonny, her heartbeat picking up pace. She had to admit she did like him, a lot, and more than she probably should considering their age difference, not to mention his occupation as an armed robber. By rights, she should have been afraid of him, only she wasn't, and she couldn't quite understand why seeing as she'd been downright terrified of her brothers and their reputations weren't too dissimilar. Not that she stood a chance with him now; Bianca had all but seen to that. She hadn't imagined the disgust written across Jonny's face; it had been there as clear as day. The very notion of a romantic fling taking place between them had repulsed him to the very core.

'Can I get another drink, or are the two of you planning on standing around chatting all day?'

Terri huffed out a breath, and pulling back her shoulders, she forced her expression to become closed off. By the time she had made her way over to where Jonny was sitting, she'd pushed all thoughts of romance to the back of her mind, exactly where they belonged. If Rina could put on an act and pretend that everything was okay then so could she. After all, she'd had a lot of practice; she'd survived living with her family, had lost count of how many times she'd plastered a smile across her face when all she'd wanted to do was sob her heart out, more often than not terrified that

Michael's hatred of her would one day go too far. And as Jonny had already stated, it wasn't as though she or Rina had any other choice in the matter, they had to be strong whether they wanted to be or not.

* * *

Tracey Hardcastle was in her element. She loved having her grandchildren around her, not that her grandson Mason wanted to spend much time with her any more. He was far too old for sleep-overs, had been for years, and as much as he would pop over to see her whenever he found the time, it just wasn't the same as when he'd been a little boy and had hung on to her every word. He'd grown up, that was half the problem, and hanging out with his old nan wasn't cool or hip or whatever it was the youngsters called it these days. Not that Tracey considered herself to be fit for the knacker's yard just yet. She may be fast approaching her seventieth birthday, but she still had a lot of energy, she and her husband Max both did, they liked to keep active, thoroughly believing that it kept them looking and feeling much younger than they actually were.

'That's it.' She smiled as her eldest granddaughter whisked sugar, flour and eggs together. I've got a feeling these are going to be some of the best cakes we've ever baked.'

Ten-year-old Sorina beamed up at her. She looked like her father Jamie, just as her younger sister Adelina did too. From what Tracey could make out, the girls hadn't seemed to have inherited much from their mother Georgiana or Georgie as she was more commonly known, other than their height. All three were petite and in Tracey's opinion both Sorina and Adelina were as cute as a button, not that she was biased or anything.

'You all right, Mum?' Breezing into the kitchen, Jamie made a beeline for his daughters and as they squealed with delight, he picked them up and spun them around, causing drops of cake batter to land on the floor, kitchen counter, and their clothes, much to Tracey's annoyance. As she batted him away from her, a scowl was etched across her face.

'Leave it out,' she scolded. 'What are you playing at? Look at the bleeding mess you're making of my kitchen.'

'Nana said a bad word,' Sorina giggled.

'Yeah Mum,' Jamie chastised, a playful look in his eyes as he made a big show of pretending to cover his daughters' ears. 'You just said a bad word in front of the girls.'

Tracey rolled her eyes. Jamie was a fine one to talk. Out of his daughters' earshot, he was forever effing and blinding. 'What are you doing here?' she asked. 'I thought the girls were staying with me this weekend?'

'They are.' Clearing his throat, Jamie looked over his shoulder in time to watch Ricky and Max head into the lounge. 'Me and Rick just wanted to have a quick word; we've got something to tell you.'

Narrowing her eyes, Tracey tilted her head to the side as she studied her youngest son. 'About?'

Without answering, Jamie jerked his head towards the door, indicating for Tracey to follow him.

'Girls.' Tracey forced her voice to sound a lot more cheerful than she actually felt. 'You keep stirring and Nana will be right back.'

'What's going on?' she demanded once she'd firmly closed the lounge door behind her.

Ricky rubbed the palm of his hand over his face. He looked shifty, Tracey decided. She clasped her husband's hand tightly, concern at the forefront of her mind. 'Has something happened?' She motioned towards the Chesterfield sofa. 'Do I need to sit down for this?'

'It might be a good idea,' Jamie sighed, oblivious to the look his brother shot him.

Tracey took a seat, her heartbeat picking up pace. 'You're not ill, are you?' she asked, looking between her sons, scrutinising their complexions for any signs that they were unwell. 'Or is it your nan, has something happened to her? Oh God, it has, hasn't it?' she cried. 'She's dead.' After a shaky start, Tracey and her ex-mother-in-law Patricia had become firm friends in recent years. Tears filled her eyes. 'I only spoke to her yesterday and she was fine, complaining as usual about the corns on her little toes. We'd always joked that she'd receive her telegram from the King; she was going to have it framed and put it up on the mantlepiece.'

'It's not Nan,' Ricky was quick to interrupt. 'I wouldn't be surprised if she outlived all of us.'

'Then what is it?'

'It's…' Jamie paused then giving a gentle smile, he lifted his shoulders into a shrug. 'It's Dad.'

'Your dad?' Screwing up her face, Tracey shook her head. 'I don't understand,' she said, turning to look at Max as if to gauge his reaction. 'What about him?'

'Well.' Ricky rubbed at the back of his neck. 'Do you remember Bianca Murphy?'

Tracey snorted. 'I'm hardly likely to forget her, am I,' she said, rolling her eyes.

'She had a daughter, Dad's daughter.'

'And?' Tracey urged. She'd already known that Bianca Murphy had given birth to Terry's daughter; it had been the talk of their estate for months. 'What's any of that got to do with me?'

'Well, we met her,' Jamie announced. 'She's been staying with the Taylors at the pub.'

Tracey's eyes widened and taking a sharp intake of breath, she collapsed back on to the sofa. It wasn't so much the fact that her sons had met with their half-sister that shocked her – after all, they were adults and it was their right to do as they saw fit – it was more the fact that once again, she was plagued with thoughts of her former husband. Not in a million years would she have imagined when she'd woken up that morning that Terry would be on her mind. She hadn't thought about him in years, hadn't needed to. He was nothing more to her than a distant memory and although they may have had some good times during the time they'd been married, the fact he'd been a liar, a cheat, and not forgetting a downright monster was not something she wanted to relive anytime soon.

'She's not what you'd expect Mum, she's actually all right, she's like us. From what I can make out she's got nothing of the Murphy family in her.'

Ricky broke Tracey's reverie and as she looked up, she shook her head. 'Well, if she takes after your father then I feel sorry for the girl. And we all know how Raymond turned out; he was a nutcase.' She gave a shiver. 'If he'd had his way, he'd have killed us, all of us, even Mason and he was only a baby at the time.' As soon as the words left Tracey's mouth, she wanted to kick herself. Terry's daughter didn't deserve to be saddled with Terry and Raymond's shortcomings any more than her own sons did.

Ricky and Jamie shot each other a look. As usual, a sense of unease washed over them whenever their half-brother Raymond's name was brought up.

'I'm sorry. I was out of line,' Tracey apologised, holding up her hands. 'And I'm happy that you finally got to meet her, Terri, isn't it? Her name.'

'Yeah,' Ricky answered. 'She was named after Dad.'

'Well,' she sighed. 'You know what this means, don't you?' She got to her feet, keen to get back to her granddaughters before they ended up making even more of a mess of her kitchen. 'It's only fair that you introduce her to your nan; she is her granddaughter after all.'

* * *

Once Tracey had left the lounge, Jamie turned to look at Max. 'She took that better than I was expecting.'

Max Hardcastle nodded. In his mind, his Tracey had taken the news exactly how he would have expected her to. She didn't have a bad bone in her body. He looked between Ricky and Jamie studying them for a moment, concern etched across his face. 'What's this trouble between you and Frankie Gammon that I've been hearing about?'

Ricky sighed. 'The ponce has been taking liberties; he tried to muscle in on our patch.'

'Yeah, that's what I heard. And where does Archie Taylor come into this? Why did Gammon top him?'

Jamie shook his head. 'Gammon didn't top Archie.' He allowed his words to sink in for a few moments before continuing. 'It was Michael Murphy who took him out.'

Max narrowed his eyes, the muscles across his shoulder blades tensing. It had been his testimony in court that had helped put the Murphy family, along with his former friend Kenny Kempton, behind bars. As much as his actions had gone against the grain considering the criminal underworld he'd lived in, becoming a grass had been an easy decision to make. The women they had held captive, who had been forced to sell their bodies on a daily basis, had deserved justice and Max had been determined that they get it. 'I should have known his name would come into this somewhere, he's been a bit too quiet and for too long if you want my opinion. The entire family are scum, and as for that Bianca Murphy,' he growled, nodding his head towards the lounge door that his wife had exited through just moments earlier. 'If she starts any trouble,' he warned, proving once and for all just how protective he was of his wife, 'I'll have her fucking guts. That's if your mum doesn't get there before me. You know as well as I do what she's like once her back is up and there's a lot of history between her and Murphy, the kind of history that could very well see blood spilled.'

Jamie couldn't help but chuckle. His mum may have been a diamond, but she also had quick a temper on her, one that he, his brother, and Max were all wary of.

Fishing out his mobile phone from his pocket, Ricky looked down at the device. 'Talking of Bianca Murphy. We have to go,' he told his brother. 'Carter has just messaged me. From the looks of things, the skank has been kicking off again.'

* * *

Ten minutes later, Ricky slammed his foot on the brake and brought the car to a skidding halt. He yanked the keys out of the ignition then threw open the car door.

'Oi,' he shouted out.

Bianca Murphy spun around and on seeing both Ricky and Jamie climb out of the car she promptly turned on her heel and hitched her handbag higher up on to her shoulder.

'Oi,' Ricky shouted out a second time. 'I'm talking to you Murphy.'

Her fists clenching at her sides, Bianca came to a halt. As she turned around again, she was reminded once more just how much they looked like their father. There and then her heart began to beat faster. There was no getting away from the fact that they were Terry's sons; they were his doubles, same strong jaw line, same startling, blue eyes that seemed to have a knack for looking into your very soul. She plastered a wide smile across her face. She wouldn't mind having a bit of fun with one of Terry's boys, and if they were anything like their father then she knew she'd be in for a good time. 'What can I do for you?' she all but purred.

The scowl across Ricky's face deepened, his lips set into a thin line. 'We'd like a word.'

'Two actually,' Jamie interrupted. 'First of all, stay away from Terri, she doesn't need a skank like you giving her grief and secondly...'

Bianca burst out laughing. She should have known her daughter would put on a sob story. Not that she'd had any idea her girl was actually in contact with her brothers; she'd always been under the impression that Ricky and Jamie wanted nothing to do with her, she'd certainly never seen any form of interaction between them. 'Don't give me all of that old fanny,' she laughed. 'Since when were you and my daughter the best of pals? You've never so much as given her the time of day. Don't tell me' – she slapped her forehead as though it had just occurred to her – 'it was Jonny Carter who got on the blower, telling tales. You know he's giving her one, don't you? And the silly little cow believes he'll stick around. Only I know for a fact they never do,' she said with a measure of bitterness. 'No.' She pursed her lips together and shook her head. 'Once he's had his fill of her, he'll soon fuck her off out of it. Let's just hope that when the time comes, she hasn't got a bellyful of arms and legs.'

The nerve at the side of Ricky's jaw pulsated. 'That's your daughter you're talking about,' he spat. And as for Jonny Carter, if there was any truth to Bianca's accusations he'd come down on Jonny like a tonne of bricks. In fact, Carter or not, it would be safe to say that once Ricky had finished with him, Jonny wouldn't dare look in Terri's direction again.

Bianca shrugged and smoothing down her hair, she pushed out her breasts and licked her tongue across her lips. 'Forget about

Terri,' she said, giving a wink. 'There's a nice little pub just up the road. Maybe we could have a drink or two, and get to know one another properly. It's about time we let bygones be bygones; we could have a catch up, reminisce about your dad.'

A look of disgust flickered across both Ricky's and Jamie's faces.

'I'm not my old man,' Jamie spat. 'He might have been happy to fuck anything with a pulse, but I've got standards and I can tell you now and in no uncertain terms I'd rather pluck my eyeballs out with a rusty spoon than go anywhere with a tramp like you.'

Bianca's smile froze, her forehead furrowing. 'Oh, I see,' she snapped, crossing her arms over her chest. 'I suppose you think I'm not good enough to be seen with. Well, if that's the case, you can both piss off back to wherever the fuck it is you came from. Oh and you can say hello to your mum from me, and while you're at it, you can tell her to expect a visit; we've got some unfinished business that needs taking care of.'

She'd been about to continue on her way when Ricky yanked her roughly around to face him.

'Oi, what's your game?' Bianca shrieked as she tottered forwards, her hands held out in front of her in an attempt to stop herself from falling face first onto the pavement. 'You bastard. You could have caused me some damage; I could have broken my ankles in these heels.'

'Pity it's not your neck,' Jamie mumbled under his breath. 'Would do us all a favour.'

Ricky took a menacing step closer. 'Leave my mum out of this,' he hissed in her ear. 'Otherwise, things are going to turn really nasty. And where's that brother of yours? Where's he hiding out?'

Raising her eyebrows, Bianca ran her tongue across her yellowing, furred teeth. 'How should I know? We're not joined at the bloody hip.'

Jamie narrowed his eyes. 'Bit strange how you knew exactly which brother we were referring to.'

Bianca's face paled. 'Lucky guess.' She shrugged, about to turn away again.

'Could have been,' Jamie continued. 'Either that or you already know what he's done, what he did to Archie Taylor?'

'What are you talking about?' Bianca shook her head, her eyebrows scrunching together. 'Michael had nothing to do with Archie Taylor's murder.'

The muscles across the brothers' shoulders tensed. 'You'd best tell Michael that we're looking for him,' Ricky growled. 'And remember,' he said, stabbing his finger dangerously close to Bianca's face. 'Stay away from Terri and my mum otherwise we'll come down on you so hard that you're gonna wish you'd never been born.'

15

Beads of sweat broke out across Mason Tempest's forehead, not that he appeared to notice. With a determined grunt he heaved a bar weight up to his chest, the muscles in both his forearms and biceps burning as he pushed himself that little bit further.

He'd been coming to the gym for years and working out had become an integral part of his routine. He often enjoyed coming late in the evening, preferring to work out in solitude when the gym was relatively quiet, if not deserted. He was rarely in the mood to converse with fellow gym members and in fact could think of nothing worse than being forced to make small talk, especially seeing as he wasn't interested in forming friendships; he already had a small circle of close friends, mates who he could rely on to have his back if and when needed and vice versa.

Dropping the weight to the floor, he leaned forward, resting his hands on his thighs, taking in lungfuls of air in an attempt to steady his racing heart. He straightened up, snatched his water bottle off the bench press, wiped the back of his hand across his clammy forehead then took several sips of water, swallowing the cool liquid down, quenching his thirst. Once finished, he returned the bottle to the bench and pushed his ear pods into his ears. Immediately, music filtered through and grabbing his phone, he turned up the volume before getting himself back into position and wrapping his fingers around the iron bar.

A sudden movement from behind Mason made him pause. As far as he'd been aware he was the only person at the gym, not that he could say he'd taken much notice when he'd entered. He'd been so focused on making his way to the weights area, dumping his bag and getting stuck in that he'd barely taken note of anyone else around him. Turning his head, he frowned. 'What do you want, and how the fuck did you get in here?'

Frankie Gammon grinned, his heavy jowls wobbling with the motion. Surrounded by his firm, he fully believed himself to have the upper hand. He would even go as far as to say that since he'd taken Tempest unawares, it was pretty much game over, that his lads would soon smash Mason Tempest's cocky attitude into oblivion. And the quicker the better as far as he was concerned.

'I asked you a question,' Mason spat, yanking out the ear pods and slipping them into the pocket of his shorts. 'What do you want?'

Frankie took a step closer and flicking his head towards his minions, he motioned for them to move forward and take care of business. He had no interest in actually conversing with the prick before him; why waste time with pleasantries when there was a job to be done?

Mason gripped onto the bar weight, using it as a shield of sorts, his knuckles turning deathly white. The fact he was severely outnumbered didn't even register in his brain; his survival instinct had kicked in, and with a vast amount of space between himself and the exit, he knew he'd never be able to make a run for it, not that this was ever his intention; he'd never backed away from a fight in his life and didn't intend to start now.

A fist shot out, clipping him on his jaw. There hadn't been much weight behind the punch but even so, Mason ever so slightly stumbled back. Before he knew what was happening, he was surrounded and as fists began to fly, he held on to the weight for dear life.

Panting for breath, Mason gave an incredulous laugh. 'Seriously,' he stated as adrenaline began to pump through his veins. 'Is that the best you've got?' Bouncing on his feet his face became flushed and his eyes almost bulged out of their sockets, bringing further testament to just how angry he was. 'This is what you wanted, isn't it?' Mason roared as he began to swing the iron bar from side to side as though it weighed nothing. 'For me to lose my rag. So come on, who wants it? Which one of you cunts wants to have it toe to fucking toe?' As soon as the words left his mouth, he swung the weight through the air, focusing on the man nearest to him. And as the weight collided with its intended target, over and over again Mason smashed the heavy iron object over the man's head, spraying himself, the floor, and the walls in bright red blood.

Frankie's skin turned ashen, his gaze darting down to the unconscious form of the man on the floor. The fact a large gash could be clearly seen across his skull, revealing an unhealthy amount of bone and tissue, was more than enough to make him feel nauseous. He began to heave, his eyes becoming so wide they were almost popping out of his head and as Mason took another menacing step towards him, the bar weight in his fist still swinging backwards and forwards and dripping blood, Frankie elbowed his firm members out of the way in his haste to escape.

'Yeah I thought as much,' Mason hollered after him. 'You fucking cowards.'

Once he was sure he was alone again, Mason discarded the weight and rubbed the palm of his hand over his face, still barely able to get his head around the fact that he'd been set upon, that Frankie Gammon actually had the audacity to turn up at the gym and presume that he could take him out. Lightly dragging his thumb over his bottom lip, he looked down to see blood smeared across the tip. 'Bollocks,' he spat, dabbing at the oozing split. Gathering up his belongings, he swaggered towards the door then exited the building, without so much as giving the injured man laid out on the floor a second glance. He didn't even know if he was alive or dead, not that he particularly cared either way; to be more precise, he didn't give a shit. Why should he? The geezer was nothing but one of Gammon's henchmen, more than likely a drug dealer, one of the no-good pricks who'd been peddling pills at the school gates, a waste of fucking space in Mason's eyes.

Unlocking his car, Mason took a seat behind the wheel and rummaged around in his gym bag for his mobile phone. His dad was going to go ballistic, not to mention his uncle Jamie; they were already gunning for Gammon and he had a feeling that if he hadn't already, then after tonight's escapades, Frankie had all but signed his own death warrant. He may as well as dig his own grave and it was only a matter of time before his dad and uncle eventually caught up with him and when they did, no amount of begging would stop the inevitable from happening. In other words, it would be safe to say that Frankie Gammon was the equivalent of a dead man walking.

* * *

As it turned out, ballistic was an understatement when it came to describing the fury that rippled through Ricky's veins. After being told what had happened in the gym he was so livid that he'd screamed and hollered for over twenty minutes, so much so that Jamie had had to physically restrain him from going after Gammon there and then and battering the life out of him. Each and every time Ricky looked at his son, the familiar sense of anger would once again resurface and he'd begin shouting the odds all over again.

'I'm going to kill him,' he spat as he grasped Mason's jaw, tilting his face from side to side, inspecting the damage. 'I'm going to rip his head clean off his shoulders.'

'Dad.' Mason pulled himself free and cocked an eyebrow. 'I don't know why you're getting so worked up; I'm hardly the epitome of the walking wounded, am I. They landed a couple of lucky punches and that's about it. I've walked away with far worse on a night out and not even batted an eyelid.'

Ricky snarled. Lucky or not, the sentiment had still been there; Frankie Gammon had attempted to harm his son, his only son might he add. It was at times like these that he wished he'd never quit smoking. He reached into his pocket and pulled out his nicotine gum, scowling as he popped a piece into his mouth and began to vigorously chew. Not that he'd actually wanted to quit; it wasn't as though he'd been what he'd call a heavy smoker anyway. It had been his wife Kayla's nagging that had eventually made him give up and despite his initial reservations he did actually feel healthier for it.

'He's right,' Jamie sighed. 'It could have been a lot worse. They probably weren't expecting Mase to fight back.'

'And that,' Ricky growled, 'is exactly my point. What if he hadn't have been able to fight back? What if they'd knocked him unconscious, or he hadn't been able to ward Gammon off? We could have been identifying his body about now. And that's another thing,' he said, pointing a stiff finger towards his son. 'Make sure you lay low for a few days, and do not under any circumstances let your mother see you looking like this, I'll never hear the end of it,' he groaned.

Mason screwed up his face. He had no intentions of turning up at his parents' house; his mum would throw a hissy fit, and the last thing he needed or wanted for that matter was to see her upset in any way, shape, or form. She detested violence, thoroughly believing it to be pointless. Unfortunately for her she'd married into a family where violence was an everyday part of life. 'I won't,' he reassured his dad as he gingerly reached up to touch his lip. 'And don't worry, I'll send a couple of my pals over to the gym, they'll do a thorough clean up, get rid of any evidence.' He shrugged. 'And if needs be they'll dispose of the body an' all.'

Ricky nodded and as he began to pace the length of the taxi office, a part of him was still unable to get his head around the fact Frankie Gammon believed he could take him and Jamie on. Something didn't feel right about the whole set up; the problem was, he couldn't put his finger on what that could be.

'Look.' As if sensing his brother's inner thoughts, Jamie shook his head. 'You don't reckon Gammon has backing, do you? And I'm not talking about that lowlife Michael Murphy either. It's just...' His voice trailed off as he studied Mason. 'No offence Mase,' he said, holding up his hands and giving his nephew a small smile. 'But it's common knowledge you're a loose cannon, that you're not quite right up here,' he said, tapping his temple. 'And for the life of me I just can't work out how Gammon thought he'd be a match for you, regardless of how many pricks he'd brought with him to help fight his cause.'

Ricky nodded. Those had been his exact thoughts too. 'I think you could be right,' he admitted. 'Either that or Gammon is working for someone. And let's face it, this is no small beef, no wannabe hood rat trying his luck. No, whoever it is they've got a grudge to bear. This is personal. I can feel it in my gut.'

Jamie sighed and chewing on his thumbnail, he looked into the distance, his forehead furrowing.

'Question is though,' Ricky continued, oblivious to the turmoil going through his brother's mind. 'Who has got this much of a problem with us that they'd go to all of this trouble just to see us brought down? Why not just come out with it, have it out with us man to man? Why the need to play games, because that's what this is, someone's toying with us. They want us to be looking over our shoulders, wondering when or where the next attack will come from. And we've seen this before,' he added, stabbing his finger in his brother's direction. 'This is exactly the same as when Kenny Kempton orchestrated the arson attack on Max's car showroom,' he said. 'And you know it.'

The words hung heavy in the air and as Jamie rubbed at his temples, Ricky failed to notice just how quiet his brother had become.

* * *

Frankie Gammon's face was deathly white, and his breath that streamed out in front of him was ragged. He was scared and wasn't afraid to admit that fact. Raymond Cole had instructed him to end Mason Tempest's life and it should have been an easy task, a case of creeping up on Tempest mob handed, battering the life out of him and job done. What he hadn't been banking on was for Mason Tempest to be a complete and utter lunatic. Oh, he'd heard the rumours about him, had known the kid wasn't quite the full shilling, but to actually see him in action had unnerved Frankie far more than he was ever prepared to let on. The kid was stark raving mad; no wonder he and Raymond Cole were related. The pair of them were a couple of bonafide nutters if ever he'd seen them.

At the front door to his flat he took a deep breath, almost afraid to enter his own home.

'You can be the one to tell Cole that Tempest is still walking around as large as life,' one of his firm members, Warren Oates, grumbled as he fingered the large swelling upon his cheek that would soon turn to a bruise.

Frankie turned his head, the scowl he gave enough to make Warren snap his lips closed. He didn't need reminding that he was a failure, and even more than that he didn't need Warren to tell him that Raymond was likely to go mental once he learned that Mason Tempest had got the better of him and not just him alone but also three of his firm members, one of whom was more than likely dead if the state of his split skull was anything to go by.

Entering the flat, Frankie paused at the threshold. Other than the occasional knocks and bangs that came from the water pipes, the flat was deathly silent and if he hadn't known any better, he would have sworn the property was deserted. Cautiously, he walked the length of the hallway, his entire being on red alert. Where was Cole? He'd said that he would be waiting eagerly at the flat for news of Tempest's demise.

He stepped inside the lounge, the hairs on the back of his neck standing upright as goose flesh covered his skin. The room was in darkness and if it wasn't for the bright red, glowing cherry on the end of Raymond's cigarette, Frankie would have never known he was there.

'Well?' Raymond barked out. 'Is it done?'

Frankie swallowed deeply, and as his eyes adjusted to the darkness, his mouth opened and closed in rapid succession. How was he supposed to answer? Should he just blurt out the truth, tell Raymond that he hadn't been successful, make himself sound like even more of a loser than he already felt?

A sudden movement from Raymond was enough to make Frankie gulp, his heart racing so erratically that he feared it would stop beating altogether. 'We ran into a problem,' he gushed, the words tripping out of his mouth so fast that his brain was barely able to keep up.

'What kind of problem?' Raymond growled, the menace in his voice reverberating around the small room.

Frankie swallowed again, his mouth becoming so dry that he had to force his lips apart. 'Tempest,' he said. 'He's a nutcase, a lunatic. He went for us, smashed a bar weight across one of my lad's heads.'

Throwing his head back, Raymond roared with laughter as though he'd just been told an amusing joke. In all of his life, Frankie had never heard anything so chilling. He gave a half smile, unsure if Cole actually expected him to join in.

'So the kid's got some balls.' Raymond nodded as though impressed. He patted Frankie's shoulder, his strong fingers digging into Frankie's flesh, making him wince. 'That will make it all the more satisfying to see him brought down then. Maybe next time I'll make his old man watch, make him witness his only son's demise.' He winked.

As Raymond left the flat, Frankie stared after him. Horror spread throughout his body and mind. Cole wasn't only unhinged, he was evil, he had to be. What kind of man would force a father to bear witness to his own son's death?

* * *

With just a few minutes to spare before the pub closed for the night, Jamie pushed open the door and walked inside. As he approached the bar, Terri wiped her hands on a towel and flashed him a welcoming smile.

'What are you doing here?' she asked. 'You've left it a bit late to order a drink. We've just rung the bell for last orders.' She gave a light laugh and shook her head at her mistake. What with everything that had gone on of late, she'd almost forgotten that he and Ricky actually owned half the pub now and that they could order themselves a drink whenever they wanted to.

Jamie shrugged, and glancing around him as though he were on the lookout for someone, he rested his forearms on the bar, his shoulder blades remaining rigid. 'I didn't come here for a drink. I just wanted to know if that lowlife Gammon has given Rina any more grief?'

Terri gave an involuntary shiver and shook her head. 'No, thank God.' She sucked in her bottom lip. 'Did you really mean what you told Rina, that you believe he'll stay away from the pub? That you don't think it's likely he'll turn up and demand protection money or try to threaten us again? Like Rina said, we were there, we were witnesses to Archie's murder. What are we supposed to do if he comes back for us?'

Giving a casual laugh, Jamie shook his head. 'He wouldn't fucking dare.' He screwed up his face, his eyes hardening in an attempt to cover up the lie he'd just told. After tonight's events, who knew what Gammon was capable of and if he could go after Mason then Rina and Terri would be even easier targets. 'He might give it all the mouth and think that he's something he isn't out there in the street,' he continued. 'Especially when he's surrounded by those muppets he calls his firm, but when it comes down to it, he's nothing but a coward. He wouldn't have the bottle to step foot in here.'

'I hope you're right,' Terri said as she turned to look at Rina. 'She's been through enough as it is without Gammon putting in an appearance, half scaring her to death and threatening her with all and sundry.'

Remaining quiet, Jamie glanced around him again, chewing on the inside of his cheek as he did so.

Narrowing her eyes, Terri studied him. He seemed on edge, she noted, not quite his usual self. 'Are you okay?' she asked as she followed his gaze. 'Has something happened? Where's Ricky tonight? You've not had a falling out, have you?'

Jamie snapped his gaze back to Terri, his eyebrows lifting. 'No. Why would you ask that?'

Terri shrugged. 'It just seems odd that's all; I thought you did everything together.'

'He's not my keeper,' Jamie shot back, his voice holding a note of irritation. 'I am allowed out and about on my own.'

'I was only asking.' Terri rolled her eyes. 'I didn't think you'd be so touchy.'

'I'm sorry.' Jamie held up his hands. 'I didn't mean to snap, it's just been one of those days.' He rubbed the palm of his hand over his face. 'Mason was attacked tonight; he's all right,' he was quick to add. 'No real harm was done, but as you can imagine, it's riled me up.'

'Was it Gammon?' Terri's mouth dropped open, her eyes darting around her, half expecting Frankie Gammon to appear out of nowhere and start attacking them.

'Could have been,' Jamie lied a second time. He leaned forward and lowered his voice a fraction. 'Was there anyone else from Gammon's firm who you might recognise? Anyone who might have stood out more than the others?'

Terri frowned and thinking the question over, she shook her head. 'No, I only recognised Michael. Why?'

'So you don't recall seeing anyone with a scar?' Jamie swallowed deeply and as he ran his index finger from his eye down to his cheek, he watched her reaction closely. 'And I'm talking about a big fuck-off scar, not a scratch, not something that would fade over time. You wouldn't be able to miss it, it would stand out, would make him noticeable.'

'No.' Terri shook her head again and crossing her arms over her chest her face was a mask of concentration. 'It doesn't ring any bells.'

'Are you sure? Think back,' Jamie urged. 'Have you seen anyone who matches that description?' He paused for a moment and turned his head, his hard stare scrutinising each of the patrons in turn. 'Maybe he wasn't even with Gammon, he could have come in alone. In fact, it wouldn't surprise me if the bastard had been in here observing everything that went on. He'd get a kick out of that.'

'No,' Terri reiterated. 'It doesn't sound like someone I'd forget in a hurry.' The hairs on the back of her neck stood upright. 'What's going on?' she asked, concern getting the better of her. 'Who are you even talking about. Is it someone you know?'

Deep in thought, Jamie looked down at the bar, chewing nervously on his thumbnail, as the nerve at the side of his eye pulsated.

'Jamie.' Terri raised her voice slightly. 'Answer the question because you're starting to scare me now. Has something happened? Should I be worried? Are me and Rina in danger?'

Looking up, Jamie shook his head. 'Nah of course not, it's nothing like that.' He pushed himself away from the bar and made to leave before promptly spinning back around. 'But if you do see someone who matches that description then let me know.' He gestured to his cheek, emphasising his point in regard to the scar. 'Not Ricky, me, okay? Are we clear on that?'

Terri nodded and as Jamie made his way back outside the pub, her gaze followed him. Despite his reassurance that there was nothing for her to worry about she couldn't help the shiver of fear that ran down the length of her spine. He was worried; he might not have said as much, he hadn't needed to, his stance alone had been enough to tell her that something was wrong, seriously wrong. And why all the secrecy, she pondered. Why wouldn't he want Ricky to know? He was hiding something, she decided. He had to be. But for the life of her, Terri didn't know what that could be.

As Terri went back to work, she couldn't help but take a peek at the last lingering customers as they downed their drinks before setting off home for the night. She tried to think back. Could she have seen the man Jamie was referring to and not taken any notice of him? Not that a scar of that magnitude would be something she'd be likely to forget in a hurry, and from what Jamie had said it wasn't something the man would be able to conceal either. Certain that she hadn't seen anyone fitting that description, she began collecting the empty glasses, a lot more conscious of who was around her than she'd been previously. As much as Jamie hadn't intended to frighten her, he'd done just that. If she was being honest with herself, his entire demeanour had unnerved her to the point that she was in half a mind to give Ricky a call and ask him what was going on. He knew Jamie a lot better than she did and was bound to know if something was bothering him. It was only the fact she'd given Jamie her word not to mention anything to their eldest brother that stopped her from taking her mobile phone out of her pocket and dialling his number. Still, she thought to herself as she slid the bolt across the door once the last customer had left, whatever the issue was, it was bound to come out sooner or later; secrets very rarely stayed a secret for long. She could only hope and pray that when the truth eventually did come out that she wouldn't be within her brothers' close proximity. She had more than a sneaking suspicion that despite being brothers, Ricky and Jamie wouldn't hold back when it came to laying into one another, that they knew each other's weaknesses only too well and wouldn't be afraid to use them, no matter who got hurt in the process.

* * *

Lighting a cigarette, Raymond inhaled the smoke deep into his lungs before lazily exhaling through his nostrils. From where he'd parked his car, he had the perfect view of the pub and what was more, he couldn't be seen, not unless someone actually went out of their way to turn into the side road where he'd parked and considering the road led to a dead end, that wasn't likely.

He often came to watch Terri as she worked, using it as an opportunity to suss her out, not that he'd ever allowed himself to get too close; he didn't want to frighten her off and more importantly, he didn't want her to inform Ricky or Jamie of his presence. Not when they'd left him fighting for his life in a ditch beside the side of the road. It was only by some miracle that he'd survived; in fact, he wouldn't be surprised if they'd assumed he'd died, that he'd succumbed to the injuries they had left him with. He lightly trailed his fingers down the length of his scar, his expression hardening as he watched the youngest of his brothers step outside the pub and make his way over to where he'd parked his own car. And it was a flashy motor too, not that he should have expected anything different from Jamie, he'd always been a flash bastard. Even as a youngster he'd had a mouth on him, had thought that the sun had shone out of his arse. Raymond continued watching his every move; he could take him down right now if he so wished, he could plunge a blade into Jamie's back and he wouldn't have even known what had hit him. Not that he would of course; where would the fun be in that? No, it would be too quick, he reasoned, and if nothing else, Raymond wanted to see his siblings suffer for their wrongdoings just as he too had been made to suffer. He'd waited a long time for this moment, years in fact, but it would be worth the wait and he was going to savour every moment of bringing them down, he would make sure of that.

Turning his gaze back to the pub, he watched as his sister said goodnight to one of the customers before firmly closing the door. She was a pretty little thing, the image of their late father, the same father who had barely wanted to spend any time with his illegitimate son. In Terry's eyes, Raymond had been nothing more than a dirty little secret; he'd been so far down his father's list of priorities that he'd barely been a given a second or third thought, a fact he'd been made well aware of.

A smile tugged at the corner of his lips and tossing the cigarette butt out of the window, he started the ignition; it was a pity really that Terri would find herself a pawn in his sick game, but in the circumstances, what was else was he supposed to do? He had a grudge to bear, an anger inside of him that consumed his every waking thought and if he had to use Terri to get to his half-brothers then he was more than prepared to do just that. In fact, if need be, he was prepared to bring down each and every one of the Tempests. After all, it was the price they had to pay, their comeuppance for kicking him to the kerb, for making him feel worthless.

As he drove out of the car park, Raymond gave the pub one last seething glance before stepping his foot down on the accelerator. As far as he was concerned, he hadn't even begun to dish out his revenge yet, but when he did, when he finally came for them, they would all know it, each and every last one of them, if it was the last thing he ever did.

16

A week later, after Archie's body had been released for burial, they laid him to rest in Rippleside Cemetery in Barking, Essex. He'd had a good turn out too. The church had been standing room only and there were so many floral tributes that it had taken Terri and Rina at least thirty minutes just to stop and look at each of them.

And just as Terri had predicted she would, Rina had fallen to pieces. The brave face she'd put on leading up to the funeral had all but evaporated. Not only had she sobbed her entire way through the service, but she had almost become near hysterical when it had been time to inter the coffin into the ground.

'I can't,' she'd cried in the car as they made their way back to the pub for the wake. 'I just can't live without him.'

'Yes, you can,' Terri had reassured her. 'You're strong.' She crossed one shapely leg over the other, the jet-black heels she wore accentuating her long, tanned, bare legs. 'And Archie would want you to carry on,' she said as she clasped Rina's hand in hers. 'He wouldn't want to see you upset like this and you'll have me to help you. I promise that I'll be with you every step of the way, that I will help you to get through this.'

Dabbing at her eyes, Rina waved her hand dismissively. 'You're young,' she sniffed. 'Before you know it, you'll want a home of your own, maybe even a family of your own and I won't hold you back.'

If the circumstances had been different, Terri would have thrown her head back and roared with laughter. She highly doubted she would ever want those things. She'd never even had so much as a boyfriend, at least not a serious one anyway. And who in their right mind would want the Murphys as in-laws?

All too soon the car was pulling up outside the pub. The sheer volume of cars parked in the car park was enough to tell them that the pub would be packed to the rafters, the mourners and well-wishers all keen to get a glimpse of the grieving widow. Ricky and Jamie had even gone as far as to employ bar staff for the night. They had insisted that Rina was to have the night off so that she could pay her respects to Archie without needing to worry about the running of the pub.

Climbing out of the car, Rina took a large breath, her steps faltering as she neared the entrance. 'I don't want to do this,' she wailed, anguish written across her face as she gripped onto Terri's arm so tightly, she was in grave danger of cutting off the blood supply.

In a quandary, Terri glanced towards the pub, her eyes falling upon Jonny Carter. She gave him a pleading look, almost sighing with relief when he began to make his way over.

'Come on Rina.' Without needing to be asked, he instinctively slipped his arm around Rina's shoulders and hugged her to him. 'There are a lot of people inside who want to make sure you're okay. We'll find you a seat, and make sure that you've got a drink and if you need a bit of time out, a bit of space, then we will make sure you have that too. How does that sound?'

Rina nodded and as she allowed Jonny to lead her inside, Terri blew out her cheeks, thankful that the situation had been defused before following on behind. Minutes later, they were seated at a table with glasses of wine set in front of them. Not much of a wine drinker, Terri grimaced as she sipped at the liquid. Rina had told her that it was an acquired taste and if Terri was being truthful, she couldn't see herself ever coming to enjoy the drink; it was too bitter and too strong in her opinion.

Before she knew it, however, Terri had downed the entire glass, and as a second filled glass miraculously materialised in front of her, she picked it up and swallowed down a large mouthful. Already, the alcohol had gone to her head, and she was fast on her way to feeling tipsy. She'd slow down after this one, she told herself. She didn't want to get too drunk, especially today of all days.

* * *

By the time Terri was on her fifth glass of wine, all thoughts of staying sober had well and truly gone out of the window. Unsteadily, she got to her feet, swaying in time to the music blasting out from the speakers.

Bypassing her brothers who were standing at the bar, their expressions hard, their watchful eyes following her every move, Terri made a beeline for the table where Jonny was sitting. The alcohol had made her feel even more confident and now was the perfect time to make her move on him. Not only that but Rina was right, she did like him; why should she allow Bianca to ruin any future dalliances between them? As far as Terri was concerned, they would make a good couple; they both came from notorious families, her a Tempest and him a Carter; it was a match made in heaven, or hell, whichever way you wanted to look at it.

Coming to stand behind Jonny, she leaned forward and slung her arm around his neck, allowing her loose dark hair to cascade across his cheek whilst she breathed in his scent. He smelled so good, she mused, and he looked so handsome dressed in black trousers and a pristine white shirt. The thought of being so close to him made her giggle like a school girl.

'Are you trying to get me killed?' Jonny hissed, glancing in Ricky's and Jamie's direction. 'Your brothers are right there.'

'And?' Terri slurred, her fingers grabbing onto Jonny's arm to stop herself from falling to the floor. 'They're not my keepers, why would they even care?' She gave a hiccup and screwed up her face. 'Until recently, we'd never even spoken to one another and they've hardly behaved as brothers should. They've never looked out for me, have they.' As the music changed, she broke into a wide grin. 'I love this song,' she declared. 'Dance with me,' she urged, pulling Jonny to his feet.

Disentangling himself from her embrace, Jonny cast another cautious glance towards her brothers. 'What do you mean they've never looked out for you? Who do you think it was who told Bianca to back off? It was your brothers, that's who. They care a lot more than you think.'

Terri squashed her lips together, her forehead furrowing. 'Don't be daft.' She giggled again and yanked on his arm, pulling him even closer until their bodies were so close Terri could feel his heartbeat, and it was beating fast too, just as hers was. 'I like you.' She grinned up at him. 'A lot.'

Gently prising her fingers away from him, Jonny sighed. 'I think you've had a bit too much to drink. Maybe you should sit down, have some water.' He looked towards the bar and motioned to one of the bar staff for a glass of water.

Terri pouted. 'I'm not a child.' A smile tugged at the corners of her lips as she twirled a lock of hair around her finger. 'You even said so yourself,' she added, batting her eyelashes at him.

Jonny groaned. It was true; just one glance in her direction was enough to tell him that she was no child. She had a pert backside and legs that seemed to go on forever and even more than that she was just his type, or at least she would have been if it wasn't for the fact that he didn't want her brothers breathing down his neck. It was highly unlikely that Ricky or Jamie would give him their blessing, that they would tell him to crack on. In fact, if the expressions across their faces were anything to go by, Jonny wouldn't be surprised if they were on the verge of charging over and laying into him.

'Like I said.' Jonny glanced around him again, more than aware that their interaction was gaining an audience. 'I think you've had a bit too much to drink.'

About to laugh off his comment, Terri's eyes widened. She didn't feel so well; her head was swimming and if she didn't know any better, she would have sworn there were two Jonnys standing in front of her. Slamming her hand over her mouth, nausea washed over her, and the more she tried to swallow the urge down, the more she wanted to vomit. 'I think I'm going to —' She was unable to get the rest of the words out before she promptly bent forward and vomited onto the floor, narrowly missing Jonny's shoes in the process. Mortified, she sank to her knees and held her head in her hands as tears filled her eyes.

'For fuck's sake,' Ricky roared as he barged Jonny out of his way. 'Why did you let her get into this state?'

Jonny's eyes popped open. 'Me?' he shouted, stabbing his thumb into his chest. 'Why the fuck are you blaming me? I wasn't the one who plied her with booze.'

'Oh darling.' As Rina came forward, she knelt beside Terri and lifted her hair away from her clammy forehead. 'What a mess you've gotten yourself into, eh?'

'Yeah, you can say that again,' Jamie groaned, wrinkling his nose as the acrid stench of vomit filled the air.

'What and you've never had too much to drink before?' Rina snapped, giving him a knowing look.

Jamie had the grace to look away.

'Yeah, I thought as much,' she retorted. 'I've seen the three of you so paralytic that you didn't know what day it was let alone have any idea how you were going to get home, so don't you dare stand there pointing fingers.' She went back to smoothing the hair out of Terri's face, all the while whispering words of comfort. 'Well come on,' she urged, looking up at the three men. 'Don't just stand there; help me get her up off the floor.'

With little effort, they got Terri to her feet, not that it did anything to help put an end to the room spinning, and as Terri lurched forward again, she emptied the contents of her stomach a second time. 'I'm sorry,' she wailed, tears filling her eyes. 'I don't think I should have had that last drink.'

'Or maybe the last four drinks,' Jamie added, wrinkling his nose again.

Rina glared. 'You're not helping matters.' Turning her attention back to Terri, she waved her hand dismissively. 'It's happened to the best of us, sweetheart.' She turned to look at the three men. 'No doubt she'll have a raging hangover tomorrow,' she mused. 'And if I so much as hear one of you,' she warned, wagging her finger between them, 'say that she only has herself to blame, I'll start swinging for you. Like I said we've all been there at some point, some more than others.' She gave Jamie a pointed look. 'So which one of you is going to help me get her upstairs?

'I will.' Staring Jonny down, Ricky tucked his arm through Terri's, all the while daring Jonny to argue the case.

Terri looked up and giving Ricky a lopsided grin, it took all of her effort to keep her eyes open. 'You're so lovely,' she declared. 'Unlike him.' She jerked her head in Jonny's direction and scowled. 'He wouldn't even dance with me.'

Ricky clenched his jaw. 'For fuck's sake,' he muttered under his breath. 'She's in an even worse state than I first thought.'

* * *

The next morning, Terri rolled over in bed and opened her eyes, feeling momentarily disorientated. As a wave of nausea swept over her, she groaned. Why was the room spinning and why did her head hurt so much? She hadn't had that much to drink, surely? Gingerly pulling herself into a sitting position, she squinted at the sunlight filtering through the net curtain, her hand clutching her forehead. A thought suddenly occurred to her and throwing back the duvet, she stared down at her semi-naked form, her eyes narrowing into slits. She had no recollection of getting into bed or how she had even managed to climb the steep staircase. Rina wouldn't have been able to carry her, she knew that much, at least not without help. In fact, the last thing she could recollect was sitting with Rina at the wake. They'd had a few glasses of wine; she could even remember feeling a little tipsy and since she hadn't eaten that day, the alcohol had gone straight to her head, but even so, she couldn't have been that drunk, could she? Looking around her, Terri's gaze fell upon the wardrobe, her forehead furrowing even further. The dress she'd been wearing to the funeral hung neatly on a hanger, far too neatly for someone who couldn't remember even getting into bed. And if she hadn't been the one to hang the dress then who had undressed her?

As memories of the previous day began to resurface, she brought her hands up to her face. 'Oh God,' she grumbled aloud. 'No, no, no.' Had she really made a move on Jonny Carter? She must have done; she could vaguely recall him turning her down. Shame coursed through her, and she was in half a mind to lie back down, throw the duvet over her head and stay there for the duration. How would she ever be able to show her face in the pub again? She'd made herself look like a fool, a laughing stock. And Rina, oh God, poor Rina. Didn't she have enough to contend with without Terri making life even more difficult? She was supposed to have been taking care of Rina, not the other way around.

'Are you awake?'

Terri opened one eye and shaking her head, she dived back under the duvet. How could she face Rina now? She'd let her down.

Rina gave a gentle laugh. 'I'm guessing you're going to need these.' She placed a glass of water on the nightstand then handed over two tablets. 'They will help with the headache.'

Terri groaned and pushing herself up again, she popped the pills on the back of her tongue and washed them down with the water. 'And what about the shame?' she asked, her husky voice low. 'Will they help with that too?'

'Unfortunately not,' Rina laughed.

Flopping back on to the bed, Terri covered her eyes. 'I'm so sorry Rina.'

'What for?' Sitting on the edge of the bed, Rina gently pulled Terri's arm away so that she could look her in the eyes. 'You did nothing wrong.'

'But I got drunk,' Terri protested. 'I ruined the wake.'

Rina waved her hand in the air. 'If anyone ruined the wake then it was those brothers of yours.'

Terri's eyes spang open and scrambling up the bed, she pulled the duvet up to her neck. 'What happened?'

Rina paused. 'Let's just say they didn't take too kindly to you and Jonny Carter having a...' She paused a second time, as if unable to find the right word. 'A chat,' she finally volunteered.

Terri's eyes widened to their utmost. It had been more than a chat. She'd practically thrown herself at him and had been one step away from actually dragging him up the stairs to her bedroom. 'No.'

She shook her head, feeling even more ashamed of herself. 'Please tell me they didn't get into an altercation.'

Giving a sad smile Rina sighed. 'It got pretty heated at one point. Tempers were beginning to flare.'

'They went for him, didn't they?' Clutching her head again, Terri closed her eyes in distress.

'It came close,' Rina confirmed. 'And I think they may have actually got one or two jabs in before they were pulled apart.'

'They had no right,' Terri seethed, jumping out of bed and shrugging on one of Rina's old dressing gowns before wrapping it around her. 'How could they do that?'

'They were looking out for you, darling. It's what brothers do.'

Terri opened her mouth to answer when a snippet of the conversation she'd had with Jonny filtered into her mind. Ricky and Jamie had told her mum to back off. They had actually gone out of their way to warn Bianca to stay away from her. Why would they even do that? She didn't mean anything to them, did she?

Rina got to her feet and patting Terri's shoulder, she smiled. 'Food for thought, eh. Maybe they care about you more than you think. In fact, I'd even go as far as to say that you've got them eating out of the palm of your hand.'

As Rina left the bedroom, Terri's mind reeled. This was what she'd always hoped for, wasn't it? A family who wanted her in their life, a family who cared about her. Heading for the bathroom, Terri was still unable to get her head around the fact that her brothers had actually lashed out at Jonny. If Rina hadn't told her about the altercation, she would never have believed it possible. Would never have believed that she was important enough for someone to come to her defence and not once, but twice.

* * *

Jonny Carter made his way inside the pub. At the bar, he stuffed his hands into his pockets and gave an awkward smile. 'How's your head doing today?'

Terri looked up, alarm filtering across her face. Jonny was the last person she'd been expecting to see. In fact, she wouldn't have been surprised if he'd decided to avoid her until the end of his days. She wouldn't have blamed him either; she'd embarrassed them both, herself even more.

'You were pretty smashed last night,' he teased. 'Fuck me, I thought I was bad, but by all accounts the way you were knocking the drinks back, anyone would think they were going out of fashion.'

There and then, anger washed over Terri. 'I'm glad you find it so amusing,' she spat, her cheeks turning pink. Collecting the glasses, she turned to walk away from him, her entire body bristling. As annoyed as she was, he did have a point and a valid one at that. She'd been so drunk she hadn't been able to see straight, let alone think coherently, and she had been knocking back the drinks, she must have been. Why else would she have thought it a good idea to practically throw herself at him? Drunk or not though, it made no difference; he'd still turned her down, had still made her look like a fool in front of the entire pub. Conveniently she chose to ignore the fact that she too had also contributed to making a show of herself by drooling all over him one minute then vomiting over him the next, or as good as anyway. 'What do you even want Carter?'

Jonny sighed. 'Look, about last night. Maybe it was the drink talking, I dunno.' He held up his hands. 'But—'

'Don't say it.' Terri gulped, her cheeks turning even redder. She swiped a lock of hair away from her face and turned away from him. 'I already know what you're going to say.'

Narrowing his eyes, Jonny studied her. 'As flattered as I am,' he continued, regardless of the fact she'd told him to stop. 'I wouldn't be any good for you. In my line of work...' He shook his head as though trying to find the right words. 'Let's just say that I'm already on borrowed time. I could be nicked at any given moment and you're a nice girl, you don't want someone like me in your life, you deserve better.'

Terri's face fell. The fact he was doing his best to let her down gently stung. 'You condescending bastard, not to mention arrogant.' Pushing her shoulders back, she pulled herself up to her full height, all the while barely able to look him in the eyes certain that he would be able to see right through her, that he would know deep down her intentions had been real, that she did want him. 'Like you said.' She glowered. 'It was the drink talking, so from where I'm standing there's no need for this.' She gestured between them. 'Now, if you don't mind, I've got work to do.'

Jonny lifted his eyebrows and giving an incredulous laugh, he pointed to the purple swelling across his jaw. 'Well in that case you need to give your brothers the heads-up. I took a right hander for you. A bit of compassion wouldn't go amiss.'

Terri swallowed deeply, her gaze lingering upon his jawline. From where she was standing it looked as though he'd received a lot more than a couple of jabs; in fact, if the bruise was anything to go by, she wouldn't be surprised if her brothers had really laid into him. Placing the empty glasses on the bar, she gave a nonchalant shrug. 'I'm sure you've had a lot worse,' she answered in an attempt to hide her true thoughts before moving along the bar to serve the next customer.

'Hey,' Jonny called after her, his voice a low growl. 'What the fuck is your problem?'

As Terri turned back to look at him, she swallowed deeply again. As much as she hated to admit it, he'd just hit the nail on the head. What exactly *was* her problem? Other than feeling remorse and embarrassment, she didn't have one, not really. All she wanted to do was forget the whole debacle and that also included forgetting just how handsome he was, or how much she liked him. From now on, she was determined to keep Jonny Carter at arm's length, to pretend he meant nothing to her, that his handsome face didn't make her heart flutter, or her legs go weak at the knees. 'I'm busy.' She motioned to the customer standing in front of her. 'I'm sure that Rina will be along in a minute to serve you.'

Jonny's forehead furrowed, his strong jaw becoming rigid. 'Do you know what,' he fumed. 'This is a fucking joke. Cheers for that, for this,' he corrected, pointing to his jaw. 'Next time I won't bother.' Pushing himself away from the bar, he shook his head before walking away. At the entrance, he rocked back on his heels, his body involuntarily stiffening. 'You don't need to start throwing punches again,' he spat, shooting Terri a scowl over his shoulder as Ricky and Jamie entered the pub. 'I'm done here.'

'What did that prick want?' As he reached the bar, Ricky jerked his head behind him.

Terri slammed the till closed, two pink spots appearing on her cheeks. 'Let's get one thing straight,' she all but barked out. 'I'm warning you now,' she said, looking between both Ricky and Jamie. 'You are not my keepers. You don't get to tell me what to do, neither do you tell me who I should or shouldn't be friends with. I'm a grown woman and more than capable of making my own decisions.'

Jamie raised his eyebrows and as he nudged his brother in the ribs, he threw him a wink. 'Is that what they call it these days? Friends?'

Terri glared and pushing herself forward, she was on the verge of losing her temper. She was as much a Tempest as they were, and they would do well to remember that fact if they knew what was good for them. She wasn't entirely green around the edges; they seemed to forget that she'd been raised by the Murphys, that she knew how to take care of herself; she'd had no other choice on the matter. Fair enough, she may not have been a match for them when it came to their standing within the criminal underworld, nor did she share their notoriety and if she was being entirely honest she wasn't so sure that she wanted to but that didn't mean she was a walkover. Her temper was just as quick as theirs, and she could hold her own when she needed to; she'd had enough practice over the years.

'Yes,' she snarled. 'Friends. So why the fuck you felt the need to lay into Jonny Carter, I'll never know. And I can tell you something else for nothing: do yourselves a favour and back off.' She turned away and giving a big sigh, she turned back to look at them, her expression softening. They had tried to look out for her, she reasoned to herself. And as much as she was annoyed with them, their hearts had been in the right place or at least she thought they were. 'But thank you, anyway.'

A wide grin spread across Jamie's face. 'See, she knows the score,' he declared. 'And as it just so happens, there's been a development, one that just might be of an interest to you.'

Terri's ears pricked up. 'What kind of development?'

'Frankie Gammon and your uncle.'

'What about them?' Terri held her breath, her body stiffening.

'We're going after them, tonight,' Ricky volunteered. 'We've finally got an address for Gammon; turns out the house in Dagenham was a front, just some shit hole he uses as a meeting place, a place where he dishes out the shit he sells. His real home is a flat on one of the estates and from what I've been told, Michael Murphy is a frequent visitor.'

'The question is...' Jamie shrugged, the hint of a grin tugging at the corners of his lips. 'Are you in or are you out?'

Terri didn't need to be asked twice. Of course she was in, there was no question about that. She wanted to see Michael pay for what he'd done almost as much as they did, if not even more. She held out her hand. 'Phone,' she snapped.

Jamie dug his hand into his pocket then paused, his forehead furrowing. 'Why?'

'Come on, hand it over,' she beckoned, ignoring his question.

Reluctantly handing over his phone, Jamie placed the device into her hand, watching her every move as she scrolled down his contact list. Coming to Jonny Carter's phone number, she pressed dial. 'Now apologise to him,' she demanded. 'You were out of order and unless it's escaped your notice, if we're going to bring Michael and Frankie Gammon down then we're going to need him. He's added muscle and just remember, I know what Michael is like; he can be a slippery fucker when he needs to be.'

As Jamie wandered off to take the call, Ricky shook his head. 'You're deluded if you think that he'll apologise.'

Moments later, Jamie walked back over to them. 'Are you happy now?' he said, slamming the phone on the bar. 'Carter will be loving this.' He groaned. 'No doubt he'll tell all and sundry that he made me grovel for his forgiveness.'

Terri gave a triumphant grin. 'You were saying?' She smiled sweetly at Ricky, a knowing look in her eyes.

17

Later that evening, Terri was a bundle of nerves. Not only had she gained two elder brothers, but she'd also acquired a paternal grandmother, one she hadn't even known existed before now. At Ricky and Jamie's insistence, she'd finally agreed to meet her, and to say that she was nervous would be an understatement of epic proportions. What if Patricia took an instant dislike to her, or what if she was expecting a carbon copy of Bianca to walk through the door? The scenarios and the what ifs were endless, so much so that by the time Jamie pulled up outside his mother's house, Terri felt sick to her stomach and was in half a mind to tell him that she'd changed her mind, that she couldn't go through with it, that she wanted to go home and be with Rina, her safety net.

At the front gate, Jamie paused. 'About Nan...' he began.

Terri's heart pounded inside her chest and glancing towards Tracey Hardcastle's home, her eyes widened in alarm. 'What about her?'

Jamie paused again. 'She's...'

He'd been about to continue when the front door was flung open and Tracey stepped outside the house. 'I thought you'd got lost,' she berated her son. 'If you'd have left it any longer you would have missed your nan; Max was getting ready to take her home.' Turning her attention to Terri, she gave a welcoming smile. 'Well come on the pair of you, get yourselves inside.'

Stepping across the threshold of Tracey's home, Terri gave a shy smile then remembering her manners, she shoved out her hand. Unlike the Murphy family home that she'd grown up in, Tracey's house was spotless and it was more than evident that she took pride in keeping her home tidy. Not only did the scent of furniture polish fill Terri's nostrils, but there was also a hint of something else too. Red wine perhaps, and unless she was very much mistaken, roasted chicken, sautéed potatoes, and a variety of different vegetables. It was enough to make Terri's mouth water, especially as she'd been brought up on fast food and greasy takeaways. Both her mother and grandmother had been hard pushed to boil an egg; they were far too lazy to cook or bake and if the food they bought couldn't be heated in a microwave then they weren't interested. In fact, it was only thanks to Rina that Terri had been taught the basics and that she could confidently cook herself a meal, something else she thanked the tiny woman for. 'Thank you for allowing me to come by. I wasn't so sure if I'd be welcome...' Her voice trailed off, apprehension getting the better of her. By rights, Tracey should despise her and Terri was only too aware of that fact, considering she and her father had been married when he'd committed adultery and that the affair had resulted in her conception.

Tracey Hardcastle stared down at the outstretched hand, a soft smile creasing her face. 'Get away with you,' she said, pulling Terri in for a warm hug. 'No need for formalities around here. Whether you like it or not, you're family sweetheart and that means you're welcome any time.'

Inside the lounge, Tracey motioned towards an elderly woman sitting on the Chesterfield sofa, her white, fluffy hair resembling a halo perched on top of her head. 'She's a bit hard of hearing,' Tracey explained with a raise of her eyebrows. 'So it might be best if you speak up.'

'Pat,' Tracey said, nodding towards Terri, her voice loud. 'This is Terry's daughter.'

'Who?' Patricia shouted back. Cocking her head to one side, her expression was one of confusion.

Fast on her way to losing her patience with her former mother-in-law, Tracey rolled her eyes. 'Terry, your son,' she yelled. 'For Christ's sake Pat, turn your hearing aid up and you might hear what I'm saying for once. It drives me round the bloody bend,' she said to Terri. 'It's forever whistling and she's oblivious to it.'

'I know who Terry is,' Patricia retorted, giving Tracey a scowl. 'I might be hard of hearing but I haven't lost my marbles just yet.'

'Well, this is his daughter.' Nodding towards Terri a second time, Tracey gave the younger woman a reassuring smile. 'I did tell her you were coming.' She tapped her head and leaned in closer, lowering her voice as she did so. 'She more than likely forgot. She's becoming quite forgetful of late,' she said, giving Patricia a concerned glance. 'It's her age you see. You're not quite as young as you used to be, are you Pat,' she shouted again.

'Oi.' Patricia bristled, her lips pursed together as though she were sucking on a lemon. 'I heard that, you cheeky mare and I'll have you know I've got the memory of an elephant. I don't forget anything.'

'She has selective hearing too.' Tracey winked. 'Isn't that right Pat? You only hear what you want to hear.'

Patricia waved her daughter-in-law away from her. Tracey may have gone on to re-marry after Terry's death, but she'd still been his wife, and the only daughter-in-law Patricia had ever had. As she went on to study her granddaughter, Patricia's eyes lit up. 'Well come closer, let me have a proper butcher's at you.' Tilting her head from side to side as she looked her granddaughter over, Patricia grinned. 'Of course you're my boy's daughter, you've got his look about you, the Tempest look. You're his bleeding double if ever I've seen one, only far prettier.'

Terri gave an uncertain smile. 'Well I hope that's a good thing?' she asked, looking around her, her gaze falling on the youngest of her brothers.

'Of course, it is.' Patricia beamed. 'Tracey,' she instructed. 'Fetch the photo albums, and while you're at it, get the girl a drink, oh and get the good glasses out an' all, those posh ones you keep hidden away in the back of the cupboard, you know the ones I mean. The ones I bought for you, not that I've ever seen you get them out, let alone put them to use.'

Rolling her eyes at the quip, Tracey made her way over to the cabinet where she kept the photo albums. 'She'll be the bleeding death of me,' she mumbled under her breath, giving her son a playful wink.

'So what's your poison?' Patricia continued. 'How about a drop of brandy, or a glass of wine, or I'll tell you what, how about a nice Baileys? We've still got some left over from Christmas, haven't we?' she asked, turning her rheumy eyes back to Tracey.

'Oh no, I don't want to put you out,' Terri was quick to answer, her gaze snapping between Tracey and Jamie.

'Yeah leave it out Nan,' Jamie groaned, screwing up his face. 'She doesn't want to look through hundreds of photos of people she doesn't even know.'

'Nonsense.' Ignoring her grandson's comment, Patricia patted the empty seat beside her. 'It's her family history, it's where she comes from. Of course she would want to take a look at them.' She squinted up at Terri, a grin spreading across her face, causing her dentures to look far too big for her mouth. Sucking them back into place with a loud click, she patted the seat again. 'You'd like to see some photos of your dad, wouldn't you?'

The look on Patricia's face melted Terri's heart. She was so tiny and so fragile that she couldn't say no. 'I'd love to,' she said, ignoring the second groan that came from Jamie. Taking a seat beside the elderly woman, Terri flashed Jamie an apologetic smile and as he impatiently tapped at his watch, reminding her that they needed to leave, she lifted her hand in the air. 'Five minutes,' she mouthed to him.

'Now this' – Patricia grinned as she turned the first page of the photo album – 'was your dad when he was a baby. And let me tell you, he was a handsome little devil even then. Everyone fell in love with him and even the midwife who delivered him told me she'd never seen such a beautiful baby.'

Terri couldn't help but smile. Up until now the only images she'd seen of her father were the ones she'd found on the internet when she'd typed his name into a search engine. And even then, the news reports covering his death had chosen photographs of him looking downright menacing. 'You're right.' She grinned, studying each of the photographs. 'He was handsome.'

* * *

Wandering through to his mother's kitchen, Jamie scowled. He should have known it would be a bad idea bringing Terri to see their nan. And he had a nasty feeling that the quick visit he'd anticipated could very well end up lasting hours if his nan had her way. Leaning against the kitchen worktop, he slipped his hand into his pocket and pulled out his mobile phone, his finger hovering over the dial button. They were already late and if he knew his brother as well as he thought he did then he was bound to kick off. Ricky was a stickler for time keeping, always had been, it was one of the main bones of contention between them. 'Looks like we're going to be a while,' he grumbled. 'Nan's got the photo albums out.' Moments later he pulled the device away from his ear as Ricky screamed and hollered down the phone, almost deafening him in the process.

'What are you doing hiding away in here?'

As his mother entered the kitchen, Jamie hastily ended the call and rammed the phone back into his pocket. 'You know I can't stand all of that sentimental bollocks,' he complained, nodding his head in the direction of the lounge.

Tracey flashed a sad smile and as she collected the glasses from the cupboard, she sighed. Unless she was very much mistaken, she had a feeling that it wasn't so much the photographs her youngest son was averse to but more so that he didn't want to listen to any talk surrounding his dad. It hadn't escaped her notice that her sons rarely spoke about their late father; they didn't even have any photos of him displayed in their homes. There were plenty of her and Max taken on the various family holidays they'd taken over the years but when it came to Terry it was almost as if they were trying to erase all trace of him from their lives. So much so that she highly doubted Jamie's daughters even knew who he was. Right from the get-go the girls had called Max grandad, and he had been the only grandfather figure they had known. Out of her three grandchildren it was only Mason who remembered Terry; he'd actually witnessed his grandfather's murder and could still to this day recall hearing the gunshot, followed by harrowing screams. Despite being only a little boy at the time, a mere baby, the murder was ingrained into his memory.

'Can't you have a word with Nan?' Jamie added, screwing up his face. 'She's not going to want to look through the albums; she doesn't even know who anyone is.'

Tracey sighed. 'Your nan's heart is in the right place; all she wants to do is show Terri her family, where she comes from. And you and Ricky were right,' she said, changing the subject. 'She is lovely. In a way she reminds me of the two of you and I can see Sorina in her too, they both have that little mole right there.' She pointed to the corner of her lip. 'I had no idea it actually came from your dad's side of the family. And did you see your nan's face? She's in her element; I've not seen her look this happy in years. And you know how hard your nan can be to please, she'd be able to find fault with Jesus Christ himself. So don't spoil it all by throwing a paddy. Let your nan spend a bit of time with her granddaughter, she's not getting any younger you know. She's well into her nineties and well,' she said, throwing her youngest son a sombre look, 'we don't know how much longer we'll have her with us for; when they get to this age, they can go downhill all too quick.'

Jamie rolled his eyes. He highly doubted that his nan would be going anywhere, at least not for a few years yet. She was far too stubborn for a start.

'And you all look so alike,' Tracey continued. 'I can hardly get my head around it.'

'You said yourself that Dad's genes were strong.' Jamie shrugged, opening the fridge door and taking a peek inside.

Tracey was thoughtful for a moment. 'Don't lead her astray,' she warned. 'She seems like a nice girl and what with that Tempest blood she has running through her veins... well, we all know how quick your tempers are. It doesn't take much to rile you and Ricky up, and your father was exactly the same. Even as little boys you were too bloody headstrong,' she chuckled, patting her son's arm. 'You made me want to pull my bloody hair out at times; it's no wonder that I didn't end up bald. The pair of you were forever getting up to mischief, or doing something you shouldn't be. You should be thankful,' she laughed, giving a wink, 'that you've got girls because believe me they've got to be a lot less troublesome than you and your brother were, I can tell you that much.'

Giving a half laugh as he closed the fridge, Jamie resumed his position and leaned against the worktop. His mum couldn't have been more right if she'd tried. He too was thankful that he'd been blessed with daughters. He'd end up having a coronary or turning prematurely grey if any of his kids were to turn out anything like Mason. And as much as he loved his only nephew, he'd be one of the first to hold his hands up and admit that Mason had a screw loose, that he wasn't quite all the ticket, not forgetting he could be a dangerous fucker when he needed to be which just so happened to be often. 'As if I'd do something like that. Besides, I thought you said I get my temper from you,' he teased.

'I mean it Jamie,' Tracey warned again. 'I'm not playing around; I'm being deadly serious. Do not let that girl become tainted by your father's name. He's already caused a lot of damage; he almost destroyed our family, and I wouldn't like to see that girl become another of his victims.'

'I won't,' Jamie lied. The fact he could barely look his mother in the eyes was lost on neither of them. Terri was already involved. Her uncle had murdered Archie and she had been a witness to that murder. And as his mother had already pointed out, Terri was a Tempest. Whether she wanted it or not, trouble was in her blood.

***

With the hood of his sweatshirt pulled up over his head, Frankie Gammon's beady little eyes darted around him. Other than when he and his firm had gone after Mason Tempest, he'd barely left his home since Archie Taylor's murder, preferring to lie low, hidden out of sight. He'd heard rumours that the Tempest brothers were gunning for him and despite the image he projected, by his own admission he wasn't what could be considered a tough man. And as much as he enjoyed intimidating others, without his firm around him he was a no one, a coward. He couldn't punch his way out of a paper bag and that right there was the truth of the matter. In all of his life he'd never participated in a real ruck, or rather, he'd never been in a fight that had been one on one. He'd only ever hidden behind his minions, had coerced them into doing his bidding; in the process, he'd been able to propel himself higher up the pecking order without so much as getting his own hands dirty. Oh, he could give it all the mouth, he even looked the part with his cropped hair, thick bullish neck, and heavy build, but that was as far as it ever went.

As he passed the local fish and chip shop, Frankie's stomach began to growl. He'd give anything to sink his teeth into a battered sausage with a portion of greasy chips smothered in salt and vinegar on the side. Taking another cautious glance around him, he chewed on his bottom lip. Where would be the harm in nipping into the chippie? No one had seen him, it wasn't as though he'd been spotted; the hood he pulled low over his head had been more than enough to disguise him or at least this was what he hoped anyway.

Without giving the matter another thought, Frankie pushed open the door and wandered inside, his hands digging into the pockets of his jeans, his greedy eyes surveying the glass cabinet filled with fried fish, saveloys, meat pies, and of course, the battered sausages he was so fond of.

His mouth watering at the scent of the fried food, he gave his order then leaned casually against the wall, idly scrolling through his mobile phone while he waited for his food to arrive. He was so consumed by the thought of filling his belly that he failed to notice the black, brand spanking new Range Rover that pulled up opposite the shop, the occupants intently watching his every move.

* * *

Jonny Carter leaned back in his seat, his thumb absentmindedly tapping the steering wheel. He'd spent the majority of his career as an armed robber acting as his brothers' appointed getaway driver and he was good too, better than good, he drove like a pro and as soon as he'd been old enough to climb behind the wheel of a motor, he'd taken to driving like a duck to water. There was nothing he didn't know about cars, and he made it his business to be at the top of his game; it was his livelihood after all.

In the seat beside him, Ricky switched off his mobile phone and groaned. 'Jamie's gonna be late.' He looked over his shoulder to where his son lounged casually on the back seat of Jonny's Range Rover. 'He's stuck with Nan; she's showing Terri the photo albums,' he said with a raise of his eyebrows.

Mason snorted out a laugh. 'Fuck me, they're gonna be hours then.' He glanced at his mobile phone, taking note of the time. 'You know what Nan's like once she starts rabbiting,' he said, referring to his great grandmother Patricia. 'She'll end up boring them to death.'

Turning back in his seat, Ricky continued to study the fish and chip shop, the atmosphere in the car growing thicker by the second.

Jonny sighed, the incessant thumb tapping becoming even more prominent. 'If you've got something to say then you might as well come out with it,' he said with an irritated sigh. 'Get it over and done with.'

Ricky turned his head, his expression hard. 'What, the fact you're shagging my sister?'

Jonny sighed. 'Are we talking about the same sister you wanted nothing to do with?'

His jaw clenching, Ricky narrowed his eyes.

'So don't sit there giving me all of that old bollocks,' Jonny growled. 'This sudden change of heart of yours is enough to give me whiplash, so fuck knows how Terri must feel. You left her out to dry and you know it. What fucking hope did she have with the Murphys raising her? They can't be trusted to look after an animal let alone a child. They're scum, no better than vermin and yet you were more than happy to leave her with them, for her to be dragged up.'

The fact Jonny had pulled him up on one of his biggest regrets in life grated heavily on Ricky's nerves. Admittedly in the beginning, he hadn't wanted to be a part of Terri's life but in his own way he had looked out for her, or at least he'd tried to, he'd just never told anyone, not even Jamie and they were more than just brothers, they were best mates. 'You know fuck all about me or what I've done,' he snarled.

'Don't I?' Jonny answered nonchalantly, the muscles across his forearms tensing as he turned in his seat. 'I know a lot more than you think. Did you really believe that people weren't talking, that the whispers and rumours weren't doing the rounds, that your reps would have been enough to make people keep schtum. It was common knowledge that you and Jamie wanted nothing to do with her, everyone knew it, even Terri herself. Just admit it, you couldn't stand the fact your old man did the dirty on your mum and that Terri was the result of his affair with Bianca Murphy.' He gave a shake of his head, his lips curling into a snarl. 'And you've got the front to question me, you've got the audacity to give it all the mouth as if you're something special—'

Before Jonny could finish the sentence, Ricky pulled back his fist, the expression across his face one of contempt.

'Leave it out Dad.' Anticipating the fact that his father was about to start a war between them and the Carter family, Mason leapt forward, positioning his body between the two front seats, putting an immediate block on his father's attempt to follow through with the assault. They were already fast on their way to creating a feud between the two families all thanks to the altercation at the wake and at this precise moment in time they needed allies, not a further reason for bad blood to manifest between them. 'Enough,' he yelled. 'You're angry and I get it, but throwing punches isn't going to solve anything, is it. You're meant to be pals for fuck's sake, business associates or whatever the fuck you want to call it, not enemies.'

With one last snarl, Ricky lowered his arm, his meaty fist slowly uncurling. As he straightened out his shirt, the muscles across his shoulder blades were still taut. 'You've got a big mouth Carter,' he said, stabbing his finger forward. 'Always have had.'

Mason groaned. 'Can we all calm the fuck down and just chill out for two minutes.' Not often the voice of reason, Mason looked between the two men. 'Seriously Dad,' he reiterated, silently warning his father to take heed of his words. 'Now isn't the time, is it? If you want to tear chunks out of each other, at least wait until we've dealt with that lowlife Gammon first.'

Jonny snapped his head back to look out of the windscreen, his eyebrows scrunching together. 'Where the fuck is he?' he said, peering towards the chip shop. Starting the ignition, he shot Ricky a look. 'See what you've caused now? We've lost the bastard,' he shouted, slamming his fist on the steering wheel.

Rubbing his hand over his face, Ricky's expression was set like thunder. 'Just drive,' he growled. 'He can't have got far; it's not as if he's likely to outrun us is it, the fat bastard can just about walk.'

'More like waddle,' Mason chuckled as he eased himself back on to the backseat.

As he flicked the indicator and pulled out into the road, Jonny continued to shake his head, his anger slowly subsiding. 'Believe what you want,' he sighed. 'But I haven't fucked her. I give you my word on that.'

Ricky snapped his head around to face Jonny, his eyes narrowing into slits. That hadn't been the version of events Bianca Murphy had given. She'd been adamant that Jonny and Terri were a couple, and she should know considering she was Terri's mother, no matter how estranged their relationship may have been. 'Maybe not but you want to, and we both know one way or another you always get what you want. It's one of the perks of being a Carter, isn't it?' he spat. 'All you lot ever do is take what you want regardless of the consequences. What's that saying of yours?' He screwed up his face and tilted his chin in the air as though he was trying to think. 'Oh yeah, that's it,' he mocked. 'If it's got your name on it then it's yours for the taking.'

Jonny remained silent, the sly dig at his family hanging heavy in the air. While it was true that both he and his brothers were armed robbers, and bloody good armed robbers at that, might he add, in their defence they had never burgled anybody's home, nor had they ever behaved like lowlifes and mugged anyone on the street of their belongings. Despite their chosen occupation, they did have some morals and had only ever targeted banks, high-end jewellers, or the big organisations. And when it came to Terri, he had to admit that there was also a ring of truth to Ricky's words. He did want her, not that anything was likely to happen between them now. Terri had barely been able to bring herself to look at him this morning. Not that he entirely blamed her; he'd hardly handled the situation as well as he could have done and had practically shoved her away from him, more concerned with how her brothers were going to react. And considering the grief they'd given him since then, a part of him wished he'd given in to her, had given them a valid reason to really lay into him.

'Shouldn't we to wait for Jamie?' Mason asked with a nod of his head as up ahead of them Frankie Gammon came into view.

'Nah,' Ricky growled. 'If the three us can't handle the bastard, then there's something fucking wrong. We shouldn't be in this game,' he added, shooting Jonny another glare. 'Not that some us should be in it to start with especially when driving cars is all they're good for.'

Groaning out loud, Jonny moved his head from side to side, easing the tension out of his neck, his hands itching to curl back into fists and start throwing punches. 'Give it a rest,' he said with a nonchalant shake of his head.

As Ricky opened his mouth to answer, Jonny slammed his foot on the brake, forcing Ricky to throw his hands out in front of him in a bid to stop his head from colliding with the windscreen. 'What the fuck is your problem?' Ricky yelled. 'I thought you knew how to drive?'

Giving a half laugh, Jonny flung open the car door and jumped out. 'You want to have it out with Gammon, don't you?' he said, jerking his head towards the back alley Frankie Gammon had just disappeared down.

The look Ricky gave was murderous. 'There was no need to be a prick about it,' he snarled before heaving himself out of the car and slamming the door closed behind him. 'A bit of warning wouldn't have gone amiss.'

Still grinning, Jonny shook his head. In his book there was only one person acting like a prized prick and it certainly wasn't him.

18

The scent of his battered sausage and chips was too much for Frankie to handle. Salivating, he could barely wait to get stuck in. He licked his lips, tore away the paper packaging and rammed a steaming hot chip into his mouth. Opening and closing his mouth in rapid succession in an attempt to cool the food down, he quickly swallowed before reaching into his pocket and pulling out a can of cola. Snapping open the pull ring, he guzzled down half the contents then gave a loud belch. Tentatively picking up another chip, he blew on it for a moment before stuffing it into his mouth and repeating the process all over again. He was far too hungry to wait for the food to cool down. All he wanted to do was shovel the chips into his mouth, barely even allowing himself the time to chew let alone come up for air in his haste to suppress his hunger.

Once he'd demolished the chips, he plucked out the sausage in batter, saving the best for last and took a large bite, oblivious to the layer of grease that coated his fingers, lips, and chin. Savouring the taste of the sausage as the juices exploded over his tongue, he gave a satisfied sigh. He'd always loved his grub and it would be fair to say that he had a large appetite. In his defence though, he was a big man, perhaps not in height, but more so in build, not that he believed himself to be overweight because he wasn't, maybe a bit chubby but definitely not what he would describe as fat.

He was so busy munching away that he didn't hear the sound of someone creeping up behind him. It wasn't until a hand was wrapped around his mouth and jaw and he was being roughly jerked backwards, the remainder of the sausage and paper packaging dropping to the floor in the process that he even realised he was in trouble, and unless he was very much mistaken, big trouble.

Almost immediately, Frankie was unable to breathe and as panic began to set in, his arms flailed around him. His mouth was still full of sausage, the shock of being dragged through the alleyway causing the large chunks to become caught in the back of his throat, cutting off his air supply. And as much as he felt the urge to chew or to even spit the food back out, he wasn't able to; the hand that gripped his jaw was so tight that it prevented him from doing so. And the more he tried to free himself, the tighter the grip became. His eyes began to bulge and vomit threatened to fill what little remaining space he had left in his throat.

This was it, he thought to himself, he was going to die. The thought of death made him even more afraid and as snot and tears cascaded down his cheeks and past his lips, his legs buckled from underneath him. Thick spurts of rancid vomit spewed from his nostrils and as his lungs screamed for oxygen, black spots danced before his eyes as what little air supply he had left all but deserted him.

* * *

'The bastard.' Dropping Frankie unceremoniously to the floor, Mason stared down at the vomit that trickled from between his fingers in slimy rivets. 'The dirty fucker,' he screamed, his lips curling in disgust as he kicked out at Frankie, his heavy boot connecting with his abdomen. 'He just puked all over me.'

Inspecting his soiled hand, Mason looked up and glanced around him, searching for something he could clean himself up with before bending down and using Frankie's shirt as a towel of sorts; it was his vomit after all. 'This is bollocks,' he complained as Frankie began to gasp for air, the chunk of sausage stuck in his throat finally becoming dislodged as he heaved, coughed and cried so hard that he could barely catch his breath. 'Shut up,' Mason roared, kicking out for a second time. 'And he fucking stinks,' he spat, wrinkling his nose.

'So would you,' Jonny answered, nodding down at the vomit coating Frankie's face and shirt, his expression one of revulsion. 'Not that I can say he smelled much better before in all fairness.'

'Right.' Taking out his mobile phone and shooting off a text message, Ricky nodded towards Jonny. 'Back the Range up; the quicker we move him out of here the better. The last thing we need is for him to start screaming blue murder.'

Jonny's jaw dropped. 'What do you mean go and get the Range?' he exclaimed, alarm filtering across his face. 'Like fuck am I putting him in my car.' He wrinkled his nose again. 'I've just had it cleaned.'

Ricky's eyes hardened. 'How else do you think we're going to move him?' he gritted out, the muscles in his jaw clenching. 'Take it in turns and give him a fucking piggy back ride?'

Ignoring the comment, Jonny continued to shake his head. 'I've got a job coming up next week,' he was quick to add. 'A big fucking job. My brothers are gonna go garrity if I take any unnecessary risks, or if I end up linking us to this no-good fucker. I've already told you that I'm skating on thin ice where Jimmy is concerned and if something goes wrong and we get our collars felt it'll be hard enough explaining why we've got balaclavas and shotguns in the boot of the car, let alone explaining murder on top of it. We've been planning this job for months, eight fucking months to be precise,' he fumed. 'And if I fuck up, my life will be as good as over.' He made a slicing action across his throat and gave a shake of his head, his eyes wide. 'Do you even know how hard it is to get rid of bodily fluids? They fucking linger mate, no matter how much you might think you've cleaned them. The old bill have got this stuff...' He clicked his fingers together as if to jog his memory. 'That's it,' he said, stabbing his finger in Ricky's direction. 'Luminol it's called, and no matter how much you wash the blood, piss, or vomit away it still shows up. Ultraviolet it is. I watched a documentary about it, was pretty interesting.'

'Thanks for the science lesson.' Ricky rolled his eyes. 'But that's not going to help us move him to the warehouse, is it.'

'Nah I think you've got that wrong.' Scratching his jaw, Mason gave a thoughtful nod. 'I thought it was only blood they could detect. A pal of mine, Taylor Richardson,' he said to Ricky. 'You remember him. We went to school together. Tall, lanky, one eye bigger than the other, proper fucking nutter, he tried to take one of the teachers out with a cricket bat.'

Ricky lifted his eyebrows. His son was a fine one to talk about nutters. 'Yeah, vaguely.' He waved his hand dismissively, keen to get to the crux of the story. 'What about him?'

'Well that's how he ended up in Pentonville, the filth used that stuff.' He gestured towards Jonny. 'Apparently his clothes were covered in some geezer's blood that he'd topped, and he reckons he'd washed them an' all, and more than once,' he said with a raise of his eyebrows, 'but the blood still showed up. In the end they threw the book at him, sentenced him to life.' He shook his head and huffed out a breath. 'He should have just burnt the clothes, poured petrol over them, then whoosh job done; I mean, that's what any other normal person would do, isn't it?' he said, looking between his father and Jonny. 'Or at least that's what I would have done in the same situation.'

'Yeah well,' Jonny grumbled. 'It's still a big risk if you ask me. And one I'm not prepared to take. It's all right for you,' he said, nodding his head in Ricky's direction. 'But you're not the one who's gonna end up getting it in the neck are you.'

'I don't believe this.' Ricky rubbed at his temples. 'Are the pair of you all right?' His eyes blazed. 'Have you both lost the fucking plot? First of all,' he said, addressing Jonny. 'Feel free to correct me if I'm wrong but you're more than likely planning to torch the motor after the job. So why you're giving me all of this grief for the life of me I can't work out. And secondly, there won't be any old bill because this fucker's body,' he spat, nodding down at Frankie, 'is never going to be found, is it? We're hardly going to dump the bastard on the side of the road for all and sundry to find him. So do us all a favour, stop wasting my time and go and get the fucking car.'

'Hold up a minute.' Jonny's voice began to rise, his gaze darting towards the entrance of the alleyway where he'd parked his car. 'I still didn't agree to any of this. Where's Jamie?' He glanced back towards the entrance again. 'Why can't he take him?'

'Because he's not here, is he,' Ricky roared, throwing his arms up into the air in exasperation. 'Or do you suggest we just stand around waiting for him to turn up, which might I add, could take hours. Anyone could walk down here.' He glanced up and down the alley, checking for himself that it was still deserted. 'Have you even thought about that? Has it actually registered in your head yet that we're standing in the middle of a public walkway with this fat bastard on his knees covered in vomit. One word from this fucker and the old bill will be called for, and we'd be caught bang to rights. And as for your precious job well there won't be one if you're banged up for attempted murder, will there?'

Jonny swallowed and as Frankie began to cry even harder,

mumbling over and over that he didn't want to die, he resisted the urge to kick out at him just as Mason had done moments earlier, not that he wouldn't have taken satisfaction from seeing the ponce rolling on the floor in agony. Reluctantly, he pulled out his car keys. 'You can chuck him in the boot.' He scowled, screwing up his face again as Frankie began vehemently shaking his head, his body trembling so violently that he looked as though he were having some kind of seizure. 'Like fuck is he going anywhere near the seats though; they'll be a bugger to clean.'

'Right.' Ricky huffed out a breath, his gaze hardening as he looked down at Frankie. 'Now we're actually starting to get somewhere.'

* * *

The smile across Terri's face was so wide that her jaw ached. Climbing into Jamie's car, she pulled the seat belt across her chest, clicked it into place, then turned to wave out of the window.

'She's so lovely,' she gushed. 'I don't know what I was so nervous about. Bless her, she's a sweetheart.'

Shaking his head, Jamie chuckled. Although to be fair, their nan had mellowed over the years, not that this meant she'd become completely docile with old age, she still had a harsh tongue on her, one that she wasn't afraid to use, especially when it came to himself, Ricky or Mason. 'She's all right, I suppose,' Jamie remarked, flicking the indicator and pulling out into the road. 'Although if you'd have met her years ago you might think differently. Her and my mum used to have some right ding dongs I can tell you that much; they despised one another.'

'No.' Terri's mouth dropped open, her forehead furrowing 'I don't believe you; they seem so close.'

'Honest to God,' Jamie answered. 'They might be close now but years ago they were more like enemies. Things were pretty ugly between them, and nine times out of ten Nan was the instigator; she more or less disapproved of everything Mum did. Even me and Ricky came under her scrutiny; she gave us hell.' Digging his hand into his pocket, he pulled out his mobile phone and glanced down at the screen, swearing under his breath. 'Looks like they've started without us,' he groaned, looking up into the rear-view mirror before hastily performing a three-point turn and driving in the opposite direction.

'They've got Michael?' Terri lifted her eyebrows, hope spreading through her veins.

'Nah,' Jamie said as he pushed his foot down on the accelerator. 'Gammon.'

Terri nodded. Becoming quiet, she stared out of the side window, the oncoming cars nothing but a blur as they whizzed past.

Jamie glanced sideways. 'Are you sure you're going to be able to handle this?'

Her lips set into a thin line, Terri nodded. 'He's as much responsible for Archie's death as Michael is, so what do you think?'

'If you want me to be honest, then I don't know.' Jamie shrugged, casting her a second glance. 'This isn't some game we're playing. A man is going to die tonight, and you're going to be a part of it. You'll have blood on your hands; that's not something you're gonna be likely to forget in a hurry.'

Remaining silent, Terri thought over his words. Jamie had a point. Would she be able to handle it? Would she really be able to stand idly by and watch a man die? She had to, she decided, for Archie's sake. He deserved justice; he'd lost his life so why should his murderer and those who had orchestrated the murder get off scot-free? A hard glint glistened in her eyes, and her husky voice when she spoke was low and filled with malice. 'Just watch me,' she growled. 'I can handle anything you throw at me.'

* * *

The atmosphere in Jonny's car had become slightly less tense, not that Ricky's mood had completely lifted. He was still angry and even more than that he still had a bone to pick with Jonny Carter.

From the boot of the car came loud thuds, Frankie Gammon's high-pitched cries for help becoming more and more frantic as the minutes ticked by.

'Is this bastard getting on your nerves or is it just me?' Punching the empty space beside him, Mason hollered at the top of his lungs. 'Shut the fuck up you useless pile of shit.'

'Oi.' Turning his head, Jonny's expression was hard. 'Do you fucking mind, that's my car you're punching.'

Mason grinned. 'What's the big deal? You're gonna torch it anyway.' He glanced around him. 'Shame really, it's a nice motor; I would have bought it from you for a good price.'

Turning off the A13, Jonny gave a disgruntled shake of his head as up ahead of them the signs for Barking came into view. 'Can't take the risk,' he said, casting his gaze across the dashboard. 'As nice as she is,' he said, smoothing his fingers across the glossy interior. 'She's got to go.'

Moments later, they entered an industrial area. On either side of the road several warehouses and a recycling plant came into view.

'Are you sure about this place?' Ricky asked.

Jonny groaned. 'I'm not completely wet behind the ears. I've been in this game for a long time.' He shifted his weight, making himself more comfortable, his hands casually gripping the steering wheel. 'It used to be owned by a face back in the day or at least it was until he met with a grisly end. It's been lying empty ever since. We still use it from time to time,' he added, lifting his shoulders in a shrug.

With a flick of the indicator, Jonny eased his foot off the accelerator, the tyres squelching across the tarmac as he drove towards a large warehouse situated at the far side of the property. Isolated and set apart from any other units, the warehouse was in the perfect position. 'This place was actually handpicked by Danny McKay himself,' he declared. 'And' – he motioned ahead of him – 'you can see exactly why. It can't be seen from the road and unless you even knew it was here, you'd actually drive by the place none the wiser.'

Ricky nodded. As much as he didn't want to be, he had to admit he was impressed.

'So who's this face?' As he jumped out of the car Mason surveyed the warehouse his eyes narrowing into slits. 'I might recognise his name.'

'No one,' Jonny retorted as he slipped from behind the wheel. 'He's not important, and like I said he's been dead for a long time.' He pressed the key fob, activating the central locking system, then made his way round to the boot. Turning the key in the lock, the boot sprang open, causing Frankie to blink rapidly up at them as his eyes adjusted to the sudden change of light.

'Don't hurt me,' he cried, cowering away from them, his back against the rear of the boot. 'I'll do anything you say, just don't hurt me.'

'Don't give me all of that old fanny.' Mason replied, a hint of amusement clearly evident in his voice. 'You should have thought of the consequences when Archie Taylor's life was being snuffed out, or when you were trying to muscle in on my dad's turf.'

'But it wasn't me.' Frankie shook his head, the words tumbling out of his mouth so fast that saliva dribbled from the corners of his lips and his terrified eyes almost bulged out of his head. 'I didn't kill Archie; none of this was my idea, I didn't even want to go to the boozer that night, he made me go there. It was Michael Murphy, he was the one who did it, he was the one who stabbed the landlord.'

Pushing his face forward, Mason gave a maniacal grin, his eyes lighting up with glee. 'We already know.' He winked before proceeding to drag Frankie roughly out of the car. 'Not that it makes one iota of a difference, you're still a dead man and believe me pal.' He grinned as he waved a screwdriver in front of Frankie's face. 'I'm gonna enjoy taking you down, might even take my time, really savour the moment.'

In that instant, Frankie cried even louder and as a wet patch appeared between his legs and trickled down his trousers, the sound of Mason's laughter reverberating around him filled his entire being with a sense of pure and utter dread.

19

Taking note of Jonny Carter's Range Rover parked on the forecourt, Jamie brought his car to a screeching halt beside it. Switching off the ignition, he flung open the door and jumped out with Terri swiftly following behind him.

Adrenaline pumped through his veins. It had been a long time since he or Ricky had been involved in an active feud, years to be precise, and as he made his way towards the warehouse with a determined swagger, he took his cigarettes out of his pocket and lit up, inhaling the smoke deep into his lungs.

'Well,' he called out as he entered the building. 'What has this slimy little fucker had to say for himself?'

'Not a lot.' Jonny looked up and on seeing Terri walking behind Jamie, he did a double take. 'Are you for real?' he shouted. 'What's she doing here?' He stabbed his finger in Terri's direction, the scowl across his face enough to tell them he wasn't happy that she'd been brought along for the ride. 'This is no place for a woman.'

Terri shot him a look as she made her way inside. 'I'd say that my being here isn't any of your business,' she spat back. She turned then to look at Frankie, almost recoiling in shock as she did so. His skin was clammy and drained of all colour, his top lip already split in two. The blood that smeared his lips, cheek and chin was so stark against the paleness of his skin that she felt nauseous. To top it off, he'd been tied to a chair, and if the colour of his hands were anything to go by then the restraints across his forearms and legs were so tight that Terri wouldn't be surprised if his blood supply had been cut off.

Pressing the back of her hand against her lips, Terri averted her gaze. She could feel the colour drain from her own face and the walls begin to close in, a sense of light-headedness washing over her. Taking deep breaths to steady her racing heart, she moved slightly out of the way so as not to have to look at Frankie's face, nor witness the pleading look in his eyes. She couldn't cave in, not now, not in front of her brothers and Jonny. Time and time again she'd told them that she could handle whatever they threw at her, that she could watch a man die. Only now she wasn't so sure and as Frankie's screams reverberated around the warehouse, she was in half a mind to cover her ears, run out of the door and never look back.

'Where is he?' Ricky's voice was full of venom, the blade in his hand sharp as he began to prise off another of Frankie's fingernails.

'I don't know,' Frankie screamed, his voice reaching a crescendo as the nail was ripped from its bed. 'Please,' he wailed. 'I don't know anything.'

Ricky's expression hardened and gripping a third finger in his fist, he flicked the knife under the nail. 'I'm not going to ask you again,' he growled. 'Where is Michael Murphy?'

'I don't know,' Frankie screamed again, beads of cold sweat coating his forehead. 'I swear to God I don't know.'

Mason began to laugh. 'Wrong answer.' As his father ripped away the fingernail, he bounded forward, a screwdriver gripped tightly in his fist. Plunging the makeshift blade into Frankie's eye, he gave it a twist for good measure. 'I love it when it does that,' he chuckled as Frankie's eye imploded on impact, leaving behind nothing but an empty socket.

It was more than Terri could take and just one look at the screwdriver in her nephew's fist complete with Frankie's eye still attached to it was enough to make her want to pass out. Swaying unsteadily on her feet, the warehouse began to swim, her eyes barely able to focus on anything around her.

'Woah.' Racing forward, Jonny gripped her around the waist before she dropped to the floor. 'I think you need some air,' he whispered in her ear, low enough so that only she could hear.

Terri nodded and clutching at her head, she allowed him to lead her outside. Her legs felt like jelly, and her lips numb. More than anything though, she was annoyed at herself; she'd shown weakness, had proved to her brothers once and for all that she wasn't cut out for their world.

Taking a seat on a wooden pallet, Terri held her head in her hands, the bitter cold wind that blew around them doing nothing to ease the dizziness she felt.

'I remember my first time.' Jonny dug his hands into his pockets and gave a small smile. 'Admittedly it wasn't quite as gruesome, but it was still brutal. Three blokes shot between the eyes at close range. I thought I was going to throw up.'

'But you didn't.' Terri's voice was small as she looked up at him, her face still deathly pale.

'Nah.' He gave another smile. 'My brothers would never have let me live it down and considering the fact they'd only been roped into committing the murders because of me, because of something I'd done, well as you can imagine it wouldn't have gone down too well. I'd owed someone some money and it was either take a hammering or kill those men. And Tommy, my eldest brother, well he was all about loyalty, everything he did was for the family. He wouldn't have let me take the pounding no matter how much I might have deserved it.' He gave a laugh and shook his head. 'Not that he wouldn't have been averse to giving me a right hander himself, mind. It was just that no one else could do it if you know what I mean. Like I said, he was loyal through and through.'

Terri gave a smile, the colour slowly returning to her cheeks. 'You miss him, don't you?' she asked. 'You talk about him a lot.'

Jonny gave a shrug and as he turned to look away, he gave a sad smile. 'He was a big part of our lives, what's not to miss?'

'I've let them down, haven't I?' Referring to her brothers, Terri nodded towards the warehouse, her expression one of regret. 'And I've let myself down even more.'

'I suppose that's what happens when you're the youngest in a family,' Jonny sighed. 'You have a lot to live up to.' He gave a slight shrug. 'I still remember the first time I ever got into the ring. I was only a kid, and the boy I was fighting was twice my size; if truth be told, I didn't stand a chance of beating him. And when he gave me a right hook, right here,' he said, pointing to his jaw. 'I almost burst into tears; I'd never been hit like that before. You see, being that much younger than my brothers, they didn't go as heavy on me as they did each other. On a daily basis they'd try to knock seven bells of shit out of one another, it's what happens when you come from a big family and well there were six of us, but when it came to me, they'd go easy on me, maybe because I was the baby of the family.' He shrugged again. 'I don't know. But the point I'm trying to make is that I was still a Carter, my family had a rep, and I was expected to be just like them. I wasn't given any other choice than to toughen up. Same goes for you. You're a Tempest whether you like it or not, and sometimes you have to fake it until you make it.'

'So you think I'm weak too?' Terri averted her gaze, not wanting to look at him.

Jonny shook his head. 'No, you're just not used to this world, at least not yet anyway.'

Terri didn't answer. As much as he was trying to reassure her, he was wrong. She was used to it, she'd lived with the Murphys, she'd seen deprivation first-hand.

'Look.' Taking a seat beside her, Jonny glanced over his shoulder at the warehouse. To their relief Frankie's screams had quietened down; if he wasn't already dead then it was only a matter of time until he took his last breath. 'I just wanted to clear the air between us.'

Terri closed her eyes, the urge to cry washing over her. What with witnessing the torture of Frankie Gammon, she didn't think she could handle Jonny turning her down a second time and all on the same night. 'It's okay.' She shook her head. 'You've already said it once, you don't need to say it again. It was stupid of me. I should never have—'

Placing his finger upon her lips to silence her, Jonny shook his head. 'What I said before, you know at the pub, well it was partly the truth. I'm not naïve enough to think that I'm invincible, that I'll never be caught, that my family's good luck won't run out one day. You know that I could go down, right? That I don't live a nine-to-five life, that I'm never going to turn over a new leaf and go straight. I am what I am; my life was mapped out for me before I could even walk or talk. There was only one path I was destined to take and that was to follow my brothers into the family business. And that means it's not going to be easy.' He gestured between them. 'I could be around one minute and gone the next, and who knows for how long.'

Terri nodded, understanding exactly what he was trying to tell her. That his future, their future if they had one, wasn't guaranteed, that months or maybe even years down the line she could very well find herself alone. As Jonny sighed, she leaned her head against his shoulder. Even covered in Frankie's blood, he still smelled good. And in a roundabout way he was right, if they were ever going to stand a chance then she had to get her head out of the clouds and learn to toughen up whether she wanted to or not.

The door to the warehouse opened. They sprang apart and as Ricky stepped outside, Jonny got to his feet. Giving Ricky a nod, he flashed Terri a small smile before making his way back inside.

* * *

'Are you okay?' Taking a seat beside Terri, Ricky kicked out his long legs as he made himself as comfortable as he possibly could on the wooden pallet.

Terri nodded. 'I just…' She glanced behind her. 'I just needed some air.' She took several deep breaths. 'Is it done, is he…?'

'Yeah,' Ricky answered, turning his head slightly to look at her. 'It's done, he's dead.'

Terri nodded again. She'd expected to feel euphoria; instead, she felt sick to her stomach. Jamie had been right, this was no game they were playing, a man was dead, and she had participated in his death. Fair enough, she hadn't physically lashed out at him, but she'd still been a part of it.

'Look, if you can't handle this no one would think differently of you if you walked away.'

'I can handle it,' Terri was quick to answer. Whether she wanted to or not she had to see this through to the bitter end, for Archie's sake; she owed him that much. 'It's just…' Her voice trailed off and she hugged her knees to her chest. 'I just wasn't expecting it to be so brutal.' She gave a shiver; Frankie Gammon's screams still rang loudly in her ears, and she had a feeling they would continue to do so for a long time.

Ricky laughed. 'It was never going to be all about hearts and flowers, sweetheart. Whether you like it or not, this is the real world, darling, and taking a life is brutal. But Gammon deserved everything he had coming to him and if it hadn't been us who'd wiped him out then sooner or later someone else would have done it.'

As she digested Ricky's words, Terri nodded. It was true. Frankie Gammon had been as much to blame as Michael, so why should she feel sorry for him?

A moment of silence followed and blowing out his cheeks, Ricky raised his eyebrows. 'So you and Carter, eh?'

'I didn't think I was that obvious?' Terri's cheeks turned red. 'I was hoping that no one else had noticed how much of a fool I'd made of myself.'

'Would have been pretty hard to miss it,' Ricky grumbled. 'And as for Carter, he's walking around like some lovesick puppy. What the fuck have you done to him?' He wrinkled his nose then held up his hand. 'On second thoughts, don't answer that, I don't want to know.'

It was Terri's turn to laugh and as she playfully elbowed Ricky in the ribs, she smiled. 'Don't tell me you're about to go all big brother on me again?'

'I wouldn't fucking dare,' Ricky answered, returning the grin. 'You've made it quite clear that you're more than capable of taking care of yourself. But Carter of all people.' He rubbed at his forehead. 'You do realise that he's a dickhead.'

Terri laughed even harder. 'I knew it,' she giggled. 'You are. You're about to give the big brother speech.'

'I'm just giving you a heads-up,' Ricky protested.

'Well thank you for your concern.' Terri smiled. 'But I like him. He's...' She paused for a moment, trying to find the right word. 'Nice.'

'Yeah, if you say so,' Ricky sighed. 'If you want my opinion, nice and Jonny Carter don't belong in the same sentence.' He looked into the distance again. 'Look, I'm not trying to come across heavy or try to tell you how you should live your life, or even try to put a dampener on things. Believe me, I've made enough mistakes of my own over the years so I get it; all I'm trying to do is look out for you.' Pausing, he turned to look at her. 'I spoke to you when you were a little girl, did you know that?'

Terri shook her head, her expression one of concentration as she tried to think back to when she'd been a child.

'You must have only been about five or six at the time. You were in a shop.' He gave a gentle smile. 'I bought you some sweets, you could barely even reach the shop counter, and those bastards who were supposed to be caring for you had deemed it acceptable to allow you to roam the streets alone.'

Terri's eyes widened. She could recall talking to a man once, he'd had dark hair and the bluest eyes she'd ever seen. She'd convinced herself he'd been her dad. Not for a single second had it occurred to her that he could have been her brother. 'I think I remember. You smelled of Matey bubble bath.'

Ricky chuckled. 'Probably. Mason loved it as a kid and I think Kayla pretty much bought out the supermarket.' He smiled. 'We were bathing in the stuff for months. I couldn't wait to see the back of it in the end. It hardly did my street cred any good, I can tell you that much,' he laughed. 'There was me trying to look tough, collecting debts and whatnot, and all the while I reeked of Matey.'

Terri burst out laughing. 'I can imagine.' She looked into the distance, a wistful expression creasing her face. 'I used to love that bubble bath, not that my grandparents bought it often, they'd rather waste their money on booze and cigarettes than on something I loved. I think that's probably why it stood out to me.'

Ricky gave a sad smile. 'I'm sorry.' He lifted his shoulders. 'I should have been there, me and Jamie both should have. It's just.'

He blew out his cheeks. 'I'm not trying to make excuses; I was in the wrong and I'll hold my hands up and admit that fact. But after my dad, well our dad,' he corrected. 'When he died me and Jamie had to take care of our mum, she was our priority, she was in pieces and so broken that at one point we actually thought she'd lost the plot, that Terry's death had tipped her over the edge. It wasn't a good time for any of us. Not that the bastard actually deserved her tears; he'd betrayed her trust in more ways than one.'

'You mean the brothels?' Terri probed.

'No not just the prostitution racket.' Ricky shook his head. 'There were the affairs, the lies. He'd never been a good husband or even a good father come to that, not really. He only wanted me and Jamie around when we were of a benefit to him, when we were doing his bidding, his dirty work.' His shoulders stiffened and he clenched his jaw. 'While me and Jamie were vying for his attention, he was too preoccupied spending quality time with that nutter Raymond.'

Terri narrowed her eyes. 'Who's Raymond?'

Ricky turned his head, paused for a moment, then sighed. 'Raymond is our brother, half-brother. Or rather he was.'

'Was?' Terri exclaimed.

'Yeah.' Looking down at the blood covering his hands, Ricky shrugged. 'It's a long story,' he answered in the way of an explanation. 'But anyway, getting back to Carter.' He forced a smile. 'I just want you to know exactly what you're getting yourself involved with. Carter is into some pretty heavy shit, stuff that would make even my head spin. Bank robberies are the Carter family's specialty. That means if he ever gets his collar felt he'll be going down for a long time, and I'm not talking about a couple of years, I'm talking decades. The old bill will more than likely try to pin every robbery within a hundred-mile radius on him and his family.'

Terri nodded; she already knew this. Jonny had warned her

more than once that his line of work could mean if caught, he'd be sent down for a long time. Not that she cared; she liked Jonny, could even see herself having feelings for him. Where was the point in worrying about something that may never happen? 'But they're good at what they do, they've never come close to being caught.'

'True,' Ricky conceded. 'I just want you to be aware of what could happen later down the line and seeing as Jimmy Carter is leaving the family business and the planning of any future robberies will fall on Jonny boy's shoulders,' he said, jerking his head behind him to where Jonny, Jamie, and Mason were cleaning up the crime scene. 'There's always a first time for things to go tits up.'

'I'm sure he'll be careful,' she said as the three men walked out of the warehouse, their clothes and hands still stained with Frankie Gammon's blood. Her eyes were drawn to the carrier bag Mason was carrying. Instinctively she knew that she didn't want to know what was inside; no doubt it would be a body part, something that would be sent to her uncle in the way of a threat, warning him of what was to come.

Ricky got to his feet and giving Jonny a pointed look, he nodded towards Terri. 'I don't like it, and I'm probably never going to like it, but for now I'll swallow my tongue.' He blew out his cheeks and ran his hand through his dark hair. 'I suppose I've got no choice but to accept it. But just remember this, because believe me this is the only warning I'm giving you: do anything to hurt her and I mean anything, and I will have you. Are we clear on that? I will hunt you down and I will bury your body somewhere so secluded that you will never be found.'

Jonny gave a nod in return. 'Understood.'

Oblivious to the new development between Terri and Jonny, Jamie screwed up his face. 'What's going on?' he asked, looking around him.

'I'll fill you in on the way home.' Ricky threw Terri a wink then dug out his car keys. 'Are you sure this bloke of yours knows what he's doing?' Ricky asked, referring to the man Jonny had hired to dispose of Frankie Gammon's corpse.

'He's the best in the business, we use him ourselves.'

Satisfied with Jonny's answer, Ricky turned to leave. 'Oh just one more thing,' he said, looking directly at Terri. 'If you thought this was tough then believe me, it's going to get a lot harder once we have Michael in our clutches. Have a think about that.'

Terri nodded, her expression becoming hard. She didn't need to think about anything. Michael may have been her uncle, but he meant nothing to her. She was over the worst, had witnessed her first death so to speak, and next time she wouldn't need to step outside and greedily gulp air into her lungs. In fact, she would go as far as to say that Michael's murder would be one she didn't want to miss, not in a million years.

20

Michael Murphy walked aimlessly through the house that Frankie Gammon used as his meet up. He'd already rifled through the kitchen cabinets and drawers, not that he'd found anything of interest, more's the pity. He was in the mood for a buzz, something to get him through the monotony of his day. Grabbing a can of lager, he leaned against the kitchen sink, then brought the can up to his lips and took a deep swig, swallowing the liquid down.

The fact the house was empty should have been his first indication that something wasn't quite right. In any normal circumstances, he could usually find at least one of Frankie's minions loitering around, more than likely stoned out of his nut. And now he came to think of it, he hadn't seen Frankie for a few days either.

Narrowing his eyes, Michael wandered through to the hallway, batting several flies out of his path as he went. A sour stench assaulted his nostrils and he wrinkled his nose. He'd noticed the smell as soon as he'd entered the house, not that he'd taken much of an interest; the house always stank. Mould, excrement, and ground-in dirt were the usual culprits, not to mention the stale body odour that came from Frankie himself.

At the foot of the stairs, he took note of a carrier bag, the buzz of bluebottles becoming even louder as they congregated around the bag. The hairs on the back of Michael's neck stood upright and glancing around him, he gave an involuntary shudder, almost too afraid to take a peek inside.

Say what you want about him, but by his own admission, Michael was no fool. Something was wrong, he could feel it in his gut. Inching closer to the bag, he held his hand over his nose and mouth, the rancid stench becoming even stronger. Tentatively, he reached down, his breath becoming ragged as he tried not to gag.

Moments later, he peered inside, his eyes almost popping out of his head as he did so. The sight before him was enough to send him careering to the floor and as he scrambled several feet backwards, his feet kicked out at the bag in his haste to escape.

A whimper tore from his throat, and the beer he had guzzled spewed out of his mouth as he went on to empty the contents of his stomach. Gasping for breath, Michael could only stare in horror as Frankie Gammon's head rolled out of the bag and came to a halt just inches away from his feet. Frankie's skin had taken on a mottled green hue, one eye staring towards him, the other a gaping black, blood encrusted hole.

There and then Michael heaved even harder, his heart pounding so hard and so fast that he actually believed he was going to keel over. Unsteadily Michael got to his feet and pressing his back against the wall, he side-stepped around the head before staggering out of the house and running as if his life depended on it, without so much as giving the meet up a backward glance.

* * *

Raymond Cole chewed absentmindedly on his fingernail; his eyes narrowed into slits as he stared at Frankie Gammon's decomposing head set on the coffee table before him.

After sending one of Frankie's firm members to collect the head, Raymond had fallen into silence. He needed time to think, needed to work out his next move.

From across the other side of the room, Michael cleared his throat, the quietness of the flat beginning to give him the creeps. 'What are you thinking?'

Raymond looked up, the hint of a grin tugging at the corners of his lips. 'I'm thinking that it's not looking good,' he answered, nodding back down at the head, amusement clearly audible in his voice. 'And unless I'm very much mistaken, I'd say that he's as dead as a fucking dodo.'

Michael screwed up his face, Cole's idea of a sick joke making him feel nauseous. A familiar sense of panic began to engulf him. Whoever had targeted Frankie could come after him too. 'I need protection,' he whimpered. 'What if I'm next?'

Raymond gave a dismissive wave of his hand.

'I mean it.' Becoming more animated, Michael looked around him. 'They took Frankie out, so what's stopping them from coming for me an' all?'

Raymond's eyes narrowed, the sly grin he gave enough to make Michael shudder. 'I suppose you do have a point.' Leaning back in the chair, he spread open his arms. 'I mean, you were the one who killed Taylor.' He glanced back to the head and lifted his shoulders. 'And if they can do this to poor Frankie,' he said with a dramatic sigh. 'Then what exactly are they planning to do to you?'

The colour slipped from Michael's face. 'You have to help me,' he pleaded. 'I'll do anything, just name it and I swear I'll do it.'

Raymond's shoulders relaxed. 'Anything?' he asked casually.

Michael nodded so furiously that he was in grave danger of causing himself some harm. 'Anything, I swear on my mother's life.'

Raymond chuckled. 'We both know that you don't give two shits about your mother.'

'On my life then,' Michael was quick to answer, his hands steepled in front of him.

Placing his feet on the coffee table, Raymond swiped Frankie's severed head to the floor then crossed his ankles. 'I've got a little job for you to do.' He grinned. 'One that is going to blow my brothers' minds. In fact' – he winked as he reached up to touch the scar on his face – 'I only wish that I could be there to see their faces when the shit finally hits the fan, when they come to realise that I mean business.'

* * *

Pulling back her shoulders, Terri held her head up high. With her dark hair hanging loose, she was dressed in her heels that accentuated her long legs, and a navy blue, short sleeved, fitted trouser suit. She crossed over the road and with a newfound confidence, made her way across the forecourt of the Carter brothers' scrapyard. Not that she was daft enough to believe that they actually dealt in scrap metal. Like her brothers' taxi firm, the yard was nothing more than a façade, a front for the real business.

The sound of dogs barking stopped her in her tracks. Not that she was actually afraid of them. Her uncle Kevin kept dogs, and as intimidating as they looked, they were actually as soft as anything. Continuing on her way, she reached a portable cabin, and gave a tap on the door before pulling it open.

A hushed silence fell over the occupants and as they all turned to look at her, their reactions were priceless. 'Can I come in?' She offered a smile.

Jonny cleared his throat and with a jerk of his head, he indicated for her to enter. 'The rest of you can clear off,' he barked out to his nephews.

Jonny's youngest nephew lounged back on a sofa. Like his uncles and great uncles before him, he was a handsome man with a mop of dark hair, cheeky grin and an attitude to match. 'Nah you're all right.' He grinned. 'I think I'll stay here; the view's a lot better in here than out there.'

'Tommy.' Jonny made to get out of his seat, his eyes hard.

Once young Tommy had left the office, Terri burst out laughing. 'Tommy?' she queried. 'Was he named after your brother?'

'He's Tommy's grandson,' Jonny explained as he swiped some paperwork off a chair and gestured for her to take a seat. 'So to what do I owe this pleasure? Not that I'm complaining, mind. Believe me, you're a welcome distraction, and a lot better to look at than any of that lot,' he said, nodding towards his nephews on the forecourt.

Terri sighed and sitting down, she placed her handbag on the floor and crossed her legs. 'It's Michael.'

'What about him?' His forehead furrowing, Jonny perched his backside on the edge of the desk.

'It's just, well.' Sitting forward, Terri clasped her hands together. 'I had an idea and I wanted to run it past you first.'

'Go on.'

'Well...' She paused for a moment. 'Me and Michael, we've never really seen eye to eye; in fact, I'd go as far as to say that he despises me. But I was thinking what if I told him I wanted to meet, or if I was to get a message to him through my mum...'

Jonny held up his hand, cutting her off. 'Not gonna happen,' he said, shaking his head, his expression serious.

'Yeah but—'

'No.' Sighing, Jonny clasped hold of her hand. 'It's too dangerous; who knows what that mad fucker is capable of? He could hold a knife up to your throat, could use you as leverage.'

Terri gave him a look and as she squeezed his hand, she shook her head. 'You said yourself that I should fake it until I make it and I want him to pay for what he did to Archie.'

'Then let Ricky and Jamie take care of him,' Jonny butted in. 'They've been in this game since they were kids, they know what they're doing.'

'And I don't.' Terri's face fell.

Huffing out a breath, Jonny rubbed a hand over his face. 'It's too dangerous,' he repeated.

'Then how about I lure him to the pub? You and my brothers could be waiting for him.' She gave him a pleading look. 'I need to do this,' she cried, sinking back into the chair. 'We can't let Michael get away with what he did.'

'He's not going to get away with it.' Relenting somewhat, Jonny studied her. 'Look, why don't you run it past your brothers and if they agree with it then...' He shook his head again, the look on his face telling her that no matter what Ricky or Jamie said, he still didn't agree to her putting herself in harm's way. 'Then I'm in. Okay.'

Terri flashed him a smile and as he pulled her to her feet and wrapped his arms around her, the smile slipped from her face. Talking the situation through with Ricky and Jamie would take time, time that they didn't have. An idea formed in her mind; she didn't need her brothers' permission, she could still lure Michael to a meeting place, could still dish out her own form of retribution.

* * *

Bianca Murphy lit a cigarette from the butt of her previous one. She was dressed in an old, oversized, stained T-shirt that she wore to bed, her hair resembled a bird's nest on top of her head, and underneath her eyes, streaks of dried mascara were smeared, giving her the appearance of a panda. A rather large, unpleasant panda.

Engrossed in a daytime television show, she chuckled out loud. Where they got these contestants from, she'd never know; half of them looked a state. Oblivious to her own attire, she continued watching, only taking her eyes away from the screen to stub out the cigarette in an already overflowing ashtray.

'Get that, will you?' she shouted out as the doorbell rang.

Moments later, the bell rang again and throwing up her arms, she began to heave her heavy frame off the sofa. 'I suppose I'll get it,' she grumbled, her gruff voice loud. 'Just like I do everything else around here.'

Bianca flung the door open, an all too familiar scowl etched across her face.

'Hello, Mum.'

The look on Bianca's face was one of shock and as her mouth hung open, she blinked rapidly as though she were seeing a ghost.

'Are you going to invite me in?'

Bianca nodded and stepping aside, she stared at her daughter. 'So you finally came home then, did you? Don't tell me.' She crossed her arms over her chest, and flashed a smug grin. 'He dumped you, didn't he? Just like I said he would. It's your own fault,' she chastised. 'I said that you were too frigid for your own good. Men don't want a woman like that, they want to have a good time, have a bit of fun. And I can tell you something else for nothing, you'd better not be in the club because if you are then first thing tomorrow morning you'll be down that clinic getting rid of it.' She paused for breath, her eyebrows scrunching together. 'Here, hold up a minute, he's a Carter ain't he?' Her eyes lit up. 'Well you know what that means, don't you? He's got some dough and if I know anything about the Carters then it'll be a lot of dough. On second thoughts, keep the kid and rinse him for every penny he's got.'

Terri held up her hand. 'Mum, I'm not pregnant.'

'Oh.' Bianca's face fell. 'Oh well,' she sighed. 'Better luck next time and make sure the next fella you shack up with has got some cash in his back pocket, because I can tell you now, I won't be supporting you. My days of running after you are long gone.' Making her way back into the lounge, Bianca flopped onto the sofa and reached for her cigarette packet, her beady eyes raking her daughter over. 'You look well,' she begrudgingly pointed out, a hint of jealousy notable in her voice. 'Not that I should say I'm surprised. You do have my genes.'

Terri rolled her eyes. 'I look like my dad,' she pointed out.

Bianca ran her tongue over her teeth. 'Yeah well,' she sniffed. 'It was me who carried you, I do deserve some credit. Anyway.' She flapped her hand. 'What do you want?'

Terri gave an incredulous laugh. 'Cheers for that, Mum and it's nice to see you too.' She glanced around her. 'Is Michael home?' she asked, cocking her head to one side and making sure to keep her voice neutral.

'Not at the moment.' She stabbed her cigarette forward. 'And if you want my advice, steer clear of him; he still hasn't forgotten the fact you lamped him one.'

'He was going to attack me,' Terri was quick to answer. 'While you stood by and did nothing, might I add.'

Bianca had the grace to look away. 'He would never have hurt you; he loves you. You're his niece.'

Terri raised her eyebrows and getting to her feet, she glanced around her, her nose wrinkling at the stale stench permeating the house. 'You're right,' she said, giving a wide smile. 'Good old Uncle Michael, he would never hurt me.' She inched closer to the door.

'Why don't you tell him to pop by the pub? I could buy him a drink, clear the air between us, let bygones be bygones.'

'Yeah all right,' Bianca answered, her gaze going back to the television. 'And if I come with him, do I get a free drink as well?' she added as an afterthought.

Not bothering to answer, Terri opened the front door. 'Don't forget to tell him,' she called out before stepping outside and gently closing the door behind her.

* * *

Mason Tempest was fast on his way to becoming paralytic drunk. Having spent most of the afternoon knocking back shots of vodka and Red Bull, he slung his arm around a blonde woman. Blondes weren't his usual type but seeing as she'd put it on him, who was he to turn her down? Not only that, but after recent events, he'd gone off brunettes, was too scared they could turn out to be another long lost relative. As for the woman currently hanging off his arm, he couldn't even remember her name, not that it mattered in the grand scheme of things, he supposed. He had a raging hard on and as he adjusted the crotch of his jeans, he copped a feel of her backside.

'Oi,' she giggled as she tottered beside him on dangerously high heels. 'Not here; wait until we're somewhere a bit more private.'

In high spirits, Mason exited the pub and dug his hand into his pocket, pulling out his phone. 'Are you coming back to mine?' he asked, already dialling the number of his dad's taxi firm.

The woman gave a second giggle. 'Or we could go back to mine.' She twirled a lock of blonde hair around her finger, a coy look spread across her face. 'It's only a five-minute walk away.'

'Sounds like a plan.' Cancelling the call, he stuffed the device back into his pocket. 'After you then.' He motioned for her to lead the way, taking the opportunity to ogle her backside. She'd better not turn out to be some old dog once the drink had worn off. Still, he reasoned, even if it was a case of the beer goggles clouding his judgement, it wasn't like he was planning to stick around for the long haul. No, once he'd given her one, he'd have it away on his toes. The last thing he wanted or even needed for that matter was to be saddled with a bird questioning his every move. Nah fuck that, he'd much rather be single, footloose and fancy-free as the old saying went.

As they turned the corner of the street, Mason narrowed his eyes. 'I thought you said your place was only up the road?'

'It is.' The woman grinned. 'It's just up there.' She pointed into the distance then linked her arm through his, making a point of pushing her large breasts up against him. 'It won't take us long, I promise.'

Mason glanced around him. He wasn't so drunk that he didn't have a feel for his bearings, and they'd definitely been walking for more than five minutes; it was more like ten minutes and considering there weren't even any houses or flats around them, something didn't feel quite right. 'Are you having a laugh?' He pulled his arm free and squinted down at her. 'Are you on the game or something? Because let me tell you something now sweetheart, you've picked the wrong man. I've never paid for sex in my life and I sure as fuck ain't going to start now.'

The woman shrugged and stepping several feet away from him, she gave an apologetic smile. 'Sorry,' she said. 'But I was skint and could do with some extra cash. I've got a baby to look after.'

As Mason narrowed his eyes, confusion spread across his face. He opened his mouth to answer when a heavy object crashed into the back of his skull. He sank to his knees, his eyes rolling to the back of his head before he fell face first on to the pavement with a loud thud.

The woman held out her hand and as Michael Murphy placed

two crisp fifty-pound notes into it, he gave her a wide grin. 'Was nice doing business with you,' he chuckled.

Snatching the money, the woman looked down at Mason. 'What are you going to do to him?' she asked, chewing on her bottom lip, concern etching across her features. Although it would be fair to say it was a bit too late for her to feel any form of remorse, she'd already done her part, had already been paid to lure the man somewhere desolate.

Michael laughed and tapping the side of his nose, he gave her a wink. 'That's for me to know and for him to find out.'

The woman sighed and as two men heaved Mason off the floor and threw him into the back of a van, she tucked the money into her handbag and gave a shrug. 'Shame,' she said as she began to walk away. 'He was a looker an' all.'

Michael laughed even harder. 'Was being the operative word,' he called after her as he climbed up into the front seat of the van and slammed the door closed behind him before speeding away from the kerb.

21

From across the bar, Rina Taylor studied Terri. It hadn't escaped her attention that the younger women seemed on edge. Nor had she failed to notice that each and every time the door to the pub opened, Terri would look up, her body tensing, as if she was expecting to see someone walk through the door.

'Are you okay?' Rina asked, catching hold of Terri's arm. 'Is something bothering you?'

Terri gave a carefree laugh. 'Don't be daft. Why would something be bothering me?'

'I don't know.' Rina cocked her head to the side. 'You just don't seem yourself today.'

Waving off Rina's words, Terri busied herself polishing the glasses. Wandering off to serve the next customer, Rina couldn't help but keep a watchful eye on Terri. Her intuition had never let her down before, and there was definitely something wrong, she just couldn't quite put her finger on what it could be.

She almost gave a sigh of relief when Jonny walked through the door and as he made a beeline for Terri, she couldn't help but smile. They were a match made in heaven despite the age difference between them. Not that ten years was such a big gap, she reasoned. Archie had been older than her by several years; in fact, she knew many couples who had an age difference and they seemed happy enough.

'Rina.' Digging his hand into his pocket, Jonny pulled out a twenty-pound note. 'Can I get my two favourite barmaids a drink?'

'Get away with you,' Rina retorted. 'We all know that you only have eyes for one person, and it definitely isn't me.'

Jonny chuckled and giving over his order, he leaned casually against the bar. 'Yeah you could be on to something there.' He threw Terri a wink. 'So,' he asked, lowering his voice. 'Did you have a word with Ricky and Jamie?'

'No not yet.' Placing the glass she was wiping back underneath the bar, Terri picked up the next glass and began to vigorously polish it. 'Maybe you were right.' She shrugged. 'It was a stupid idea.'

Jonny narrowed his eyes. 'That wasn't what you were saying earlier. In fact, I'd go as far as to say you looked pretty adamant that you wanted to go through with it.' He grabbed her hand, forcing her to stop polishing. Even from where he was standing, he could see that the glasses were already sparkling. 'Please tell me you haven't done something reckless, that you didn't put yourself at risk?'

Terri screwed up her face and as the door opened, she snapped her head around to take a look, a fleeting glimpse of worry crossing over her features.

'What the fuck have you done?' Jonny shook his head, his voice a low growl.

Giving an awkward smile, Terri shrugged. 'I already told you; Michael isn't going to get away with what he's done. He needs to pay, and I'm not prepared to wait around for Ricky and Jamie to get their arses into gear and put a plan of action into place. So' – she lifted her chin in the air, defiance flashing in her eyes – 'I went to see my mum, told her I want to meet Michael, told her I'd buy him a drink and you know what a bunch of freeloaders they are, he'll snap my hand off if he thinks he's getting free booze.'

'So you think you'll be able to take him on then? That you'll be a match for him? He's a nasty piece of work; which part of that don't you understand?' he said, tapping the side of his head. 'Do you really believe that he's going to come in here, have a drink and then quietly leave again? That he'll want to kiss and make up, or that he'll suddenly grow a conscience or even take it into account that you're his niece, his blood. You know what the man's like, he'll have a hidden agenda. He pimped out women for fuck sake, trafficked them into the country, kept them held as prisoners, lived off immoral earnings. He has no morals, he's a fucking weasel, a lowlife, and to the right person or wrong person, whichever way you look at it, he's a dangerous fucker.'

Terri shook her head, her eyes blazing. If her back hadn't been up before it certainly was now. 'I already know all of this, I know what he did, what he's capable of. I lived with the man for four years and certainly don't need you to tell me what he's like.' Gripping on to the bar, she took several deep breaths, doing everything in her power to keep her temper in check, to stop herself from exploding and giving Jonny an ear bashing that he wouldn't forget in a hurry. 'All I'm trying to do is what the three of you should have done right from the very beginning. So what if you disposed of Gammon?' she spat, lowering her voice so that only he could hear. 'It's been weeks since Archie was killed, but Michael's allowed to walk around without a care in the world. This should have been resolved long before now.' She threw her arms up into the air and shook her head, despair flowing through her veins. 'And for the life of me I don't understand what you are all waiting for. Why you haven't gone after him yet. I'm starting to wonder if any of you genuinely cared about Archie because you're good at giving it all the mouth but when it comes to putting words into actions you do nothing, zilch. If I didn't know any better,' she raged, 'I'd think you were all afraid of him.'

Jonny's lips curled into a snarl. 'Is that what you think?' He gave an incredulous laugh. 'That I'm scared of that tosser?'

Giving a sigh, Terri shook her head. 'No... I don't know.' She shrugged. 'I just can't work any of it out. Why aren't you dealing with this?'

'Because these things take time. They have to be planned out. What would be the point in going in all guns blazing just to make a sloppy mistake and end up getting nicked?' He made to grab for her hand only for Terri to throw him off.

'Well, I don't have time,' Terri retorted. 'This isn't one of your bank jobs. A man died and if the three of you won't sort it out then I'm more than prepared to do so.'

As he pushed himself away from the bar, anger clouded Jonny's face. 'For fuck's sake Terri,' he shouted, rubbing at the back of his neck, his expression a mixture of disbelief and fury. 'What the fuck is wrong with you? Have you got a death wish or something? Or maybe you'd rather spend the rest of your life eating porridge, because that's exactly what's going to happen if you're not careful.' With those parting words, he stormed from the pub, leaving Terri to stare helplessly after him.

'What's going on?' As Rina sidled up beside Terri, she crossed her arms over her chest, concern creasing her face. 'What's got into him?' she asked, nodding towards the door Jonny had exited through. 'Have the two of you had a row?'

Terri shook her head, her earlier anger rapidly subsiding. She was in the right, wasn't she? They were taking too long in bringing Michael down. As she replayed Jonny's words over in her mind, she gave a shudder. What if she was wrong and he was the one who was right? What if what he'd said was true and she was playing a dangerous game? 'I think maybe I might have made a mistake,' she said, looking down at Rina. 'A big mistake.'

* * *

Mason slowly opened his eyes. His head was pounding; no, it was more than pounding, it hurt like a bitch. Blinking, he looked around him, unable to fathom out where he was. His throat was dry and God his head. He made to reach up and touch the back of his skull. Unable to move his arms, he frowned. What the fuck was going on?

Narrowing his eyes, he stared down at the cable ties that held him in place. No wonder he couldn't move, he was being restrained. Confusion washed over him. What had happened to him? He could remember the pub, could recall knocking back the drinks, and plenty of them. Could recall the blonde woman; she'd practically thrown herself at him. And then what had happened? He tried to rack his brain; they were meant to be going back to her place, weren't they?

'So he finally rises.'

Mason snapped his head up.

'You've been out cold for hours. I was starting to get a bit concerned, thought maybe the lads had hit you a bit too hard.'

Mason swallowed. Despite the man's words, his voice didn't hold an ounce of emotion. He tugged on the restraints, the plastic ties biting into his flesh.

'Save your energy son, you won't escape, my boys made sure of that and by all accounts you're a feisty little fucker, got a bit of a rep.'

Mason looked up again. There was something familiar about the man; it was almost as though he knew him or at the very least, recognised him from somewhere. 'Who the fuck are you?' he spat out.

Raymond laughed and shaking his head, he gave a long sigh. 'Come on, even you're not that dense.' He studied him for a moment. 'Don't tell me that you can't see the resemblance.' He reached up to touch his dark hair and gave the strands a tug. 'Think hard,' he said. 'Dark hair, blue eyes. Who do I remind you of?'

His mouth dry, Mason gulped. 'My dad.'

'Bingo.' Clapping his hands together, Raymond grinned. 'There are no flies on you, are there, eh?' He got to his feet, his large frame towering over Mason. 'Your dad, not forgetting that uncle of yours. They tried to kill me, left me in a ditch by the side of the road.' He fingered his scar. 'Left me with this as a constant reminder of them.'

'Raymond?' Mason volunteered. 'But' – he screwed up his face in confusion – 'I thought you were dead?'

'The one and only.' Holding up his hands, Raymond laughed. 'And as you can see, I'm very much alive and kicking, no thanks to your old man.'

'For now,' Mason muttered under his breath. Taking this as an opportunity to look around him, he frowned. The room he was being held in looked familiar. Bare concrete floor, peeling wallpaper complete with patches of mould, dusty outdated fireplace, battered, rusting can of petrol sitting in front of the window. Gammon's meet up, it had to be. 'So I take it you found the present I left for you?'

Raymond's laughter stopped, a nerve at the side of his eye twitching. 'If you're referring to Frankie Gammon's severed head, then yeah I did.'

Mason grinned. 'Was a bugger to cut off, but being the sick fuck you are, I thought you'd appreciate it.'

The eye twitching increased. 'I can see that you and me are cut from the same cloth. In fact.' He moved in closer, as though he were studying Mason. 'I can see a lot of myself in you, when I was a bit younger of course.'

'I don't think so,' Mason snorted, his face twisting in disgust. 'You tried to kill my mum and nan; I'd never harm a woman.'

Raymond waved his hand through the air. 'They were nothing but collateral damage. No, it was your old man I was really after, both him and Jamie, let's not forget that mouthy prick.'

As he tugged on the restraints again, beads of cold sweat broke out across Mason's forehead. 'You won't get away with this,' he spat. 'My dad's gonna kill you.'

'Maybe,' Raymond answered as he lifted a crow bar above his head. 'But' – he gave a sad smile and kissed his teeth – 'I highly doubt it.' He pulled back his arm and as Mason slammed his eyes shut, bracing himself for the blow, Raymond chuckled. 'Don't worry, I'm not going to kill you, at least not yet anyway. No.' He brought the bar crashing down on Mason's shoulder, and as he screamed, the loud crack was more than enough to signal a broken bone. 'I'm going to make your dad watch me kill you. Going to make him get down on his knees and beg me to save your life and do you know what,' he asked, his grinning face just inches away from Mason's. 'I'm going to enjoy every last second of blowing his world far apart.'

* * *

'She's done what?' Jamie's eyes were as wide as saucers. 'Has she lost the fucking plot?'

'Yeah, you'd think so,' Jonny grumbled as he took a seat at the brothers' taxi office. 'She's too fucking headstrong if you want my opinion. Got too much of that Tempest blood flowing through her veins.'

'Yeah well.' Jamie grinned. 'To me, that sounds like a problem for you to deal with. You were the one who wanted her.'

Jonny rolled his eyes. 'Can we get back on track?' he said, looking between Ricky and Jamie. 'She is your sister after all; she's as much your problem as she is mine.'

'Half-sister,' Jamie corrected.

'Sister,' Ricky said, giving his brother a pointed look. Rubbing his hand over his jaw, he gave a shake of his head. 'Murphy's not stupid; I doubt he'd turn up at the boozer.'

'That's not the point,' Jonny exclaimed. 'The fact of the matter is she still took it upon herself to turn up at the Murphy family home. I mean' – he spread open his arms – 'surely to fuck she must have known how dangerous that would be.' He tapped his temple. 'Michael killed Archie, so what the fuck would he have done to her? She's hardly a match for him, is she, and you know as well as I do that hitting out at a woman is all that prick is good for.'

Ricky sighed. 'True.' Sitting forward, he placed his elbows on the desk and rested his chin on his clasped fingers. 'So what do we do now?'

'End this,' Jonny volunteered. 'Take Michael out of the game.'

'This plan of Terri's.' Jamie flicked his head towards Jonny. 'You've got to admit it wasn't a bad one. Lure the bastard to the pub and then nab him. Like you said, if he thinks she's offering him an olive branch then his defences will be down. Only, when he turns up as happy as fucking Larry, thinking he'll be shouting the odds, we'll be there waiting for him.'

'It's still a big risk.' Jonny shook his head.

'Not really,' Ricky said. 'There'll be four of us; he won't stand a chance.' Leaning back in his seat, he pulled out his phone. 'That reminds me, have you seen Mason? He hasn't been answering my calls.'

Getting to his feet, Jonny shook his head.

'You know what he's like.' Picking up his car keys, Jamie grabbed his jacket off the back of the chair. 'He's probably out shagging some sort.'

'Yeah probably,' Ricky answered with a frown before pocketing his phone. 'Right, come on then, it's about time we had a little chat with that bastard Michael.'

* * *

Chewing on her thumbnail, Terri couldn't help but keep a watchful eye on the door. How could have she been so stupid? If Michael was to turn up now, what would she do? She would never be able to overpower him; even armed with a weapon, she highly doubted that she'd have the upper hand.

As the door to the pub opened and Jonny, Ricky, and Jamie walked through, she snapped her spine a little straighter. She should have seen this coming and shooting Jonny a glare, she shook her head.

'I should have known you'd go running to them. Well go on,' she said, addressing Ricky and Jamie. 'Do your worst, tell me how stupid I am, how I put myself at risk.'

'Yeah, you did.' Jamie gave a nod. 'And it was fucking stupid... but despite all of that, it was a good plan.'

Terri's jaw dropped. 'What?' she asked, looking between the men and hardly believing her ears.

'It could actually work,' Ricky agreed. 'And,' he conceded, 'it's not like Michael has shown his face since the murder. We've even put the feelers out, let it be known that we're gunning for the bastard, and no one has seen hide nor hair of him. So, if we can get him here under false pretences, it might just be our best shot at taking him out.'

Terri's face lit up. 'I knew it could work.' She grinned.

'So...' Slipping onto a bar stool, Jamie looked around him. 'Now all we have to do is get him here.'

Terri nodded. That could be the hard part. Taking into account Michael's hatred of her, getting him to the pub might not be quite as easy as she'd first anticipated.

22

Mason's breathing was ragged. Each and every time he either inhaled or exhaled, pain shot through his rib cage. His ribs were broken; it didn't take a genius to tell him that, and unless he was mistaken, the breaks weren't limited to just his ribs either. He had more than a sneaky suspicion that his collarbone, his wrists, and at least five of his fingers were also broken and perhaps even his skull had suffered a fracture if the blinding pain across the back of his head was anything to go by.

He felt dizzy and sick, and his voice was hoarse. He'd screamed so much and so loud that it felt as though he were swallowing razor blades, not that the attack upon himself had relented in any way, shape, or form; if anything, it had got worse. He was going to die; he was only twenty-four and his life was over, he knew that as well as he knew his own name. His dad wasn't going to find him in time and despite Raymond's threat to kill him in front of his old man, he had a feeling that he'd be dead long before that ever happened.

Mason had always assumed that he had anger problems, that he wasn't able to control the red mist that descended over him, but Raymond's fury was on another level. He was a sick bastard, he had to be. He, his dad and Jamie were brothers, they were family, and yet Raymond wanted to destroy them, and not only destroy them but he wanted to make them suffer in the process. It was inconceivable to Mason. Fair enough, he didn't have any siblings, but he did have cousins, and not in a million years would it ever enter his head to harm Sorina or Adelina. He loved them, he'd die for them, and no matter what, they were his blood.

A movement from behind Mason made him wearily close his eyes, his body becoming limp; it was all he could to limit the damage being caused. 'You're a sick fuck,' he choked out. 'My dad's going to kill you for this.' He'd been saying the same thing for over two hours, not that it made any difference, still the assault continued, still Raymond beat him senseless to the point he thought he was going to actually pass out.

Michael Murphy was in his element. For the past hour he'd been pretty much begging Raymond to let him have a go at Tempest. There was a lot of bad blood between himself and the Tempest family and despite the fact the little prick sitting in front of him wasn't the Tempest brother he was after, in his mind it made no difference. At the end of the day, they were all the same, all trappy little cunts with too much to say for themselves.

He unbuckled his belt and pulled the leather through the loops. Holding the length of thick material between his fingers, he tested the weight of the buckle. Oh, this was going to hurt, and he wouldn't be surprised if it split the bastard's skin wide apart. He just hoped the fucker screamed, really screamed.

Swishing the belt through the air, Michael closed his eyes in delight, savouring the moment. Just as he'd hoped he would, Mason Tempest howled in pain. It was like music to his ears, and as he flicked the belt a second time, he allowed himself to smile. He was enjoying himself; years of pent-up rage was being released.

In rapid succession, he flicked the belt a third and a fourth time. The bastard had better not croak on him, not when he was enjoying himself so much.

* * *

Bianca Murphy was in the mood for partying, not that she was in the position to do so. She had roughly two pounds in her purse, not even enough to buy herself a drink.

'Oh, go on Mum,' she begged. 'Lend us a score.'

Bianca's mother shook her head, her smug grin intensifying the more her daughter asked. 'Not on your nelly.' She placed her hand over her ample stomach, her eyes not leaving the large flat screen television. 'I'm not made of bleeding money you know.'

'How about a tenner then? I promise I'll give it back.'

'What, like the last lot of money you had off me? You promised to give that back an' all but never did.'

'I will this time, honest I will,' Bianca continued to whine.

'No. Ask your father.'

'Dad.' Turning her attention to her father, Bianca batted her eyelashes at him. 'Lend us a score.'

'Get out of it.' Slamming his newspaper closed, Bianca's father heaved himself out of his armchair. 'You should get a job,' he chastised. 'Do an honest day's work, then you'd have a bit of cash in your pocket.'

'What, like you do?' Bianca retorted. 'You've never even had a job.'

'That's because I'm on the sick.' He tapped the side of his nose. 'So keep that out of it.'

Bianca sulked. All she wanted was a drink or two, to let her hair down and have a good time. Anyone would think she was asking for the earth the way they were carrying on. Huffing out a breath, she glanced towards the window; it was still light outside, giving her plenty of time to get herself dolled up. 'Come on, Mum.'

'I said no. Ask your brother. Michael's never short of a bob or two, and you are his favourite,' she said with a nod.

As an image of her daughter sprang to her mind, a crafty glint shone in Bianca's eyes. Terri had said that she would buy her and Michael a drink, maybe she'd even stretch to two drinks. Jumping up from the sofa, she snatched up her mobile phone. She and Michael may not have been as close as they used to be, but she could still wrap him around her little finger when she needed to. 'Yeah, you're right,' she announced, flouncing out of the room. 'I'll ask Michael.'

* * *

To Michael's annoyance, Mason Tempest had blacked out. Rethreading his belt, he surveyed the damage he'd caused. Thick red welts, the majority of which were either bleeding or weeping, zig-zagged across the man's body, the heavy metal buckle causing the most damage. It probably stung like a bitch. Not that he particularly cared; as far as he was concerned, the kid deserved it; the fact he was a Tempest had been enough to seal his fate. As for the welts there was no particular pattern to them, he'd been so incensed that he'd just lashed out, marking the man wherever the belt should happen to land.

His phone began to ring and taking it out of his pocket, he saw his sister's name flash across the screen. He had half a mind to let it ring off, only, knowing Bianca, she'd more than likely continue calling until he eventually answered. It was a particular trait of hers; she didn't like being ignored.

'What?' he growled into the phone.

A cruel grin spread across his face. So the little bitch he called a niece had finally seen the light and turned up at his mother's house. Slowly, he prowled around Mason Tempest's broken body, observing the injuries he'd inflicted. He'd get a kick out of turning up at the pub, knowing that he'd been the one to kill Archie Taylor and not Frankie Gammon. And not only that, but the fact he'd played a part in destroying Terri's nephew was enough to make his heart sing. He had one over on the little cow. He knew something that she didn't, and he knew for a fact that both her half-brothers and her nephew were going to be wiped out, that Raymond Cole wouldn't stop until he'd seen their blood spilled and they ceased to exist.

'Yeah all right.' He continued to grin. 'We'll go and have a drink and if she apologises to me then I might even let her back into the family.'

Ending the call, Michael turned back to look at Mason. He'd never felt so empowered; it was heady stuff, something he would treasure for the remainder of his life. He'd found his place in life and to be a part of something so colossal was downright exhilarating. To the right of where he was standing was a can of petrol. Picking it up, he unscrewed the lid and gave the contents a quick sniff; it was almost enough to make his eyes water. With a jerk of his hand, he splashed the liquid over Mason's head, grinning to himself as he did so before sauntering out of the room. He'd be surprised if the kid even made it through the night.

'I'll be back later,' he shouted out. 'Try not to kill him before I get back; I don't want to miss all the fun.'

* * *

Terri drummed her fingers across her mobile phone. Minutes earlier, she'd sent her mother a text message, not that she actually expected a response.

'Anything?' Ricky asked.

Terri shook her head. She was beginning to feel nervous. What if Michael didn't take her up on the offer of a drink or what if he turned up when Ricky and Jamie weren't there? The plan would be foiled.

Her phone lit up, indicating a new message. As she snatched the device up, Terri's heart was in her mouth. 'It's Mum.'

'Well?' Jamie asked.

Reading the message, Terri placed her hand upon her chest. 'They're on their way,' she said, looking up, the colour draining from her face.

'Good.' Taking out his own phone, Ricky attempted to call his son again. His forehead furrowing, he ended the call. 'He's still not picking up.'

'Because he's too busy shagging,' Jamie retorted with a roll of his eyes.

'What, for this long? It's been hours. Surely to fuck he can't still be going at it.'

Jamie raised his eyebrows. 'Speak for yourself; we're not all a two-minute wonder.' He winked. 'Just send him a message and tell him to call you as soon as he's finished.'

'We need to warn Rina.' Chewing on her lip, Terri nodded in Rina's direction.

'I'll do it,' Jonny volunteered. 'It'll be better coming from me.' He gave Rina a glance, his lips curling up into a soft smile. 'She's always had a bit of a soft spot for me.'

'Do you really think this is going to work?' Terri asked. 'That Michael won't suss the plan out?'

Thinking it over, Jamie shrugged. 'Only one way we're going to find out, isn't there? We'll wait back there.' He gestured to the hallway behind the bar. 'And as soon as they turn up, give us the nod.'

* * *

Once the men had got into position, Terri made her way across the bar. 'I am so sorry Rina,' she said. 'I didn't mean to get you involved and I wish there could have been another way.'

Rina's eyes were hard. 'No need to apologise. That bastard murdered my husband; I'd like to kill him myself.'

Terri gave a sad smile. She understood where Rina was coming from; she felt exactly the same way. Michael had broken Rina's heart. Archie had been the love of her life and they should have had the rest of their lives to look forward to. Their dreams and hopes for the future were in tatters, forever to remain unfulfilled all thanks to her uncle's wicked deeds.

'We'll have him out of here as soon as we can. Ricky and Jamie will have the car on standby. It'll be so quick that I doubt anyone will even notice,' she added, nodding around the bar.

Rina gave a laugh, her gaze remaining firmly fixed on the door. 'Believe me darling, no one here will be calling the police. The Murphys are hardly the pillar of the community, are they? As far as this lot are concerned, it will be one less Murphy to contend with in their book.'

Terri didn't answer; what was she supposed to even say? Until recently, she'd been a part of the very same family that the community despised. She'd always known that they were tolerated rather than liked, but she hadn't realised just how deep the loathing and hatred went.

As the door opened and her mother and uncle walked inside with a cocky swagger, Terri stiffened.

'Remember to smile,' Rina reminded her as she inched closer to the hallway. 'Don't do anything to make them suspicious.'

Forcing a smile, Terri clasped her hands together in a bid to stop them from trembling. As much as she knew her brothers were waiting in the wings, being in Michael's presence terrified her. 'Hello Mum.' She turned her head, the smile still frozen in place. 'Hello Michael.'

* * *

'Hello Michael,' was the cue that Ricky, Jamie and Jonny had been waiting for. As soon as the words left Terri's mouth, they bounded forward and just as Terri had predicted the situation would go down, it all happened so fast that before anyone could register what was happening, Jamie and Jonny had bundled Michael out of the pub and into the boot of Jamie's car.

It was Ricky who had dealt with Bianca, and before she'd even had the chance to scream blue murder, he'd dragged her behind the bar, and threatened her in no uncertain terms with a violent, grisly end if she so much as opened her mouth. Then he'd promptly threw her out of the pub.

On the drive to the warehouse where Frankie Gammon had been murdered, Terri felt sick to her stomach. She swore to herself that she wouldn't cave in, not again; she couldn't let her brothers down a second time. No matter how gruesome his murder was, or how much her instincts told her to come to his aid, at the end of the day, it made no difference. Michael was a monster; he needed to be destroyed.

'Are you okay?' As he reached out to grab her hand, there was a hint of concern in Jonny's voice.

Terri nodded. 'I will be.' She offered him a small smile then blew out her cheeks. 'I just want to get this over and done with. I want life to go back to how it was before.'

'You and me both.' Jonny squeezed her hand. 'But' – he jerked his head towards Jamie's car up ahead of them – 'that wasn't what I meant.'

'I know what you meant,' Terri reassured him. 'And I'll be fine, I promise. I'm going to see this through to the bitter end.'

As the car came to a halt, Terri unclipped her seat belt then taking a deep breath, she stepped outside. She heard her uncle before she saw him. The language spewing out of his mouth was so vile and abusive that she knew she'd done the right thing by luring him to the pub.

'You bastards,' he continued to roar. 'You no-good fucking cunts.'

His eyes locked with Terri's, the hatred he felt towards his niece more than evident. 'And as for you, you're the biggest cunt of them all. I wish you'd never been born; your mother should have aborted you; she should have flushed you down the toilet like all the other bastards she had torn out of her belly.'

As Ricky and Jamie turned to look at her, gauging her reaction to Michael's heinous words, Terri crossed her arms over her chest, her expression remaining unfazed. 'It's nothing I haven't heard before,' she told them, stony faced.

It was at that moment the penny finally dropped. She could see the different emotions pass across her brothers' faces. Disbelief, disgust, anger, but most of all guilt. It was as though it had finally sunk into their brains that this was the treatment she had endured at the Murphy family's hands, and even more than that, that they had been happy to leave her in the care of people who had used and abused her, people who had let her down time and time again.

* * *

Almost immediately, the beating began. It was both ferocious, and merciless. Through it all, Terri didn't look away, not once. It was almost as though she were detached from the situation, as though she were there in body but not in mind.

Gasping for air, Michael held out his hand. Blood dripped from his fingertips onto the bare concrete, his head a swollen mass and his eyes so bruised that he could barely open them. 'You can kill me,' he choked out.

'Oh, I will do, there ain't any doubts about that,' Jamie roared, kicking out again.

'You can kill me,' Michael said again. 'But I'll have the last laugh. He's coming for you; he's going to destroy you.'

A silence fell over the warehouse.

'What did you just say?' Ricky hissed, raising his fist.

Michael attempted to smile, his teeth coated in red. Spitting out a mouthful of blood, his chest wheezed. 'He's coming for you.'

'What the fuck is he talking about?' Jonny looked between the brothers. 'Who's coming?'

As Michael collapsed on to his side, he began to cough, a deep hacking cough that left him gasping for air. 'Your brother,' he choked out. 'Raymond.'

Ricky snapped his head around to look at Jamie, his eyes narrowed into slits and his forehead furrowing. 'Nah.' He shook his head. 'That's not possible.'

The fact Jamie could barely look him in the eyes was all the affirmation Ricky needed and bounding forward, he grabbed his brother by the front of his shirt, their faces so close to one another's that they were almost touching.

'What is he talking about?' he growled, his eyes not leaving his brother's face. 'We both know it can't be him because you killed him. Tell me you killed him, Jamie?'

Jamie looked away and as Ricky threw him away from him, he rubbed the palm of his hand over his face.

'It's not what you think,' Jamie said, his voice so low that Ricky could barely hear him. 'I wanted to kill him, but I couldn't. I couldn't do it, all right.'

Staring at his brother as if he'd grown a second head, Ricky rubbed at his temples. 'For twenty years,' he growled, 'you led me to believe that that mad fucker was dead, when all along you knew he was alive, and not just fucking alive' – he gave an incredulous laugh, barely able to get his head around the sudden turn of events – 'but planning to destroy us.'

'I'm sorry.' Jamie looked down at the floor.

'You're sorry?' Ricky spat. 'You had the front to take the piss out of me, to tell me that I was the weakest link, that I wouldn't have been able to kill the mad bastard when all along it was you who couldn't do it. I can't believe what I'm hearing.' He shook his head. 'I seriously can't get my head around any of this.'

From behind them, Michael began to laugh again. 'He's going to bring you to your knees. He's already made a start, already taken something away from you, something of value.'

Ricky tilted his head to the side, his face becoming deathly pale. And as a shard of fear shot up the length of his spine, the tiny hairs on the back of his neck stood upright. Digging his hand into his pocket, he pulled out his phone and pressed redial. 'Come on,' he shouted. To his utter despair, once again, the call went straight to Mason's answer phone.

'No.' Jamie shook his head, the colour draining from his face just as Ricky's had moments earlier. 'No, no, no,' he repeated. 'He hasn't. Not Mason?'

Grasping a handful of Michael's hair in his fist, Ricky bellowed into his face, 'Where is my son?'

Michael gave a sickening grin. 'You're too late,' he laughed. 'He'll be dead by now.'

'Where is he?' Ricky roared again.

Michael continued to laugh. 'I always knew that I'd make you pay for what you did to me. It's because of you I was banged up, because of you that I spent the prime of my life behind bars. And as for your boy...' He gave a sickening grin. 'He screamed Frankie's house down. Fuck me did he scream. On and on it went. It was more than enough to give us a headache. I'm surprised Raymond didn't cut his tongue out.'

Ricky was so enraged that his body shook, the anger inside of him so fierce he could feel it oozing out of his pores. Over and over again, he pummelled his fists into Michael's face. His knuckles were bruised and bloody, and still he didn't stop, he couldn't, not until he'd ended Michael Murphy's life.

It was Jamie who finally pulled him away and as Michael's lifeless body fell to the floor, Ricky crouched down and held his head in his hands. His boy was gone. A lone tear slipped down his cheek; how would he ever be able to find the words to tell Kayla that their son was dead?

* * *

Terri clasped her hand over her mouth. Her eldest brother's grief was so raw that all she wanted to do was run to him and make it stop, to somehow try and ease his pain.

'No, I'm not having this. The bastard was lying, he had to be.' Getting to his feet, Ricky shoved Jamie away from him. 'Until I've seen his body with my own two eyes, I won't believe that he's gone. I can't,' he said, his voice full of emotion.

'Then we go to the house,' Terri piped out, gesturing down at her uncle's corpse. 'He said it was Frankie's house, that that's where Mason is.'

'Not you.' Jamie stabbed his finger towards her. 'You're not going anywhere near that nutter.'

'But—'

'I said no,' Jamie roared. He turned to Jonny. 'Keep her away. Do you hear what I'm telling you? Keep her away from Raymond.'

Jonny nodded.

Terri's mouth fell open, and as her brothers stormed from the warehouse, she clutched a hand to her chest. She had a bad feeling about this. If Raymond was as dangerous as they said he was, then they would need all the backup they could get, they would need the extra muscle.

She turned to look at Jonny, her eyes pleading with him. 'You have to go with them. They need you.'

'No.' He held up his hands. 'You heard what they said.'

'And since when did you take orders from them?' she asked, jerking her head behind her.

'Since it's going to keep you safe,' Jonny retorted.

Terri's nostrils flared. He seemed to be forgetting something, they all seemed to be forgetting something. She was as much a Tempest as they were. When she spoke, her voice was like steel, and her eyes as hard as flints. 'Take me to the house, now,' she spat. 'Or I swear before God, Jonny Carter, that I will start swinging for you myself. And as for them.' She jerked her head towards the door her brothers had exited through. 'Believe me when I say this, there won't be anything left for them to tear into once I've finished with you.'

23

The atmosphere in Jamie's car was strained to say the least. After a long silence, Jamie cleared his throat.

'I don't want to hear it,' Ricky said, holding up his hand and cutting his brother off before he'd even had the chance to open his mouth and speak. 'If my son is dead because you didn't tell me that that lunatic was still alive...' He shook his head, his face white with anger and his bloody fists clenched into a tight balls. 'I'll kill you Jamie, are we clear on that? I will kill you.'

Jamie swallowed. 'He's not dead. He can't be. This is Mason we're talking about, he's strong, he'd be able to easily overpower Raymond, you know he would.'

Ricky snarled. 'Believe me, you'd best hope and pray that's the case.'

Ten minutes later, Jamie pulled up outside Frankie Gammon's meet up.

'How should we—' Before Jamie could even finish the sentence, Ricky was out of the car, his heavy boot kicking out at the front door, causing the already splintered wood to swing wide open with a loud clatter.

Swearing under his breath, Jamie followed suit and raced down the pathway.

'Mason?' Charging into the house, Ricky came to a skidding halt at the door to the lounge. No,' he cried. Gripping onto the doorframe to stop himself from collapsing to the floor, he bowed his head, the colour draining from his face, his heart breaking in two. 'No,' he said over and over again like a mantra, the words catching in his throat.

Jamie's eyes widened, the fear in them more than apparent. 'No.' He shook his head, inching closer, almost too afraid to look. 'No he's not, tell me he's not,' he shouted.

Ricky looked up and turning towards his brother, his expression was murderous. 'I warned you,' he spat, the muscles across his shoulder blades clenching. 'Brother or not, I'm going to kill you for this.'

'Dad.'

Tearing his gaze back to what he'd believed to be his son's lifeless form, Ricky raced into the room, his heart in his mouth. 'I'm here.' Crouching down, he slipped his hand into his pocket and pulled out a knife, his gaze raking over his son's injuries. There were so many of them, far too many for him to count. Blood encrusted welts, some still weeping, some so deep they were sure to leave scars across every inch of his boy's torso. Not to mention the smell; his son reeked of petrol and as he brought his face closer to his son's head, the overpowering stench became even stronger. Had Raymond been planning to burn his son alive? He had to have been. It was no secret that Raymond had a penchant for playing with fire. 'I'm here, okay? It's going to be all right. I'm going to get you sorted out, going to get you help,' he said as he tore through the plastic cable ties and began massaging Mason's hands in an attempt to bring life back into them.

Mason's eyes flickered open. Every inch of him hurt and as Ricky pulled him into his arms, he whimpered, his breathing so laboured that he could barely get the words out. 'I'm sorry Dad,' he whispered. 'I let my guard down.'

'It's okay,' Ricky reassured him. 'Don't you worry about any of that. It's going to be okay. I promise.'

'Well, well, well. This is touching, I must say.'

Both Ricky and Jamie snapped their heads around.

Standing in the doorway to the lounge, Raymond spread open his arms. 'Surprise.' He grinned. 'I'm guessing that I'm the last person you ever expected to see, especially as you left me for dead.'

'You mad fucker,' Jamie hissed.

Raymond shrugged. 'What can I say?' He stepped into the room. 'Although' – he glanced towards Mason – 'this isn't quite the family reunion I was hoping for. He should have been dead for a start, but the little bastard just wouldn't die.'

Ricky jumped to his feet. 'Believe me, this ends today.'

'Too fucking right it does.' Raymond dug his hand into his pocket and pulling out a lighter, he ignited the flame and waved it through the air. 'I've waited a long time to take the pair of you out.'

Charging forward, Ricky used every ounce of his strength to knock Raymond to the floor, the knife in his fist slashing out at his half-brother. He'd rather die than stand by and watch his son burn to death. As Raymond's fists shot out in retaliation, Ricky batted him away. Even in their youth, Raymond hadn't been a match for them; he'd already tried once to get the better of them and failed, and this time would be no different, Ricky was determined of that. 'You tried to kill my son,' he roared, plunging the knife deep into Raymond's shoulder.

The loud hiss that escaped from Raymond's lips was the only sign he gave of the pain that ripped through his body. Yanking out the blade, Ricky panted for breath. 'My son,' he shouted again. 'My fucking boy.'

Raymond lifted his head off the floor and grinned, the injury to his shoulder incapacitating him somewhat. 'It's nothing more than you deserve.' He reached up to touch the wound and stared down at the blood coating his fingers. 'It's what you both deserve,' he said, turning his head to look at Jamie and throwing him the same sickening grin. 'If it wasn't for you, I could have had everything.'

* * *

Terri had almost bitten her nails down to the quick. 'Can't you drive any faster?'

Jonny raised his eyebrows. 'I'm already well over the speed limit.' He nodded down at the dashboard. 'Do you want me to end up getting pulled over?'

Terri shook her head and continued chewing. 'This Raymond,' she said, turning to look at him. 'Do you know him?'

'Nah,' Jonny answered. 'I'd never even heard of him until tonight. Didn't even know there was another brother.'

'We've wasted so much time skirting around each other.' Her voiced cracked and she hastily swiped away the tears rolling down her cheeks 'You don't think that just when we're starting to become a family, a real family,' she swallowed deeply not wanting to say the words out loud. 'That Ricky and Jamie will be taken away from me?'

Jonny gave her a sidelong glance. 'No,' he said, pushing his foot down on the accelerator. 'Trust me, I won't let that happen.'

* * *

Blood stained Raymond's shirt, the knife wound he'd suffered bleeding profusely, not that he appeared to notice.

As he was roughly dragged across the room, a maddening smile tugged at the corners of his lips. 'And I hear that we have a sister,' he continued to goad. 'Michael told me that she's got balls of steel.'

Jamie gave a light chuckle. 'What can I say,' he said, giving a nonchalant shrug. 'She's a Tempest, unlike some I could mention.'

Raymond's face clouded over. 'I'm a fucking Tempest,' he growled.

Jamie laughed again. 'Yeah, but you're not, are you, not really. No matter how much you don't want to be, you were born a Cole and you'll die a Cole, it's as simple as that.'

A smirk spread across Raymond's face. 'You won't kill me, you ain't got the bottle.'

'That's where you're wrong. I should have killed you years ago, and I take full responsibility for the fact you are still breathing, that I allowed you the opportunity to try and maim my family, but believe me,' Jamie said, leaning in closer, 'I won't make the same mistake twice.'

Footsteps from behind forced Jamie to look up and as Terri and Jonny came into view, he narrowed his eyes.

'What did I tell you?' he growled, addressing Jonny. 'I told you to keep her away from this nutter.'

'No.' Terri held her head up high, her eyes flashing with indignation. 'This has nothing to do with him. I wanted to be here; it was my choice. You can't just shut me out, not now. We're family. This is where I belong, with you and Ricky.'

Shaking his head, Jamie blew out his cheeks. 'And that's another thing,' he snarled, turning his attention back to Raymond. 'She's loyal, something else you don't know the meaning of.'

As she awaited Raymond's response, Terri held her breath. She hadn't expected him, Ricky and Jamie to look so alike, nor had she expected to see her own face reflected back in his. It was somewhat unnerving, almost as if it was a glimpse into the past and she was looking at their father. Their nan had been right, Terry's genes had been strong.

'Loyal,' Raymond scoffed. 'What about me, eh?' he roared. 'Where was your loyalty to me? Terry was my old man. I was his son, but you were happy to throw me onto the scrapheap as if I was nothing, as if I didn't matter.'

'You meant fuck all to Terry,' Jamie bellowed back. 'None of us did.' He stabbed his finger none too gently into the side of Raymond's head. 'Only you were too blind to see him for what he really was, a ponce, a nasty piece of work. Terry wouldn't have given two shits if you were alive or dead. The very moment you were no longer a benefit to him he would have kicked you to the kerb, just as he did everyone else in his life. He was nothing but a fucking leech, a treacherous bastard. And do you want to know something else?' he spat. 'I'm glad he's dead, glad that he got what he deserved. My wife suffered at his hands,' he said, referring to the fact Georgiana had been trafficked into the country for the sole use of being pimped out by Terry and his business partner Kenny Kempton. 'He left her traumatised, and for what?' he continued to shout, his lips curling in disgust. 'A bit of cash in his back pocket.'

A roar ripped from Raymond's throat and with a strength Terri had never known was even possible, he sprang forward, his arm locking around Jamie's neck in a vice-like grip as he threw him up against the wall, smashing the air out of Jamie's lungs in the process as he collided with the concrete.

'You no-good fucker,' Raymond shouted his expression murderous as he went on to smash Jamie's head against the wall. 'He was my dad.'

In the chaos that ensued, Terri's heart was in her mouth. She was no stranger to violence; she'd witnessed it first-hand growing up. But the scene that unfolded before her was something entirely different. There were no other words that could be used to describe it other than pure and utter hatred. She could feel it oozing out of her brothers' pores. It went beyond sibling rivalry, it was a deep-rooted loathing that could never be placated or brushed under the carpet, nor could the animosity between her brothers ever be erased; it was within them, and had become a part of who they were.

Streaks of blood smeared the wall and as Jamie's head was repeatedly smashed against the concrete, Terri held her breath, her eyes wide and terrified. Raymond had to be stopped before he ended up killing Jamie, before he killed them all. He was capable of it, Terri had never been more certain of anything in her life. He had a madness about him, the likes of which she had never witnessed before, and he was strong, so strong that Ricky's and Jonny's efforts to pull him away from the youngest of her brothers were futile.

In a wild panic, Terri looked around her. She needed a weapon, something, anything that would put an end to Raymond's reign of terror. From out of the corner of her eye she spotted the hilt of a blade poking out from underneath a tattered armchair and racing forward, she scooped it up. Already streaked with blood, the knife wasn't particularly large, but what it lacked in size it more than made up for it when it came to sharpness. Turning her head, she surveyed the scene, the weapon curled tightly in her fist. Unless she did something and fast, Raymond was going to destroy them all.

Her hand began to tremble. Could she really take someone's life? Could she really go through with it? She had to, she decided, she had no other choice. She was a Tempest, she reminded herself over and over again, and now more than ever she had to be strong, the lives of everyone she'd come to care about were depending on it. Bounding forward, she plunged the knife deep between Raymond's shoulder blades. It was more than enough to startle him and as he dropped Jamie to the floor, he reached behind him, his eyebrows shooting up in surprise.

Without giving the matter a second's thought, Terri thrust the blade forward a second and third time.

Raymond staggered several paces back, blood seeping through his shirt. 'You...' The words caught in his throat and as he sank to his knees, the colour drained from his face. 'You...' he tried again before promptly slumping forward.

* * *

Jamie gasped for breath, bringing his hand up to the back of his head. 'The fucker could have killed me,' he choked out, inspecting the sticky red residue across his fingers.

'Yeah and do you wanna know why?' Ricky shot back. 'Because you're a mouthy fucker. You couldn't just keep quiet and actually kill the bastard, could you? No, you had to antagonise him first, had to open that big trap of yours and give it all that,' he said, snapping his fingers open and closed, imitating a mouth.

Jamie's jaw dropped. 'Cheers bruv, a bit of sympathy wouldn't go amiss. I'm bleeding out here, I could even have concussion.' He dabbed at the back of his head again and groaned. 'I'm actually seeing stars.'

Ricky scowled. 'Don't milk it, Jamie,' he snapped. 'You're hardly at death's door, are you.' Making his way back over to his son, he crouched down beside him, concern once again at the forefront of his mind.

'He needs to get to hospital, he needs medical help, they both do,' Terri declared, giving Jamie a quick glance as she knelt in front of Mason and pressed the back of her hand against his forehead. 'He's burning up.'

Getting back to his feet, Ricky held out his hand. 'Keys,' he demanded of Jamie, then turning to Jonny, he jerked his head behind him towards his son. 'Help get him in the car,' he added, handing over his brother's car keys. 'I'll be out in a bit.'

'And what are you going to do?' Tearing her eyes away from her nephew, Terri gave her eldest brother a cautious glance. The earlier anger between him and Jamie back at the warehouse was all too apparent.

'Something I should have done a long time ago,' Ricky growled, his gaze drifting down to the can of petrol. 'Making sure this bastard doesn't come back from the dead a second time.'

'But he's still alive.' Appalled, Terri's mouth dropped open, her eyebrows scrunching together as she took note of the rise and fall of Raymond's chest. 'You can't do that,' she begged of him. 'You have to kill him first.'

Ricky's lips curled into a snarl. 'What, and you think he would have given my son the same courtesy, that he wouldn't have burnt him alive? The sick bastard would have got a kick out of it.'

Terri swallowed deeply. Maybe he had a point. The house did reek of petrol, or rather, Mason did. Could it be true that Raymond had intended for her nephew to suffer the same fate?

'Just get him to the car.' Ricky's face relaxed, his voice becoming gentler. 'Please.' He clasped her hand and gave it a squeeze, his eyes begging her to help him. 'He needs to get to hospital, he needs help. I can't lose him.'

Terri nodded and after a lot of manoeuvring, she and Jonny managed to get Mason to his feet. Even the tiniest of movements was enough to reopen the wounds that had been inflicted upon him and as they began to weep, his entire upper body became slick. Tears streamed down his face, each step causing him to cry out loud, the pain too much for him to bear. It was the most pitiful sound Terri had ever heard and making sure to keep her own tears at bay, she guided him out of the house, her voice gentle as she coaxed him to slowly put one foot in front of the other.

Gingerly, Jamie got to his feet, his hand still clasped behind his head. 'I'm sorry,' he said as he watched his brother heave up the petrol can and begin dousing Raymond in the liquid.

Ricky clenched his jaw, his eyes hardening again. 'Just answer me one question Jamie. Did you know from the off that it was this mad fucker?'

As Jamie looked down at Raymond and took note of his shallow breaths, he shook his head. 'Not in the beginning. I honestly believed Gammon was working alone. It wasn't until you suggested he could be working for someone that I began to connect the dots and even then I didn't think it was entirely possible, that he would have the audacity to come for us again, that he would be that stupid.'

Satisfied with his brother's answer, Ricky gave a nod and throwing the empty can across the room, he held out his hand for Jamie's lighter. 'This ends today,' he said again, flicking the ignition, his lips set into a hard line. 'This bastard,' he spat, 'has had his day. I won't allow for my family to suffer another minute at this fucker's hands.'

Jamie gave a solemn nod and as Ricky threw the lighter on top of Raymond's body, a loud whoosh filled their ears. Bright orange flames erupted, the fire fast on its way to destroying everything in its path. Within seconds, the searing hot flames were licking the walls, the ceiling, and the surrounding floor and as for the black smoke pouring from Raymond's contorting frame, it was thick enough to choke the life out of them.

Their hands held over their mouths and noses, Ricky and Jamie backed away. Unless they were very much mistaken, the entire house would soon be engulfed in flames, destroying not only their half-brother but also any evidence of the grisly crime that had taken place. In a way, Ricky reasoned, it was poetic justice. Raymond had a penchant for fire, and fire was the very same instrument that would finally take his life, the one and only thing to put an end to his madness.

EPILOGUE

A car accident had been the unofficial cause of Mason's injuries, or at least this was what his mother Kayla, and grandmother Tracey, had been led to believe.

As he hobbled into The Merry Fiddlers, one arm wrapped around his ribs and the other positioned across his chest in a sling, a loud cheer went up.

'Here is he, the walking wounded,' Jamie joked. 'It's good to have you back home and in the land of the living.'

Ricky threw his brother a look, silently warning him not to overplay it. Lie after lie after lie he'd told in an attempt to convince Kayla that their son's injuries had been caused by him not wearing a seat belt. Mason hadn't heard the end of it since then and once her tears had subsided and the shock had begun to wear off, she'd berated him for being so reckless, pretty much barring him from getting behind the wheel of a car ever again.

On spotting their cousin, Sorina and Adelina raced across the pub and threw themselves at Mason, each of them excited to see him after his long stint in hospital and as Mason gave a pained grunt, their mother Georgiana chastised them. 'Careful,' she warned, her accent not quite as thick as it had been when she'd first arrived in the country from Romania. 'You have to be gentle girls,' she said, alternating between English and Romanian as she tried to get her point across. 'Your cousin was in a terrible accident.'

'They're all right.' Mason continued to grin, faint bruises still littering his face as he lapped up the attention. 'It'll take a bit more than these two cheeky monkeys to wipe me out of the game.'

Standing off to one side, Terri watched the family reunion unfold. It had been her idea to throw the homecoming party for Mason. Not only was it to celebrate her nephew's recovery and release from hospital but also the demise of those who had either taken Archie's life or had orchestrated his murder. At long last, they were able to move on with their lives, and put the past to rest, not that anyone would ever forget Archie Taylor because they wouldn't, they couldn't, least of all Rina.

As she watched Rina busy herself behind the bar, Terri couldn't help but smile. She could recall Rina telling her once that she was strong, but if anyone was strong then it was Rina herself. She had a quiet strength about her, one that Terri admired and one day hoped to emulate. And Terri had a feeling that in the months and years to come, she would need to draw on Rina's courage, and maybe even rely on the tiny woman for some much needed moral support, especially when it came to Jonny Carter's chosen career, when she was bound to spend endless nights worrying herself sick that he wouldn't come home to her, that maybe this would be the time the Carters' luck finally ran out.

'Are you all right, sweetheart?'

Terri looked up and as Jonny slung his arm around her shoulder and pulled her close, she snuggled in beside him, savouring the familiar pull of him. It was hard to believe that she had been afraid of him and that the fact he was an armed robber had shocked her to the very core. She'd once been of the belief that looks could be deceptive, well so could reputations and as much as she knew that Jonny and her brothers' names were notorious and that many people were right to be wary of them, she also knew that there was another side to them too. That they were loyal to those they cared about that they had morals, and that they would never unleash their ferocious tempers on anyone who didn't deserve it.

'You know you're allowed to join in,' Jonny whispered in her ear, giving a half smile as he nodded towards the Tempests.

'No.' Terri shook her head. 'It's their private family time. I don't want to intrude.'

'What, and you're not family?' Jonny chastised, raising his eyebrows at her.

Terri bit down on her lip. He had a point, she supposed. She too was a Tempest, and she had as much right to celebrate Mason's recovery as they did, didn't she?

'Oi, Terri.' As if sensing her inner turmoil, Jamie raised his glass towards her. 'Get over here,' he shouted out. 'We're about to make a toast.'

Clasping Jonny's hand, Terri made her way across the pub.

'First of all...' Ricky cleared his throat.

'Get on with it.' Jamie made a show of rolling his eyes before giving his mum a wink. 'We ain't got all day to listen to you drone on and on.'

'Pack it in,' Tracey scolded, slapping Jamie's arm. 'Go on,' she urged her eldest son.

Throwing his brother a look, Ricky began again. 'As I was saying, first of all' – he raised his glass towards Mason – 'it's good to have you back home. As we all know, it was touch and go for a while, but you proved you're a fighter.'

'And no more driving without a seat belt,' Kayla cut in, pursing her lips together.

'That's right, no more reckless driving.' Ricky's cheeks turned red at the blatant lie he'd just told and raising the glass a second time in a bid to hide his blushes, he looked around him, his gaze falling upon Terri. 'And lastly here's to family, to our family, the Tempests.'

Terri's heart soared and as she lifted her glass, she caught Rina's eyes. 'Get over here,' she mouthed, and as Rina made her way from behind the bar, Terri hugged her close.

'I was right, wasn't I?' Rina smiled as she nodded towards Ricky and Jamie. 'All you needed was a gentle little nudge in the right direction.'

Terri nodded and as she thought over Rina's words, she came to realise just how much she had to thank the tiny woman for. Not only had Rina given her a home and the new start she had so desperately needed and craved, but she'd also taught her how to be strong, how to be confident and even more than that, she'd given both her and her brothers the opportunity to build bridges, had given them a reason to make amends.

With her glass still held aloft, Terri beamed. After a shaky start, she had a feeling that nothing and no one would ever be able to tear her and her brothers apart. They would look out for one another as siblings should, would have each other's backs. And above all else, they would be one another's greatest allies. They weren't only family; they were *her* family, the family she had always wanted. 'To us,' she chorused. 'To the Tempests.'

ACKNOWLEDGMENTS

A huge thank you to Boldwood Books for your continued support. And thank you to Emily Rushton, Candida Bradford, Arbaiah Aird, for all of your hard work. Thank you to my family and friends who spend hours listening to me as I plot out each book. Thank you to the members of NotRights book club for continuing to believe in me. And most of all thank you to the readers, your support means so much to me.

ABOUT THE AUTHOR

Kerry Kaya is the hugely popular author of Essex-based gritty gangland thrillers with strong family dynamics. She grew up on one of the largest council estates in the UK, where she sets her novels. She also works full-time in a busy maternity department for the NHS.

Sign up to Kerry Kaya's mailing list for news, competitions and updates on future books.

Follow Kerry on social media here:

 facebook.com/kerry.bryant.58

 twitter.com/KerryKayaWriter

 instagram.com/kerry_kaya_writer

ALSO BY KERRY KAYA

Reprisal

The Fletcher Family Series

The Price

The Score

Carter Brothers Series

Under Dog

Top Dog

Scorned

The Reckoning

The Tempests Series

Betrayal

Revenge

Justice

Milton Keynes UK
Ingram Content Group UK Ltd.
UKHW041905091023
430255UK00003B/126

9 781837 512706